# BONE KEY

G. P. PUTNAM'S SONS

NEW YORK

# BONE KEY

## LES STANDIFORD

F

G. P. Putnam's Sons
*Publishers Since 1838*
a member of
Penguin Putnam Inc.
375 Hudson Street
New York, NY 10014

Library of Congress Cataloging-in-Publication Data
Standiford, Les.
    Bone Key / Les Standiford.
      p.  cm.
    ISBN 0-399-14874-4
    1. Deal, John (Fictitious character)—Fiction.
    2. Contractors—Fiction.   3. Florida—Fiction.   I. Title.
    PS3569.T331528B66     2002           2002019052
    813'.54—dc21

Printed in the United States of America
10  9  8  7  6  5  4  3  2  1

BOOK DESIGN BY VICTORIA KUSKOWSKI

While Deal and I love Key West just as it really and truly exists, this is a work of fiction, and in that spirit, I have taken certain liberties with geography and place names. May they please the guilty and the innocent alike.

For their advice on matters pertaining to the grape and the vine, I would like to extend a special thanks to George Foote, Wine Educator at GuinessUDV, as well as to connoisseurs nonpareil Michael Bittel, Bob Dickinson, and Alan Diamond—their advice, their knowledge, and their encouragement have been invaluable. Any apparent fabrications in this arena are attributable to the author and certainly not to them.

This book is dedicated to Knox Burger, Nat Sobel, and Scott Waxman, three stand-up guys.

... this is a climate that is kind to bright-blooming greenery and to joys of the flesh—frisky trysts, rum, and rumpled bedsheets—and so it is that many of the citizens are well acquainted with mischief, but at a cost.

—JOHN HERSEY
*Key West Tales*

# BONE KEY

## KEY WEST

## 1931

THE STORM HAD PASSED through the Florida Straits the night before, at that time a piddling hurricane, with winds no more than seventy-five or eighty miles per hour, according to the newspapers. Gusts in everyday summer thunderstorms might reach those speeds in this part of the world. If you were a seafaring man, you understood that much, and being a Caymaner by birth, and therefore a seafarer, Ainsley Spencer understood, even if he could not read the newspapers.

He also understood that hurricanes were feckless creatures that considered no man's prayers or wishes, and disregarded probability and logic when it suited them. Take what was bearing down upon them now: a storm that had somehow done the impossible.

Just when everyone on the island had breathed a sigh of relief and muttered their good riddances, this storm retraced its steps, whirling right back through the broad channel that separated Key West from Cuba. Just as it seemed the storm would barrel into Havana Bay, it had, in an ultimate display of capriciousness, turned due north, gathering strength from the warm August waters all the while.

Now the storm carried winds twice its original strength, a real monster, barreling hell-bent toward this island of one mile by four, where the highest land lay no more than sixteen feet above the boundless waters on the calmest of days. Already Ainsley could taste salt in the sheeted rain running down his face.

The senator had called for Ainsley just after supper, asking that he bring three of his best men along. By then, the winds were howling, and most anyone with sense had taken the best shelter they could. But when the senator called, there was no saying wait or maybe, much less no. That was just the way it was, and the three men whom Ainsley had picked felt exactly as he did. He'd told June Anna where he was going and why, and she'd nodded and sent him on his way with a wordless embrace.

Now, the four of them dragged themselves down windswept Whitehead Street toward the harbor, none of them wasting energy trying to talk about the clamoring storm. Ainsley glanced up as they passed the Rexall drugstore to see the swinging sign tear loose of its standard and go flying into the ever-darkening distance. Pity the man who looked up to see that metal sail bearing down on him, he thought. Slice him in two and keep on going, that's what. Growing up in the islands, Ainsley had seen such things and worse.

He led the way past the two-story brick bank building that marked the entrance to the docks, where the wind seemed to kick up another notch now that there was nothing left to shield them. The iron gates

2

had been drawn shut and padlocked across the broad double doors of the bank's entrance, creaking and clanking against their chain in the gusts. Gates that might keep a thief out, Ainsley thought, but useless in a certain wind. He stepped off the sidewalk curb over a sodden wad of feathers that was a pigeon's carcass, but told himself it had likely been lying in the gutter before the storm's approach. Things had not gotten that bad yet.

There was a sheriff's car parked at the entrance to the docks, its headlights flaring at the group's approach. Ainsley lifted his chin into the gale and held up a hand, the rain nicking his palm as hard as buckshot. A spotlight snapped on and ran across his spattered features, then lapsed back into darkness, along with the headlights. Ainsley motioned the others forward.

In the harbor, several small boats heaved at their moorings as if they longed to leave the frothing sea and hurtle skyward. Some of the smallest craft had been hauled out to drydock, one already out of its chocks and tumbled onto its side. The hull needed a scraping, Ainsley saw. Maybe it would get one—if the boat survived the storm, that is.

The bigger boats had put out to sea, some bent on racing the storm northward toward Miami, others intending to ride it out nose to nose, where there were no pilings, no reefs, no neighboring craft to contend with. If you knew what you were about, Ainsley thought, it was not a bad way to go.

There was one freighter that remained at the dock, however, its bulk rising and falling with the erratic tides, first straining at its heavy lines, then crashing back against the mooring bumpers with a crash of waves. The *Magdelena*, Ainsley nodded. Some Spanish he could read. The name didn't fit with the thoughts in his mind, though: Instead of a woman, he saw a giant metal bull thrashing panicked in its stall.

Men were staggering down a gangway that led to the docks from a

3

port that yawned in the side of the big ship, each with a wooden crate on one shoulder and a hand on one of the swaying guy lines. There was a growing mound of crates on the dock below, fed by the antlike procession of the crew.

A man in a watch cap and slicker stood at the rail on the ship's bridge, measuring the progress intently. The captain, Ainsley assumed. A dark-browed man with Slavic features who looked like he'd be at home in the North Atlantic. Surely he longed to be untethered from this dock and out where he could deal with the storm on his own terms.

Ordinarily, a crane or cargo boom would make short work of such unloading, but in weather like this, such equipment was useless. If whatever it was had been owned by anyone besides the senator, Ainsley thought, there'd likely be no unloading going on at all.

As they crossed the docks toward the stacked crates, Ainsley felt more than heard the rumble behind him. As a heavy burst of rain swept over them, he turned to see a pair of canvas-topped trucks following in their footsteps, the lights of each flashing as they passed the sheriff's car. When the second truck had passed onto the docks, the sheriff's car roared into life, then rolled away quickly toward town. In moments it had been swallowed in the gloom.

Ainsley and his men stepped aside as the trucks rolled by. Ainsley didn't recognize the drivers, but he knew who employed them, as he knew there was no longer a need for whatever security the two in the sheriff's car might have been able to provide.

The trucks passed by the mound of crates then turned at the foot of the dock and came back to a stop beside the cargo, nosed toward town, their lights doused, engines running. The last of the crates had been stacked on the docks and the drenched crew members were making their way back up the bucking gangway toward the hold.

4

Ainsley saw that a man—small and hunched inside a yellow slicker that seemed to swallow him—had come to join the captain at the bridge. The captain said something to the man in the oversized slicker and pointed at the trucks. The man nodded and quickly clambered down a set of outer stairs onto the deck, then disappeared through a deckside door. In moments he reappeared at the gangway, pulling himself hand over hand down one of the lines to the dock.

Ainsley and his companions kept their distance as another man stepped down from the trucks and handed a satchel to the man in the flapping slicker, who opened it briefly and glanced inside. Whatever he saw seemed to satisfy him, for he turned to signal the captain on the bridge, then hurried back up the gangway with the satchel tucked to his chest.

"Let's go!" the man who'd handed over the satchel shouted to Ainsley then, and Ainsley motioned his men forward.

They had the crates loaded in less than half an hour, Ainsley reckoned, glancing out at the wind-riled harbor that receded behind him. He and his men had climbed aboard in the cargo space of the second truck, sitting now atop crates beneath the canvas that clattered with the waves of buckshot rain.

The *Magdelena* had long since steamed out of sight, and none too soon, he thought. As they'd finished loading the crates onto the trucks, a sloop had broken loose from its moorings out in the harbor to come shattering against the dock. With its mast and wheelhouse sheared away and a hole in her starboard hull, it had taken only moments for the boat to go down.

Ainsley, who felt about boats as most did about people, had watched it all as if witnessing a drowning he could do nothing to prevent. He glanced at the boats still rolling in the harbor and wondered how many of them would make it until morning.

5

There was a sudden pulsing of light on the distant seaward horizon then, followed by a rumbling sound that might have come from the storm. One of the men with Ainsley glanced over.

"What do you reckon?" he asked.

"Just thunder," said the man next to him.

Ainsley glanced out in the direction where the flash had come, thinking that in all this storming, he'd heard no thunder yet, and probably still had not. He turned back to the others and nodded.

"I reckon thunder," he said, and for the others, that was that.

What was printed on the crates was indecipherable, neither English nor Spanish. Ainsley assumed that what they were hauling was some exotic kind of whiskey, valuable enough for the senator to have brought it to port in weather such as this. He'd unloaded similar goods for his employer many times before, and often ran a tender well out into the Gulf Stream to take on shipments from captains loath to flout the laws of Prohibition. Normally, they would offload their cargo, then truck whatever that might be to a warehouse on Stock Island, where it was shipped by rail to places Ainsley did not care to know about.

The senator, whom Ainsley understood lived in some distant northern state and wielded an influence greater than anyone he'd known, including the Cayman governor himself, seldom came to Key West, but when he did, he treated Ainsley with the utmost respect. He'd set up an account for Ainsley in the very bank they'd passed on the way to the docks and had instructed Ainsley how to draw from that source when he needed.

Ainsley understood that the senator derived a great portion of his income from means that the government considered illegal, but this caused him not the slightest discomfort. He was a Caymaner and a sea-faring man, and he understood that no one governed the sea. Further-more, islands, being surrounded by the sea, existed in a sealike state themselves. Whatever the inhabitants of an island deemed right and proper for the conduct of their lives constituted the natural law. In these climes, governments were like barnacles: You put up with them, and then you scraped them away.

He felt the truck slowing and glanced out the back in mild surprise. They hadn't passed over the cut to Stock Island yet. He wondered why they were stopping.

He heard a door open and slam, then saw the man who'd handed over the satchel at the docks appear at the back of the truck. The man grabbed hold of a stave and vaulted up onto the bed beside him, an adroit move for someone of his size and bulk, Ainsley thought.

"Have 'em put these on," the man said, tossing a soggy wad of cloth into Ainsley's lap.

Ainsley glanced down at the wad, realizing it was bandannas that he held, lengths of cloth folded up into long strips a couple of inches wide. Four of them. "Blindfolds?" he asked, staring up at the man.

Water dripped from the man's chin and from the brim of his hat. "It's for your own good," he said. "The less you know, the better."

Ainsley thought about this, but he didn't have to think for long. If the senator wanted him to be blindfolded, he would be blindfolded. He turned and handed each of his men one of the folded bandannas. When they had tied the blindfolds into place, Ainsley heard a banging on the side of the truck and then they were under way again.

There were several turns and much more driving than the confines of a four-mile island would have allowed, but the journey could have included some backtracking and unnecessary turning to throw them

7

off, Ainsley thought. In any case, he made no attempt to determine where they might be going. He simply hoped to get there before the storm arrived with its full fury.

Finally, he felt the truck slowing again and sensed that they had reached their destination. "Just sit tight," the man who'd delivered the blindfolds said when Ainsley stirred.

There was a wrenching sound as if heavy doors were being opened, then a lurch as the truck moved forward again. The crashing of the rain and the wild flapping of the canvas top stopped abruptly, leaving a silence that was almost painful to Ainsley's ears.

The heavy doors slammed closed again and Ainsley felt himself enveloped by a damp mustiness, the sounds of the storm a distant rumble. "Okay," the man said, jumping down from the truck. "Take 'em off."

Ainsley did as he was told, blinking in the dim light that greeted him. As his eyes adjusted, he jumped down from the truck as well, his feet meeting a packed earthen floor.

It was a sizable room they'd pulled into—nothing as big as the warehouse on Stock Island, but able to accommodate the two trucks with plenty of room to spare. A lantern, which hung on a peg beside a pair of tall wooden doors, provided the only illumination. The windowless walls were formed of coquina, the native limestone, and the wooden roof loomed high above, barely illumined by the lantern's glow.

It seemed a veritable fortress they'd come to, but still the rain pounded hard on the roof and the heavy doors bulged and gave with the winds like a pair of weary lungs. Spray managed to find its way into the cavernous room with each inward pulse brought by the winds, and Ainsley decided that it was a most illusory kind of safety they had found. His own home was built of native South Florida pine, the strongest wood capable of being carpentered, its few windows shuttered by the same materials.

8

His home, anchored to the coral rock by deeply driven pilings no storm could budge, might be small, but it was strong, and he longed to finish this business and join June Anna that they might weather this mess together. He assumed that he and his men would make quick work of stacking the crates along the walls and then be gone. He had turned in fact to begin the organizing of his men, when an odd creaking noise sounded behind him and he turned to peer into the recesses of the room.

Two men had pried a massive iron grate up from where it had been set into the floor, he realized, and were staggering about trying to keep it from falling back into place. "Sonofabitch is heavy," one of the men said.

"Just hold on," the other one said, grunting with effort. "Help me ease it against the wall."

Ainsley turned to the man beside him with a questioning gaze. The man pointed. "Take it down there," he said, handing over a second lantern he'd got going. "Be careful with the steps."

Ainsley glanced at the man, then took the smoking lantern to the portal that yawned in the corner of the room. He passed the two men who'd pried the gate up without looking at them, mindful of their panting as he held the lantern high to illumine a dank set of steps leading down to a sizable storage area chiseled out of the coral rock. Whoever had managed the feat had accomplished something, Ainsley thought with a glance at the heavy grate. And whatever you put down there would surely be safe.

"I didn't know you could have a basement in Key West," one of the men behind him said, still breathing heavily from exertion.

"There's a couple," the other said.

"Better get a move on," the man who'd wanted them blindfolded said. He pointed at the heaving doors. "This storm's turning into a bitch." 9

Ainsley moved quickly back to the truck and organized his men into a fire brigade. They'd stack all the crates at the portal to the subterranean room, he had decided, and then set up another line down the narrow stairwell.

The process worked well in fact. Unencumbered by the rain, they had the trucks emptied in half the time it had taken to load up on the docks. Outside, the storm had worsened steadily, however, the wind battering the big double doors until the cross brace that held them closed snapped like a matchstick. The doors flew inward, slamming against the stone sidewalls, the wind driving horizontal sheets of rain halfway into the room. It took all seven of them to shove the doors closed and wedge a section of the shattered cross brace back into place.

Ainsley managed a look outside, but it told him nothing. The sky was dark by now, the visibility down to nothing in the driving storm. The *Titanic* could have been bearing down upon them from a dozen yards away, for all he knew. He wondered if he would ever make it home.

With the doors shored up, they turned their attention back to the movement of the crates into the subterranean vault. Ainsley hurried down the narrow stairwell and took up the post at the end of the line, leaving two of his men on the stairs and the last to hand the crates down.

He was a man who had spent most of his life on the open water, and while he'd spent his own share of time in the cramped holds of a score or more of ships and boats, he had never overcome his aversion to close quarters. He'd never heard the word "claustrophobia," but if the symptoms had been described to him, he would likely have admitted an understanding. Furthermore, as the foreman of this hastily assembled crew, he could have been the one to stay up top and pass the boxes down, but he knew that all the others felt as he did about such dungeon

10

places, and he would not put that on anyone else. He'd swallowed his own fears, therefore, and carried the lantern down.

"Come on now," he called up the narrow stairwell and saw the first crate come through the opening.

It was a dank, low-ceilinged space, barely enough room for him to stand his six feet straight, but wide and long enough to hold what they'd brought here, he thought. He held the lantern high and saw at the far end of the room what looked like another set of steps chiseled into the rock . . . leading up to *what?* he wondered, but then the first crate was ready for him to stack and there was no more time to see.

He hadn't counted the crates exactly, but having moved them all twice, he had a fair notion of the numbers. He stacked the crates five high—just above head height—against the near wall and built out from there, six crates abreast. He was past the point where the stairs descended quickly and, leaving room to maneuver at the foot, worked himself steadily backward toward the other flight of steps, grabbing and stacking, grabbing and stacking. Sooner or later, he thought, feeling the sweat trickling down his weary back, he'd satisfy his curiosity.

"That's all," he heard then, from Ben, his mate at the bottom of the stairs, and he paused to survey the work they'd done. He glanced over his shoulder toward the other flight of steps and saw that his stacking had hidden the far end of the cavelike room in shadow. He'd need his lantern if he wanted to see anything back there, and he wondered if he had the time to waste. Working below several feet of rock had shielded the sound of the storm, but he knew from the popping in his ears that its force could only have grown.

He reached a hand to massage his back and began to make his way toward Ben, thinking that he could live without knowing where that staircase led, when he heard a pair of explosions from above. At first, he thought it might have been the cross brace snapping again, or something crashing on the roof, but he knew at once it was nothing so benign.

Ben gave him a startled glance and began to hurtle up the steps even before Ainsley could warn him. Another explosion sounded, and another and another, and Ainsley felt himself covered by something wet at the same time he heard Ben cry out and tumble backward down the staircase.

Ainsley staggered back, gasping, wiping at the gore that drenched his face and chest. Ben lay at the foot of the stairs, his head twisted oddly, his eyes sightless. Richard lay slumped halfway up the steps where he'd been working, and Marcus's body had tumbled to a step just above. He could hear the storm pounding up there now, and could hear the big double doors crashing free once more.

Ainsley felt his legs weaken, his breathing gone wild. He heard scuffing noises at the head of the steps and stared in disbelief as the body of one of the senator's drivers tumbled through the portal, followed quickly by the second. Five men dead in moments, he thought, his mind a mad whirl. He heard an odd clinking sound, then saw what might have been brass pebbles dancing down the steps. Shell casings, he realized, and heard the click of a revolver's cylinder settling back into place.

"Let's don't make this difficult," Ainsley heard a familiar voice call, then saw the thick black oxfords of the man who'd had them blindfolded descend onto the first of the rough-hewn steps. There was a crashing noise from somewhere, and a fine, salt-laden spray rolled down the narrow staircase along with it.

The roof, Ainsley thought. With the doors blown open and the storm roaring inside after them, all that wind had to go somewhere. A roof, built to ward off forces from above, was not nearly so strong when a giant force was shoving from below.

"Come on now, boy," the man called down. He descended to the

12

second step and bent to peer into the misted cellar, his revolver raised. "We'll make this quick and clean."

Ainsley, still holding his lantern, realized he was a framed target in the little cove he'd left for himself at the foot of the steps. He tried to backpedal into the darkness, but the man had seen him and was already swinging his weapon about. There was an explosion that seemed deafening in the confined space and the sound of splintering glass at Ainsley's side. Instinctively, he flung the lantern up the stairwell.

The glass chimney shattered against the coral, and flaming kerosene splashed upward. Ainsley saw one leg of the man's trousers burst into flame and heard a cry as the man retreated up the steps.

It was altogether dark in the cellar now, a dim glow marking the portal where the heavy grate had been, a glowing square cloud in a stony sky. Ainsley heard curses and scuffing noises from above. Had it been gasoline, he thought, the bursting lantern might have done the job. But kerosene was not much better than crude oil for burning, and the man's clothing had been soaked through as well.

No, Ainsley thought, he'd likely done little more than prolong the inevitable. His right hand went to the knife he kept sheathed at his belt—a seafaring man would sooner go out without britches than leave his knife behind—thinking that he might have a chance if he could only manage to lure the man down here with him in the dark.

Scarcely had the thought come to him than he heard a tremendous crashing from above and felt a fine rain of rock fragments shower onto his head and shoulders. When he glanced up, he saw that a vague crosshatching now obscured the portal at the top of the stairs. A shadow flashed across the grid, and there came the sound of a bolt slamming home.

An involuntary shudder ran through Ainsley, as he realized. The man who'd shot at him would not be coming down those steps again, not

13

anytime soon. He stared up glumly at the heavy grate that now blocked the portal and understood that he had become a prisoner, that this room where he now stood might well have been intended for such a purpose.

"You'll die the hard way, then," came the voice from above, over the roar of the wind and the sound of roofing planks being wrenched away. Rain pelted down through the bars above him now, and a stream of water was splashing down the steps.

"The senator wouldn't do this," Ainsley shouted back, not sure if it was a threat or a prayer.

He heard a barking sound that might have been meant as a laugh. "Your senator's a dead man," the voice called down from above. "Come on up where I can see you, now. I'll end it for you quick."

The stream running down the stairs had become a set of rapids, Ainsley realized, his feet already sloshing in water on the cellar floor. He glanced around the darkness, fighting the panic that rose inside him like fire. The rock-carved room was as watertight as a cistern, and there was a hurricane up there, pouring its all down that steel-grated chute. Maybe it'd be best, a part of him said. Go up the steps with his head hung down like a packing house cow and get it over with.

But he dismissed the possibility as quickly as it came. He'd go down fighting, no matter what. He glanced up at the grating and thought he saw a shadow hovering there. The openings in the grid seemed big enough to get his hand through. If the bastard were pressed close enough to the grating, he thought, his hand tight on the handle of his knife, there just might be a chance.

"What happened to the senator?" Ainsley called.

"That's none of your concern," the man said. There was a crashing as if waves were breaking above his head and a mighty gush of water down the steps.

14    Dear Lord, Ainsley thought. If this place was close to the water's

edge and the tide rose sufficiently with the press of the winds, the cellar could be full of ocean in minutes.

The voice above him came again. "Come on, boy, we're wasting time."

Ainsley had stacked a second crate atop the first now, and had climbed onto it with his knees. If he stood, he could easily reach that shadowed portion of the grate.

"Just come on up to the light, boy," the man called, as a flashlight beam snapped on.

The backwash was enough to outline the man's silhouette now, and Ainsley knew it would be this moment or never. He rose straight from his heels, as if he meant to take flight, his arm extended rigidly, his hand around the knife handle like iron.

He felt the point of his knife glance off the heavy gratework and the flesh of his knuckles shear away, but nothing could have made him lose his grip. In the next second he heard a gasp and felt his fist burying itself in soft flesh.

There was a bright flash and a blinding explosion, and then another, but Ainsley held fast to his blade, his arm driven up through the gate past the elbow. He heard the man gasp and felt his bulk rising from the grating where he'd lurked. Ainsley twisted and pulled down hard and felt a gush of warmth bathe his arm and shoulder.

There was a groan from above him then, and the clatter of metal on metal as the revolver tumbled free. The man's weight was crushing, suddenly, and Ainsley felt the crates going sideways, his feet flying from under him, his grasp loosening on the knife as he fell. He went down on his back, hard enough to have brained himself, but there was a foot of water covering the rough-hewn floor now, enough to cushion his fall.

Still the blow stunned him. He lay momentarily paralyzed, his breath knocked away. A beam of light shot up toward the grating from the foot of the steps, he realized, and he managed to move his head enough

15

to see that the flashlight had tumbled down to rest on Ben's unmoving chest. The man who'd meant to kill him lay facedown on the grate, blood dripping from a place below his belt.

But he wasn't dead, Ainsley saw. The man's gaze was glassy, but focused upon him, and while his body was still, his hand was moving slowly across the grating like a giant white spider, inching toward the fallen revolver.

Do something, Ainsley willed himself. Run. Douse that light. Go for the gun yourself. But all he could manage was a feeble splashing of his arms in the rising water and a *huunnh, huunnh, hunnh* bleating from his airless lungs.

The man's hand had found the revolver's grip now, and Ainsley watched in fascination as his arm snaked down through the grate. He was raising the barrel slowly into position—the sonofabitch was dying at the same time he was going to kill him, Ainsley thought—when there came an awful screaming from above. Nails wrenching free of wood, thick shards of wood shattering, and a stab of pain at Ainsley's ears that suggested all the air around them had been sucked away in an instant.

Tornado, he thought. A whirlwind spawned in the midst of the storm that had lifted up the roof of the building and all the air beneath it. Then there was a mighty crash from above that made the dropping of the steel grate seem like the blow of a feather in comparison. Great chunks of the cellar ceiling rained down, one crashing down on Ben's lifeless body, knocking the flashlight askew, another boulder narrowly missing Ainsley's skull.

He rolled over in the water and thrashed madly toward the shelter of the crates, fully expecting a gunshot to drop him at any instant. But there was nothing.

He was past the place where the steps came down to the room now, one of Ben's outflung hands stretching barely a yard away, the flashlight half-in, half-out of the water nearby. Ainsley's breath had come back in ragged gasps, his heart pounding so loudly he couldn't hear the storm. He struggled to calm himself, listened for a few more moments, but heard nothing but the unearthly rumble of the storm and the cascading of water down the steps.

Finally, he ducked down and reached quickly to snatch the tumbled flashlight. In the instant that he jerked himself back out of sight, he saw something odd . . . what had seemed like a pair of arms dangling down from the grate above. He inched one eye out past the corner of the roughly chiseled wall and stole another glance.

The man's hand dangled down, the pistol no longer held there. And what he had taken for a second arm was not that at all, he realized, as he stepped out into the open, sloshing shin-deep toward the sight.

The man's eyes were still open but frozen now, his cheek flattened against one cross member, his tongue squeezed out like a tiny pink flag of surrender. A section of the roof had broken loose and toppled down on him, Ainsley realized

Had crushed him against the grate like the roach he was. A splintered shard of planking had plunged through his back and burst out of his chest where his heart would have been, if he'd had one. But there had been no such organ there, could not have been, as far as Ainsley was concerned. And whatever was that dark stuff dripping from the end of the shattered plank, you wouldn't even call it blood.

The old man awakened then, spared the reliving of what had happened next; and for that much, he was grateful. Ainsley knew that he had been dreaming, but he woke with a shudder nonetheless, for it was as much a memory as a dream, every bit of it being true. Though he had survived, it brought him no great pleasure to recall just how, as it brought him little cheer to recall the events at all.

17

The dream, or living memory, had come upon him before, at certain times in his life when great change loomed ahead. He had relived the events the night before the first of his sons had been born, and again the night before his son's son had been born, and also the night that his great-grandson, Dequarius, had come into this world.

The old man might have been relieved if he could assume that the dream was an omen of good things to come, but he had also relived those events the night that his own June Anna had died, which put the lie to good-omen foolishness, yes indeed.

What struck him when he awoke this morning, breathing hard, sweat soaking his nightshirt as briny as those nightmare waves, was how few possibilities there were, when it came to portents at least. If the dream was a harbinger of his own death, it hardly seemed worth the trouble. He was old and worn and expected to die, himself not least among those who did the expecting. His wife was gone, his two sons likewise, his grandson alive, but who knew where.

That left among the possibilities his great-grandson, a boy for whom no sane man could hold high hopes. And yet still, the old man loved him. Which is why he sat on the edge of his bed and trembled in the tropical dawn, pondering those events so long ago . . . all the while praying that it could not be a curse he'd brought upon them all, but just an old man's stubborn memory that came and went at random, that calamity no more loomed above this island now than that which chance might bring.

The wail of distant sirens broke Ainsley Spencer's reverie, and he glanced around his tidy bedroom to reassure himself of what was real, then forced himself up from his bed, willing the vision of the dead man's sightless stare from his mind. That had been then, and this was now, he told himself.

18     What a man might remember was one thing, but the events them-

selves belonged to the past. And even if he felt a certain responsibility for what had happened, it was far too late to change things now. Events that had happened once could not happen again.

His concerns should be with what could be managed, he reminded himself. Take this day in hand and do with it well.

Indeed, he thought as the sirens wailed. He would go check on his great-grandson now, though he already feared what he was likely to find.

**2**

## KEY WEST

### The Present Day

"**HOW COME SHE** didn't bring you the cork?" Russell Straight said to John Deal.

"That's only when you buy the whole bottle," Deal said, lifting his glass of red.

Russell, who'd ordered a beer, nodded thoughtfully. He had his eyes on the receding backside of their cocktail waitress. She was tall and deeply tanned, with blond hair that just tickled the collar of the parrot-print Hawaiian shirt that the Pier House staff wore. She had the shirt untucked, and the khaki shorts were standard-issue unisex, but certain virtues were impossible to disguise. Deal didn't blame Russell for staring. He was staring himself, starting to feel the different pulse of life as it was lived in Margaritaville.

Deal, who'd inherited what was left of DealCo Construction from his late father, had come down from Miami to Key West to see a man about a job, as it were. Though it was summer and well ahead of the serious tourist season, which wouldn't kick into high gear for months, the island paradise at the end of the American road—all one mile by four miles of it—was hardly sleepy.

Last evening, for instance, he and Russell, his newly promoted construction superintendent, had idled away part of the cocktail hour walking along the seawall at the Malory Docks, the city's tour-boat port, elbowing their way through a crowd of easily a couple of thousand who'd come down for the ritual viewing of the sun's fiery plunge into the waters of the Gulf of Mexico. Despite the mixture of heat and humidity that had combined to form a bank of thunderheads off to the west, obscuring the fabled sunset, there'd been no dearth of gawkers for the fire-eaters, jugglers, mimes, and bygone-era folksingers providing their own brand of entertainment at the steely water's edge.

The number of tourists had simply been reduced to the very nearly tolerable, Deal thought, glancing around the crowded bar. He had promised himself that he'd never join that weary chorus who loved to tell newcomers how much better it had been "back in the old days," before the swank hotels of the eighties, or before the highway in the thirties, or before Henry Flagler built his railroad at the turn of the twentieth century, when you could only get to the town by boat.

There had always been better days, Deal thought, anywhere you went. But even with Duval Street turned into one big market and high-profile restaurateurs turning cottages into Cafés See and Be Seen on every corner, Key West was still unique, a tropical island plopped down

21

in the middle of the Gulf Stream a hundred miles from mainland Florida, enough of its original down-at-the-heels, Casablanca-like charm intact to beat the daylights out of a pleasure trip to Des Moines, or, worse, someplace like Orlando. In Orlando, they had pirate *shows.* In Key West, you could still find actual pirates.

Russell, meantime, had wrenched his gaze from the tawny waitress and turned to Deal, mulling his lesson on corkage. "I hang around with you long enough," he said, "I'll learn all sorts of civilized stuff."

"Anything's possible." Deal shrugged. He'd shifted his gaze to something else.

From where they sat, on the second floor of the upscale but aggressively laid-back hotel, there was a good view of the harbor channel and the sunset sky beyond. Cloud banks lit up in boiling pinks and shades of lavender and teal, shorebirds twisting and diving in the foreground, a couple of sailboats thrown in for good measure . . . poor Turner, who'd done so well with England's sunsets . . . he'd just been born in the wrong place, Deal thought.

"I never figured you for a wine drinker," Russell persisted. It was easier to talk, now that the steel band on the open-air porch had packed it in. Their raucous syncopation had been replaced by piped-in piano Muzak. "Anybody'd look at you, they'd say there's a beer drinker and a half."

Deal paused, his glass halfway to his mouth. In truth, he'd been at the checkout counter of Sunset Corners up in Miami, a case of light beer in his cart, when he'd started down this other path. Iron Mike, one of the owners of the package store, caught a glance at what Deal purported to buy and insisted there was a less painful way to drop a few pounds. Mike talked, Deal listened, and the light beer had gone back on the shelf, replaced by a case of Merlot and a pamphlet-sized book on how to shed a few pounds without losing your mind.

22

The rest had been history, Deal mused, staring down at his glass. A more expensive history. He tasted the wine, then tried another sip. Maybe he *should* have asked for the cork, he thought. "I like beer," he said to Russell. "But then I went on this diet."

"For what?" Russell said. "You're not fat."

"Compared to whom?" Deal said, looking at Russell, who was wearing a T-shirt with a lifeguard emblem on its chest. He'd bought it earlier in the day at one of the tourist shops on Duval, an XXL that stretched over his massive chest and biceps like spandex.

"Basically, you're not supposed to drink," Deal continued, "but the guy who wrote the book said you could have a glass of red wine once in a while."

"Once in a while?" Russell lifted an eyebrow. They'd been in town two days now, doing little besides wait. Then again, for the amount of money that might come the way of DealCo Construction, a bit of waiting behooved him.

Deal shrugged again, a gesture he'd picked up from his erstwhile partner Vernon Driscoll. Driscoll, an ex–Miami homicide detective and now point man for D&D Investigative Services (Deal was the second D, an otherwise silent participant), could shrug in a hundred different ways, Deal had learned, each move with a slightly different meaning, everything from "Right you are," to "You are a wiseass, but I am going to wait at least thirty seconds before I take you apart." For the taciturn Driscoll, the shrug was a way of life. Deal was just beginning to appreciate the simple elegance of the gesture.

"This guy say how big of a glass?" Russell asked.

Deal shook his head. "Why do you think I went with his diet?"

Russell nodded. "I was on a diet once," he said, taking a swallow of his beer. His hand was so big you could hardly see the bottle.

"Please," Deal said. It was the kind of banter that seemed to spring

23

up in Key West, born of tropical malaise, he supposed. What the hell, he thought. He'd been busting his buns in Miami—he deserved a bit of downtime in paradise.

"The prison diet was what they called it," Russell said, unfazed. "How it worked, they fixed everything so it tasted like crap."

Deal smiled again. "You lost weight, huh?"

"I turned sideways, I was like a crack in the wall."

Deal shook his head. "How much do you weigh right now, Russell?"

Russell pursed his lips. "Two-forty maybe. Maybe two-fifty."

"You wish," Deal said. "And you're how tall?"

"Six-three. Is this a job interview?"

"You already work for me," Deal said mildly.

"I ain't going on no diet," Russell said. "You might as well leave this right where it is."

"I was just curious," Deal said.

"What you are is miserable, and looking for company," Russell said. "Get that fat-ass cop to go on a diet with you. He could stand to drop some poundage."

Deal laughed. When it came to an argument, about even the slightest things, Russell could be as tenacious as Vernon Driscoll. Maybe it was something that perpetrators and cops had in common, Deal thought.

Russell's gaze had wandered back to the waitress, who was bent over a nearby table, reaching for an empty. Deal glanced at his watch. "Stone said seven o'clock, right?"

"Was his *secretary* who said it," Russell answered. "I already told you. Far as I know there isn't any Franklin Stone."

"Oh, there is a Franklin Stone, all right," Deal said. "And there is *only* one." Flamboyant Franklin Stone, the man who'd invited Deal to Key West, owned a majority interest in the hotel where they were stay-

24

ing, as well as a goodly portion of the commercial real estate on the island.

Russell Straight made a noise in his throat that sounded like a rhino rooting something distasteful out of its muck pool. "I don't know why you brought me down here," he said. "Sit around and do nothing. That's what a cop is good for. You should have brought Driscoll along."

"He's got work of his own," Deal said. "I thought you might like to see Key West."

"Can I get you something else?" It was the waitress, smiling down at Russell.

Russell smiled back, then checked the beer in his hand. "Another one of these."

The waitress smiled. "Got it," she said, then glanced at Deal, who shook his head.

"I think she likes the cut of your jib," Deal said, as the waitress walked away.

"There's women everywhere," Russell observed, unimpressed. "I got to go to the can."

He unfolded himself from the chair and started across the room, weaving gracefully through the tightly packed tables, despite his size. Big, good-looking guy with his shaved head and chiseled upper body, you might take him for a professional athlete, Deal supposed. After all, his older brother had been, before he'd fallen in with the wrong people, anyway.

Deal had seen Leon Straight when he'd played for the Dolphins, Leon taking out the whole side of an opposing line Sunday after Sunday, before he'd gotten hurt and gotten into painkillers and things beyond. Later, Deal had seen Leon take on a helicopter full of killers and nearly win—he might have won, in fact, if the copter's shattered rotor blade hadn't happened to cut him in half.

25

He had finished his wine now, and when he glanced around for their waitress, realized that he was the only one left in the section. He waited a few more moments, watching the sun-struck clouds go from pink to purple, before he stood and moved to the bar.

The bartender, a tall guy with a mustache and the look of a guy who could play a part on a cop show in Hawaii, poured him a generous refill. "You want me to start a tab?" the guy asked.

Deal glanced at the table where he'd been sitting. "I thought we had one going."

The guy followed Deal's gaze, then tapped a finger to the side of his head as he realized. "Right. Denise." The guy gave Deal a look that might have suggested apology. "She closed her shift," he said. He turned and found a ticket on the counter behind him, made a note, then moved off as a waitress working the other side of the room hurried toward the service station with an order.

Deal saw there was a guy in a white dinner jacket behind a baby grand at the far end of the lounge, and he realized for the first time that what he had taken for Muzak was live. The guy, in his late fifties, was wearing a jet-black hairpiece that looked as much a part of him as a coonskin cap would have. He finished an energetic rendition of "Greensleeves," raising his hands in a flourish to a scattering of applause from the tables.

The Pier House crowd seemed a bit older and more coiffed than Deal remembered from his last visit, but that had been a while ago. He and Janice hadn't been married long. They'd run down from Miami on the spur of the moment, stayed three days right here at the Pier House, hardly got out of bed. But that had been another life, he thought.

He sensed someone sliding onto a stool next to him and turned to see a decidedly un-coiffed black kid in baggy painter's jeans and a loose-fitting basketball jersey settling in, propping his elbows on the bar. "How you doin'?" the kid said, jittering on his seat. When he nodded, Deal saw the handle of a comb planted in his luxuriant Afro.

Deal nodded back and reached for his wine.

"You diggin' this freak at the piano?"

Deal glanced over. The kid was a little older than Deal had first thought—in his mid-twenties, maybe—but his slight build and wide-eyed gaze belied his age. His skin was light coffee-colored, and a scattering of freckles dotted his fine facial features. He might have been a Caymaner, Deal thought, but there was no trace of the Brit in his accent. "You missed the steel band, I'm afraid. If that's who you came to see."

The kid shook his head, then licked his lips nervously. "What it is, I came to talk to you."

Deal looked at him. Out on the sidewalks you might be approached by some scrubbed and polished young man or woman who wanted to dragoon you into some resort's time-share presentation. Somehow, this one didn't seem the type. "Whatever you're selling, I'm not buying," he told the kid.

"You're Deal, right?" the kid said, both his feet pedaling the rail of his stool.

Deal glanced around, as if there might be someone sitting behind him. Could the kid have said something else? That sort of thing had happened before, given the circumstances: Deal me in, deal me out, let's make a deal.

"The builder," the kid continued, his voice insistent.

So much for mistakes, Deal thought. "That's me," he said. "What can I do for you?"

"There's something I need to talk to you about."

Deal stared. "If you're looking for work . . ."

27

The kid shook his head. "That's not it," he said. "I found something." He glanced around, then reached suddenly for Deal's arm. Deal felt his wineglass slip, then go over with a crash on the bar.

The bartender whirled from the service station, glancing in the direction of the sound. Then his gaze landed on the kid at Deal's side.

"Sonofabitch!" Deal heard the bartender exclaim as he started toward them.

"I'll catch you later," the kid said, his eyes wide. He was off his stool and out the door of the lounge in an instant.

Deal turned back to the onrushing bartender, who had caught himself by the edge of the polished countertop. His wild gaze suggested he was ready to vault the bar and follow after the vanished kid.

"Little bastard!" the bartender said.

"What is it?" Deal said, shaking his head in wonder.

"I ought to break his neck," the bartender grumbled. He picked up a rag, began to mop at the spilled wine.

"It was an accident," Deal said, picking up the stem of his shattered glass.

"That's not it," the bartender said. "The little shit goes around trying to sell phony coins he claims came up from the *Atocha*." Deal gave him a nod to show he understood. The *Atocha* was the famed seventeenth-century wreck salvaged by Mel Fisher, diver and himself a legendary Keys character. In the twenty years since the ship's treasure trove had first been opened, a healthy underground trade had developed in the merchandising of its supposed artifacts, most of them worthless counterfeits.

"Last week I caught him palming tips off the tables," the bartender was saying. "I ever catch him, I'll pop his head like a pimple."

Or maybe throw a wall up around this island, Deal thought. He held his tongue though, and simply nodded.

"You okay?" the bartender asked, sweeping glass shards into a plastic bucket.

"I'm fine," Deal said.

"Better make sure you still got your wallet," the bartender said.

Deal put his hand to his hip in reflex, found the reassuring bulk still there.

"Sorry about the trouble," the bartender said. He already had another glass in place, was pouring it near brim-full. "On me," he added, nodding at the glass.

"No harm, no foul," Deal said.

The bartender gave him a nod of his own and moved off toward an impatient waitress at the service station. Deal glanced again out the door where the kid had disappeared, tapped his wallet idly, then checked to make sure his watch was still on his wrist.

Just another Key West moment, he told himself, though he was mildly curious as to just what scam he might have escaped. The kid had known who he was and what he did for a living. His rap was bound to have been interesting, at the very least.

Deal took a sip of his wine, noting that the clouds outside had gone steely. He checked his watch again and saw that it was past seven-thirty. Still no sign of Franklin Stone, and none of Russell Straight, come to think of it. Maybe he *had* managed to insult Russell. Maybe Russell had sent the kid into the bar to get some kind of a rise out of him.

Deal signaled to the bartender that he'd be back, then traced Russell's steps to the men's room, which he found empty. Deal glanced in the mirror and gave himself one of Driscoll's moves, "Who the hell knows." Then, since he was there, he turned to one of the urinals.

When he got back to the bar, he was surprised to note that the piano player had shifted into a lower gear, actually showing some restraint as he worked over the bridge of "When Sunny Gets Blue." Deal    29 wouldn't have thought a guy who could get so involved with "Greensleeves" would even know Sonny Stitt, much less play him halfway well, but then he realized that a singer in a cocktail gown stood now by the piano, counting time, waiting to come in. The piano player glanced up, she nodded, and that's when Deal realized that all the chatter on that side of the room had died away, and for good reason.

Her voice cut the room clearly, with a husky undertone that added authority to her perfect pitch. She was a bit too far away for him to get a clear look at her face, but there was an ease about her movements—the very opposite of those of her hardworking accompanist—that suggested she knew every nuance that her plaintive lyrics conveyed and then some. When she closed out the number, applause swept the room, and a guy in a lime-green sport coat actually stood up to clap.

As the clamor died down, Deal heard a cellular phone begin to beep. He glanced behind him, wondering who the oaf was, then realized it was his own phone chirping away in his pants pocket. He snatched the thing out, pushed the answer button, and made his way quickly out into the hallway that connected the lounge to the main part of the hotel.

"John Deal," he said as the lounge door swung shut behind him.

"This is Lisa," a woman's voice came on the other end. "Franklin—Mr. Stone—asked me to call. He's so sorry. Something came up. He'd like to reschedule."

"Again?" Deal said, trying to keep his voice calm.

"I know," Stone's secretary said. "He's truly very sorry."

Deal glanced down the hallway in front of him. Where the passage dead-ended at an intersection, a tall blond woman walked by, her tan legs flashing. Denise, he found himself thinking. Their cocktail waitress. She'd switched the parrot-print blouse for a T-shirt, though, and it had taken him a moment to recognize her.

Deal turned back to the phone, trying to bury his annoyance with Lisa's employer. "You're working kind of late, aren't you?"

"You know what they say," Stone's secretary chirped. "No rest for the wicked." She sounded a little too cheery to understand the meaning of the phrase, Deal thought.

"When are we talking about?" Deal said. "I've got to get back to Miami sometime."

"First thing in the morning," Lisa said. "Mr. Stone would like to meet you in the hotel restaurant for breakfast."

Deal mulled it over. Tomorrow was Friday, and he'd intended to get back to see how the site preparation on the Port Administration Offices project was going before things shut down for the weekend. That part of the work belonged to the prime contractor for the entire Free Trade complex that would cover forty acres on Carson Island, and strictly speaking, Deal was out of the loop until all the grading and fill work had been completed.

Nonetheless, if he didn't go broke first, he was going to be building a five-story office complex on top of fill that someone else had compacted. He was hardly going to take the word of a Metro Dade inspector that his pilings wouldn't sink straight to China. And there was also the matter of scheduling. Because of one delay and another on the massive undertaking, Deal's part of the job was already six weeks past the start date he'd planned for. If he couldn't get under way soon, his own subcontractors would bail out, taking other jobs.

On the other hand, the development that Franklin Stone wanted to talk about—though a year down the pipeline, at the least—was a project that promised to be of equal, if not greater, proportions where Deal's involvement was concerned.

If the two of them could meet in the morning, Deal could still be back in Miami before the close of business on Friday. It wasn't like he

31

was going to start back tonight, in any case. His room tab and Russell's were being picked up by Stone, after all. What was one more night on the cuff in a tropical dreamworld?

"All right," he said to Stone's secretary. "What's your boss's idea of 'first thing'?"

"Seven-thirty," Lisa answered promptly. "He likes to get a jump on the day."

"Tell him I'll be there," Deal said, and hung up.

When he got back inside the lounge, he found Russell Straight on a stool at the bar, the same one the kid had taken over earlier. Just as surprising was the glass of red wine in Russell's big hand. There was an open bottle on the granite bar top beside him, and Russell was twirling its cork between his thumb and forefinger.

"Not bad," Russell said, glancing over as Deal joined him. He lifted his glass in a salute, then raised the cork to his lips. He bit down, tore it in two with his teeth, and handed the pieces to Deal. "Seems pretty fresh to me," he said.

Deal stared down at the broken cork. "You *smell* the cork, Russell. To see if it might have gone vinegary."

Russell nodded. "That's what I'll do next time." He nodded at the bottle and a freshly poured goblet beside it. "Anyways, drink up."

Deal examined the label—a French cabernet, a dozen years old. He glanced at Russell again. "How'd you come to pick this?"

Russell shook his head. "*I* didn't. Somebody had it sent."

Deal scanned the room quickly. He didn't know anyone among the green-sport-coat crowd, that much was certain. He glanced at the bartender, who had his back to them, loading drinks onto a tray at the service station. "Who was it?" he asked Russell. "Stone?"

Russell shrugged. "Bartender didn't say who."

Deal stared at Russell in exasperation. "Where did you go, anyway?"

Russell gave him a thoughtful look. "I ran into our waitress out in the hall," he said. "She had a few things on her mind."

Deal's mind flashed to the glimpse he'd had of Denise a few minutes before, headed down the hallway in the opposite direction from their rooms. Whose T-shirt had she been wearing? he found himself wondering. He looked more closely at Russell Straight. "Are you putting me on?"

Russell stared at him, deadpan. "Put you on about what?"

"Jesus," Deal said. What had it been since Russell had disappeared, all of twenty minutes? "Did you say goodbye before she left?"

Russell stared at Deal for a moment, then turned away. He used his nearly empty glass to point across the open bar, toward the stage in the far corner of the room. "That woman over there singing is good," he said.

Deal started to say something, then broke off. He hadn't been interested in their waitress in the slightest, truly he hadn't, but *still* . . .

He gave up then, following Russell's gaze across the room. "*The wind is in from Africa,*" he heard. An old Joni Mitchell song. Janice had been a major fan, had played that song—"Carey"—to death.

There was something different about this cover of the piece, though. Slowed way down, stripped of the original's perky beat. This was dark, almost dirgelike, nothing the piano player had dreamed up, that much was certain.

"*. . . my fingernails are filthy, I got beach tar on my feet . . .*"

Deal wondered if it was the right resort-town imagery for the cocktail crowd, but they seemed as rapt as ever over there. "You ever hear this song?" he asked Russell, who turned and stared at him with an eyebrow raised.

"I didn't say it was my *thing,*" Russell told him. "I was just saying she's good."

33

".. . *let's have a round for these freaks,*" she sang, nodding at the audience in front of her, eliciting some chuckles, "*a round for these friends of mine . . .*"

She turned to her accompanist with the next:

".. . *another round for the bright red devil who keeps me in this tourist town . . .*"

It brought more chuckles from the crowd, but if the piano player in the lousy topper noticed, he didn't let on. He seemed more concerned with holding himself back from bursting into a ragtime tempo.

Something about the song had caught Deal by now, some nugget of sadness he'd never paid attention to when Janice had been in her Joni Mitchell phase. Maybe it was the arrangement, or maybe it was the circumstances of his life. Or maybe, like Russell Straight said, the woman doing the singing was just damned good.

She'd moved out into the spotlight that had been centered on the piano, and Deal could see that her hair was lighter than he'd thought. A brunette, sure, but one who'd been spending some time in the sun, picking up the kinds of highlights they couldn't quite manufacture in the salon. Sequins—just a few—on her clinging white sheath, its straps bright on her tanned shoulders, and more of a profile than he'd realized at first.

".. . *but let's not talk about fare-thee-wells,*" she sang, "*. . . the night is a starry dome . . .*"

Deal checked the view out the bank of windows beside him and discovered that the sky was indeed dark by now. He found himself thinking again of Janice, his estranged wife—off to some New Age retreat in Boulder, with a quick phone call to Deal as a fare-thee-well, their nine-year-old daughter, Isabel, parked for a week with Deal's sainted neighbor, Mrs. Suarez.

34   It seemed forever that he and Janice had been on the verge. And

suddenly—though he couldn't say why, not unless it was some combination of the song, the memories of that long-ago trip they'd taken, the very ions that drifted on a languid breeze through an island town in late summer—for whatever reason, he realized how much he had lost. Some part of him had become anesthetized to it, little by little over the years, he guessed. That's how you got used to what you no longer had.

"Did you say something?" Russell Straight asked, turning in his chair.

"I don't think so," Deal told him. "Maybe I had too much wine."

"Or not enough," Russell said.

Deal mustered a smile. "One or the other."

". . . *Carey, get out your cane and I'll put on some silver,*" she sang, "*you're a mean old Daddy, but I like you . . .*"

She closed the song with a reprise of the chorus and gave her audience a bow. The guy in the lime-green coat was up to applaud again, and even Russell Straight put down his glass to clap his thick hands together a couple of times.

"You didn't like it?" Russell said, glancing at Deal, who'd been staring, transfixed.

Deal looked down at his hands. Too late for clapping now. "Sure," he told Russell. "I was just thinking about something."

"Like, why did we come here in the first place?"

It brought Deal all the way back from his reverie. "Stone's secretary called while you were gone," he said, reaching for his wine. "We're rescheduled, for breakfast."

Russell nodded. "We'll see," he said, hardly convinced.

"Whatever," Deal said. "It's been good to get out of town for a while."

"It *is* an interesting place," Russell said, checking his watch.

"You want to get some dinner?" Deal asked. He wasn't really hungry, but it seemed the thing to do.

35

Russell's eyes hooded and he glanced away. "I guess not," he said.

Deal looked at him. He'd never known Russell Straight to pass up the prospect of food. "You're not hungry?"

Russell turned back. "That's not what I said."

It took Deal a moment, then the picture of their cocktail waitress, scurrying down the hall in a T-shirt, flitted through his mind again. He sighed and held up his hands. "Sorry," he said.

"Nothing to be sorry for," Russell said, stepping down from his stool. He clapped Deal on the shoulder. "You ought to finish that wine," he said. "It's too good to go to waste."

Deal nodded. "Have fun," he said to Russell.

"Catch you in the morning," Russell Straight said, and headed for the door.

**3**

RUSSELL HAD BEEN right about the wine, Deal thought—it was a lot smoother than whatever house brand he'd had earlier. And there wasn't any point in letting it go to waste. He'd thought briefly about carrying the bottle back to his room but had decided against it. The singer had finished her set and the piano player had vacated his place as well, but he was nursing hopes for her return.

In any case, he wasn't about to slink back to his room by himself. He was on vacation. In a tropical paradise. For the rest of the night, at least. He felt the stirrings of a pleasant buzz at the base of his brain. He could probably order something to eat at the bar. He could have more wine if he wanted to. Stay right here until closing time, stare out the windows at the pretty lights that dotted the harbor down below, call in a rollaway and sleep here if he wanted, by God.

"I was wondering when you were going to show up," came the voice at his side. Familiarity there. A trace of weariness.

Deal turned, caught a flash of tanned skin, white fabric, and blond-streaked hair, found his face a foot away from that of the woman who'd been singing up onstage. He'd thought she was attractive from a distance, but up close, it was more than that. He also realized that she was older than he'd assumed, close to his own age, maybe, but it only enhanced her allure. *Pretty,* he had thought earlier. But the word didn't seem adequate, now.

He broke off his stare, turning over his shoulder to see whom she'd been talking to. There was no one else at the bar, though; even the bartender was busy at the distant service station.

When he turned back, she was regarding him with a tolerant gaze. "How's the wine?" she asked.

Deal glanced at the bottle, then back at her, shaking his head. "*You* sent this? Maybe there was a mistake."

"I don't think so," she said. She picked up the bottle to check the label. "I told Magnum there to pick a decent bottle." She pointed at the bartender with the tip of the wine bottle.

"I must have missed something," Deal said, still wondering who she thought he was.

"That *is* a fair statement," she said.

He looked at her more closely. Something familiar in her eyes, some mischief, some knowingness he'd seen before.

"Do we know each other?" he managed.

"It's *Don't* we know each other," she told him, a smile playing at her lips. "I wouldn't use the line myself, but you ought to get it right."

Deal's mental Rolodex was in a whirl now, but nothing was coming up. The number of lounge singers he'd come to know in his life stood somewhere around zero, that much he was certain of. And anyone who looked as good as the woman in front of him . . . well, it didn't seem possible he would forget.

She turned to signal the waiter, who zipped right over with an empty wineglass. "Do you mind?" she asked.

*You bought it,* he almost said, but since the bartender was already pouring, he simply nodded.

She sipped the wine, then turned to him. "Not bad," she said. She held up her glass, waiting for Deal to meet it with his own.

So what might they be toasting? Deal wondered. His early onset of Alzheimer's? The fact that she had mistaken him for someone else?

But what did it really matter? he thought. A stunning woman in a clinging cocktail dress—one who could sing like the angels—had sent him a $100 bottle of wine and had dropped by to coach him on his pickup lines. He'd be anyone she wanted him to be, he thought, lifting his glass to hers. Judge Crater, Jimmy Hoffa, the Unknown Soldier, all rolled up in one.

"I always liked that about you," she said as she lowered her glass.

"What's that?" he said. What the hell, he was thinking. Go with wherever this was flowing. Besides, it was Key West. Things like this probably happened down here all the time.

"You have no guile," she said. She stared at him, and her expression turned more serious for a moment. "I'm glad that's stayed with you."

No guile? Deal wanted to blurt that she was obviously no mind reader, but something—*his guilelessness?*—kept him from it. He was trying to think of what he might say, in fact, when she held up her finger to quiet him.

"Let's try this," she said. She had another sip of her wine, then tossed her hair and glanced away toward the distant exposed beams of the ceiling for a moment. When she turned back, her expression had changed: The stare of the been-everywhere, seen-all-that chan-    39 teuse was gone, replaced by a plaintive gaze that could have been a teenager's.

"John," she said. "I don't want to do this, not really, but I have to." She tossed her hair again, but it was a different motion this time, a young girl's indication that she was wiping away all sorts of troubling thoughts. "I'm not going to college. I'm going to New York." Sadness, sacrifice, some petulance—all the drama a teenager might bring to such a momentous declaration.

Deal stared, realization slowly creeping in. It couldn't be the same girl in front of him, but then who else could it possibly be? How much wine had he had, anyway?

"Annie?" he said finally. It wasn't really a question.

There was the hint of a smile playing at her lips now, a flicker of delight in her gaze.

"I'll be damned," he said.

"You *do* have a good memory," she said. "A little short, maybe, but good."

"Annie Dodds."

"The very one," she said, lifting her glass again.

"You've changed," he said, his tongue still trying to catch up with his racing brain.

She lifted an eyebrow. "One would hope."

Deal glanced at the cocktail dress again, trying to reconcile the memory of a gangly young woman who had favored T-shirts and cut-offs with the vision before him now. "I mean *changed,*" he said.

"I remember you being a more adept conversationalist," she said.

Deal laughed. "You caught me off guard, that's all. It has been a few years."

"Still, I'm surprised," she said, pretending to pout. "We wrote for a long time after I left."

"Maybe you should have sent pictures," he said.

She glanced down at herself, then back at him. "I've put on weight, is that what you mean?"

"I'm not sure that's the right way to put it," he told her, keeping his gaze on hers.

She smiled. "Well, you look terrific."

Deal glanced at that form-fitting dress once more. "You look transformed," he said.

She seemed to think about it. "Twenty years will do that to you," she said finally.

There was a moment of silence then. Bar glasses tinkling in the background, conversation and laughter from the green-sport-coat crowd. Annie Dodds, Deal was thinking. His high-school sweetheart, the apple of his old man's eye as well. They'd gone steady from halfway through junior year until the summer after graduation. Until the night she'd told him she wouldn't be going up to Tallahassee to join him.

Smart, pretty, tomboy tough, his equal in so many ways. He'd liked her, looked up to her, was smitten with her, he supposed. When she'd told him she was throwing over her drama scholarship and going straight to New York City, he'd understood, could actually admire her gutsiness, even at the same time he'd felt the very bottom falling out of his stomach.

They had corresponded for a while: long letters from her, all about her acting classes, the parts she landed in this and that small production, the plays she'd seen, the bright and talented people she'd met; and Deal's more hastily written replies, squeezed in between classes that seemed beyond Einsteinian, and long sessions on the practice field, where he was learning another tough lesson: the difference between being a high-school standout as a linebacker/quarterback, and a drudge on a major college practice squad.

41

By the following spring, her letters had become more sporadic, and also by then, Deal had met Janice. He couldn't remember the last time he'd written Annie. He might have told her about Janice, but then again, she might have stopped writing to him by then. Her folks had moved from Miami by the time summer rolled around. Deal certainly had thought of Annie Dodds from time to time over the years, but he had not seen her after that night she'd delivered the news that she was going to New York City, not in twenty years.

"You sounded great up there," he said, nodding toward the stage.

"Thanks," she said, following his gaze. "I had a part in a play a couple of years back, as a cabaret singer. A guy in the audience had a club." She turned back to him, smiling. "He turned up backstage one night."

"Smart guy," Deal said.

"Maybe," she said, her gaze drifting for a moment. "Anyway," she told him, coming back, "the rest is history."

"Maybe it's the beginning of history," Deal said.

"So you're as sweet as ever, too," she said.

Deal felt his ears burning. "That Joni Mitchell song," he said, searching for something to say. "'Carey,' right?"

She nodded.

"My wife used to play it to death," he said. "But I never heard it sound like that."

She smiled and lifted her glass. "Your wife?"

"Janice." Deal nodded. "And I have a daughter who's nine. Isabel."

"Nice name," she said. "I'd always pictured you with a brood."

He shrugged. "I was an only child. Maybe that's how things work."

"Maybe," she said.

"How about you? Did you ever get married?"

She matched his shrug, then finished her wine. "I read about your

42

father," she said after a moment. "I was really sorry. I should have written."

"My old man liked you," he told her. "But it's okay. I appreciate your thoughts."

"And your mom?"

"She died shortly after. She just seemed to lose interest, you know?"

"He was something else, your father."

"Something else and a half," Deal said, finding he could smile about it. There had once been a grand and glorious DealCo Construction, as there had once been a larger-than-life Barton Deal who guided that firm. If Annie Dodds had read the papers at the time of his old man's death, she probably assumed that he had died a suicide, like most people still did. He thought about setting her straight, but it was a lot longer a story than they had time for.

"So where's your wife?" Annie asked brightly, glancing around the room.

Deal swirled the wine in his glass, wondering how to respond. "She's in Colorado," he said finally. "At an ashram."

Annie stared at him. "I detect a certain judgmental quality there."

"Ashrams aren't my thing," he said. He gave her another Driscoll shrug, about a hundred code words wrapped up in that one, he thought. "We're separated," he added finally. "It's a long story."

"It usually is," she said mildly.

He thought about going further, but decided against it. Why not ask her to sing "Melancholy Baby" while he was at it? "How about you?" he said. "You're doing well?"

She glanced at the bandstand, where the piano player was back, getting himself settled, cracking his fingers in front of him like a man with important business to take care of. "It's not the Rainbow Room," she said. When she turned back to him, she was smiling. "But I like my life."

She had a final sip of her wine and slid off her stool, pausing with her hand on his arm. "So, duty calls," she said. "Are you going to be in town for a while?"

"I go back to Miami in the morning," he said. "How long's your engagement here?"

She lifted an eyebrow. "It depends on how soon I kill the piano player," she said.

Deal laughed. "Maybe I could buy you a drink, after you're finished, I mean."

She stared at him for a moment before she answered. "I wish I could, John."

He felt the pressure of her hand on his arm and glanced down. Fine-boned fingers, a cool palm, its pressure light but steady. He was trying to remember the last time someone had touched him that way. "I wish you could, too," he said, as the piano player began an overloud introduction to "New York, New York."

"You're really going to sing that?" he asked, thinking of the soulful renditions he'd heard her do.

"We worked out a compromise," she said, glancing at the stage. "He gets to choose the lead number for every set, the rest is up to me." She leaned forward to give him a peck on the cheek. "It's good to see you," she told him.

"Thanks for the wine," he said, lifting his glass.

But she was already hurrying away toward the stage, gliding between the tables like smoke.

44

**4**

IN HIS DREAM, Deal was skiing down a steep mountainside in Colorado, though there was no snow on the rocky slope and a great empty chasm yawned ahead. Still, he was digging into the gravel-strewn mountainside with his ski poles, pushing hard for more speed, his nose keen to the rushing wind like a beagle's. He had just reached the lip of the chasm for liftoff and had glanced down to see snowy slopes far below, cheering crowds lining a landing area, when it occurred to him that he had never been on skis before, knew nothing of how he'd gotten involved in this competition, and, worst of all, had at least a thousand feet to fall.

"Parachute," he called, his voice lost in the thin mountain air, jerking frantically at his chest for a rip cord that wasn't there.

"Shoot who?" someone answered, and Deal came up from his dream like a drowning man clawing to the surface.

"Russell?" Deal said, blinking at the dim light that leaked in through his undraped windows. Russell Straight stood at the foot of his bed, wearing a fresh T-shirt and shorts, a cup of coffee in his hand. "How'd you get in here?" Deal asked, still blinking away his dream.

Russell gestured toward the door. "Your door was cracked open. I thought maybe you were already out front. Then I heard somebody hollerin' about a shooting."

Deal swung his legs over the bed and glanced blearily at his door. He hadn't even managed to get the door closed when he'd come in last night? He sat for a moment, gathering his thoughts. He'd stayed on at the bar for a bit, wondering if Annie might return, but the moment she'd finished the next set, she'd ducked behind the curtains of the stage and disappeared.

The piano player hammered on, but Deal was determined to enjoy his evening. He'd finished the wine, then hailed a cab to take him across the island to Louie's, where he'd had another bottle of red with a dinner he could only vaguely remember eating. He'd walked the mile or so back to the Pier House, though along the way it seemed there had been a rest stop at an open-air bar where a Joan Baez type was singing folk songs, a bit of mournful music laced with cognac, if Deal could remember correctly.

He glanced down, saw that he was still wearing his watch. "What time is it?" he said, glancing up at Russell.

Russell shook his head. "Time to go, if we're going to run," the big man said.

"Give me a minute," Deal said, feeling a twitch in one of his eyes. He pushed himself up toward the bathroom. He shook out three aspirins from the bottle in his travel kit and filled a glass from the tap. He was standing above the toilet, urinating and chugging the water at the same time, when it occurred to him that he'd formed a kind of perpetual-motion machine and might never be able to leave that spot. He put the glass down, flushed, and pulled on a pair of swimming trunks and a T-shirt he'd left on the back of the door.

"I brought you a coffee," Russell said when he came back out. He pointed to another cup on a table that sat by the windows. The room was on the second level of the hotel, affording a somewhat more distant view of the harbor channel, the water still steely at this hour, framed by palm fronds that waved gently in a post-dawn breeze.

"Thanks," Deal said. When he bent down to retrieve his sneakers from under the table, his head felt as if it had doubled in size. He sat in one of the chairs as he tied his laces, taking enough time for his skull to deflate.

"You had yourself a night," Russell observed.

Deal glanced up at him. "I read a good book, worked out at the gym, ate some yogurt and bean sprouts at the health food store. I was in bed by nine."

"That's what I did, too," Russell said, stretching his arms luxuriantly. He gave Deal a look. "You about ready?"

"As I'll ever be," Deal said, and pushed himself up from his chair.

"You ever find out who sent us the wine?" Russell asked, as they chugged along beneath a leafy canopy formed by banyan limbs.

"It remains a mystery," Deal heard himself say. They'd been at it for about twenty minutes now and his joints were finally starting to lubricate. He wasn't sure why he didn't want to talk about Annie with Russell. Maybe it was just that his breath was still a bit hard to come by.

Russell gave him a sidelong glance. "Was probably Oliver Stone, trying to apologize for standing you up again."

"*Franklin* Stone," Deal told him. He forced himself to pick up the pace, leading the way down a sidewalk flanking a broad, brick-paved boulevard lined on both sides by stately, turn-of-the-century manor houses—like a little stretch of Savannah right here in the Tropics, he thought. A couple of the houses had been turned into law offices, he noted, another was Hemingway's former home, now a museum. Others looked as though they might still be lived in.

"I know guys living on the street would pay for what you're sweating out," Russell observed, pounding up beside him. "I wouldn't get close to any open flames if I was you."

"You're a funny guy, Russell," Deal said, trying to keep his eyes fixed on an indeterminate spot just ahead. He was beginning to feel human again, the pounding at the base of his skull abating at last. He'd finally managed to rid himself of those final dream images—tumbling head over heels, an ever-faster spiral of doom toward the frozen Colorado slopes below—but those scenes had been replaced by an equally disconcerting set of images that alternated between what Russell Straight must have been doing with their cocktail waitress last night and Deal's speculations on what Annie Dodds might look like slipping out of that cocktail dress she'd been painted into.

Once, when they'd been dating, he'd gone to Annie's house while her parents were off at a party. They'd made popcorn, sneaked a couple of beers from the bar refrigerator, watched television on the family room couch, and necked, until finally Annie had pulled away, given him an oddly solemn look, then led him up to her room.

She'd undressed by the moonlight that fell through her open blinds, guided Deal's hands to her luminous breasts . . . and then, the sound of a motor in the driveway just below had put an end to everything. They'd barely made it back downstairs in time to stash the beer bottles and arrange themselves chastely on the couch before her folks had come in—only the fact that her parents had been arguing and were too distracted to notice much had saved them, Deal thought.

48

And he still couldn't say whether his heart had been pounding more from the fear of their near-escape or the prospect of what had been about to happen between Annie and himself. He'd been a virgin at the time, and had assumed Annie was as well. But maybe that was just his guileless nature, Deal thought, remembering what she'd said to him last night.

Twenty years since this woman had seen him last, what's the first thing she remembers about him? All that had happened to him these past few years, the things he'd had to do . . . and he still came off *guileless*? Maybe he needed an image consultant, he thought, glancing at Russell Straight, who jogged silently alongside him.

There came a strange groaning sound from somewhere in front of them, and Deal swiveled his gaze back to their route. A few yards up the street, an ancient Pinto labored to a stop at the curb, its door swinging open at their approach.

"Yo, my man," he heard a familiar voice pipe up.

It was the kid who'd approached him at the Pier House emerging from the driver's seat, his hand raised to hail them. The Pinto's engine was hiccuping with preignition, as if it were threatening to bolt without its owner. Russell gave the kid a curious look, but Deal only increased his pace.

He heard scuffling footsteps behind them, then the kid's breathless voice swirling in their wake. "You guys like to work out, too, huh? This is my selfsame route. How 'bout that?"

Deal glanced over his shoulder. Despite the heat and humdity, the kid wore a long-sleeved sweatshirt with FUBU stenciled in red across its chest, along with a pair of oversized gym shorts that would have been baggy on Russell Straight. There was a golf visor jammed upside down and sideways atop his Afro, the bill angled skyward. The kid's skinny legs pumped furiously in an effort to catch up, and Deal stared incredulously at what was on his feet: dark socks reaching halfway up his calves, along with a pair of woven-leather Italian loafers, their smooth soles slipping against the pavement with every step.

"You know this guy?" Russell said, glancing at Deal.

"We've met," Deal said. He didn't want to waste breath on the extended version.

"Sorry I had to take off all sudden like that," the kid was saying, pounding at their heels now.

Deal thought of several possible responses, but delivered none.

"How you doin', bro?" the kid added toward Russell.

"Who wants to know?" Russell said. His expression suggested grave suspicion.

"I saw you guys leaving the hotel," the kid said, moving abreast of Deal now. They were less than fifty yards from where the Pinto still chugged and jerked at curbside, but already the kid seemed winded. "I was hoping we could talk someplace private."

Deal shook his head, an awkward movement while running. "I don't need any gold coins," Deal said.

"Hey, it's not about that, man," the kid said, his mouth popping for air now.

"He's got a watch, too," Russell Straight muttered. "You better breeze on, cool breeze."

"Just listen up for a second," the kid said. He reached for Deal's arm, as he had the day before, and Deal pushed his hand away. The move threw the kid off balance, his shoes sliding in a sandy patch where the pavement curved out of the residential section and into a wooded area. The kid's legs tangled, then went out from under him. He flew over the curb and landed in a tangle of bougainvillea hedge marking someone's property line.

"Ow. Shit! Motherfucker!"

Deal glanced over his shoulder, a little guilty at the sight of the kid trying to extricate himself from the clutches of the thorny bush. In truth, he hadn't meant to hurt him. "Maybe we ought to help," he said to Russell, ready to turn back.

"Are you kidding?" Russell said. "Leave him in the brier patch where he belongs."

Deal nodded uncertainly, then gave one last backward glance. The kid was out of the bushes now, panting on his hands and knees, watching like a forlorn hound as Deal and Russell moved around the curve of the tree-lined road and out of sight. Deal pointed ahead, where a sign marked a bike trail through a thick stand of Australian pines. They'd taken the trail the day before and found that it dumped out onto a stretch of road paralleling a section of public beach for a bit before circling them back toward the Pier House.

"I saw the dude outside the hotel this morning," Russell offered after a bit of quiet pounding along the narrow path. "I didn't think much of it at the time."

Deal glanced over. "Why would you?"

Russell lifted his brows. "A man needs to keep his eyes open," he said. "You never know what might happen."

Deal nodded. He might have dismissed it as an ex-inmate's paranoia except for his own sorry experiences. Truth be told, he should probably have become a bit more paranoid himself. Maybe that was the trouble with living in paradise, he thought, glancing through a screen of pines toward the palm-lined beach ahead of them. Wallow in all this beauty every day of your life, you tend to forget what might lurk in the nooks and crannies, or what crawls out once the sun goes down.

"What's all this about gold coins, anyway?" Russell asked, cutting into his thoughts.

Deal sighed. "The guy came on to me in the bar last night," he said, "while you were gone."

51

Russell looked over to see if there was any underlying message there.

"The bartender told me the kid's got a racket selling phony coins from this old Spanish shipwreck," Deal said. "He chased the kid off before he could get into it."

"Buried treasure, huh? That boy needs to get a better racket."

Deal turned his hands up in a "who knows?" gesture as he plowed on. He put on a burst that led the way out of the pines and onto the gravel shoulder of the highway, flushing a group of scavenging gulls and sending them squawking and wheeling into the sky.

The early breeze off the ocean, blocked beneath the canopy of the pines, bathed him now in a blend of intoxicating scents—salt spray, stranded seaweed, sulfur, fish parts, and gull droppings, who knew what all. It was the Gulf Stream flowing just off these shores, and like Hemingway said, you could find bits and pieces of every aspect of civilization carried along in that boiling current. The Stream was actually a mighty, mid-ocean river that ran from South America through the Caribbean, carrying its warm waters all the way to the North Atlantic, where its heat softened the stern European climate and made the British Isles habitable.

He turned his face square into the breeze and lengthened his stride, the rhythm of the run and the rush of the wind threatening to lift him out of his physical self. His earliest memories were those of the beach and staring out over these waters in permanent wonder. Poking along the ragged mangrove inlets in his dinghy, out on the swells in the *Miss Miami Priss* whenever his old man stole a day from the business for time on the bounding main.

The smells he breathed then, as now, were those of promise and adventure. Pirate ships and plunder. Sailfish, swordfish, and marlin. Distant ports of call.

*The wind is in from Africa,* he thought. Dear God. The night that Annie had told him she was deserting him, and Florida, for New York City, he'd driven out to the end of the road on Key Biscayne in a daze. He'd pulled his old man's Chrysler half off the side of the road, climbed over the barricade at the entrance to the state park, and made his way to the beach, where he stayed until morning, watching the endless sweep of the lighthouse beacon and staring out to sea, wondering how anyone might leave such a world behind.

He'd bought into it all as a kid. Atlantis. The Bermuda Triangle. Sunken treasure. Hell, he thought, a part of him still did. He shouldn't have been so hard on the kid who wanted to sell him stolen gold. Yo-ho-ho and a bottle of rum. He could have pieces of eight jingling in his pockets right now.

"You trying to make this a macho thing?" Russell called, breathing heavily as he came up on Deal's right.

Deal blinked, bringing himself back into his body. He gave Russell an apologetic look and eased off a bit. "Just got carried away, I guess."

They were well down the beach road now, he saw, clipping along the island's southeastward stretch of beach, a lonely area where an inland marsh had kept development at bay for nearly two centuries. The sun was struggling up behind a bank of clouds on the eastern horizon, a dull orb that cast a dim glow on the fringes of the thick stand of mangroves that still claimed the soggy ground.

Deal glanced across the deserted roadway toward the overgrown salt marsh, trying to imagine the string of upscale condominiums that Franklin Stone hoped to build there. Stone had already turned the former naval station downtown, where Harry Truman once kept his "Little White House," into a sprawling, gated community—dubbed Truman Town by the locals—from which he'd made a fortune.

Stone had bulldozed the nondescript wooden naval complex flat, then platted its forty-five shady acres with a gridwork of streets where he built several hundred condominiums and predesigned saltbox-style homes, all of it as neat and orderly as a town Disney might have built. In the dozen years that had passed, what had once seemed like astronomical asking prices for the residences inside the Truman gates were now commonplace. Now Stone proposed to turn the last undeveloped section of the island into another residential community, one that would dwarf the Truman project in both size and asking prices of the domiciles within.

"That's where we're going to work, huh?" said Russell Straight, who was at his left shoulder, on the ocean side now.

Deal glanced at his jogging partner. "I'm just down here to talk," he said.

"Uh-huh," Russell said. "You saying you'd hesitate one second if the man offered you the job?"

"It's a complicated project," Deal told him. "And I still haven't seen any numbers."

"Whatever the number is, gonna be a big one," Russell answered.

"Stone's still got some problems to iron out with the site," Deal said, pointing across the road. "Take a look."

They had drawn abreast of a section of the marsh that was flanked by a tall chain-link fence. A battered sign dangled from a set of padlocked gates that looked like they'd been rammed inward by a four-by-four. The salt-eaten sign was bent and dinged, but the lettering on its bottom half was still legible: WILDLIFE REFUGE, it read. NO VEHICLES.

"What's that?" Russell said.

"One of Stone's problems," Deal said. "Marshland the city declared surplus. They signed it over to Stone to get it on the tax rolls." He paused for breath, glancing at the area again. "Some local environmentalists dug up records suggesting the state still holds title. They've petitioned to block the transfer of the land."

"Sounds like a big problem to me," Russell said.

Deal would have shrugged, but it was a difficult maneuver while jogging. "Stone has as much clout in Tallahassee as he does down here," he told Russell. "He's the kind of guy who gets what he wants."

"Even so," Russell said, "you try to go to work, you could end up peeling the tree-huggers off your 'dozer blades every day."

"My point exactly," Deal said. The sun had broken through the clouds at last, and he had to squint when he turned toward Russell. "When Stone called me, he said he'd redesigned the project to incorporate the refuge into his site plan. He says the environmentalists are ready to drop their objections."

"That'd be a first," Russell said.

"Like I told you," Deal said, "I just came down to talk. Stone has a lot of interests. If this project doesn't work out, there might be others down the line."

"Every one of them with a problem?"

Deal wiped sweat from his eyes with the back of his hand, suffering Russell's observation in silence. How could he argue, anyway? Franklin Stone was a man cut from the same cloth as his own father: a larger-than-life figure who'd made a fortune by the force of his garrulous, brook-no-obstacles, take-no-prisoners personality.

The two had worked together once, back in the salad days of DealCo, when Stone had come to Miami to broker a deal for a group of Colombian businessmen who had discovered the need to build a banking tower amidst the other such skyscraping institutions on Brickell Boulevard. Being in the same room with Stone and his father had been an adventure, like climbing into a stable where a couple of barrel-chested thor-

55

oughbreds had somehow gotten quartered together—there often seemed barely enough air for anyone else to breathe, not to mention the possibility of being inadvertently crushed when one of the titans reared. Stone had tried his best to hand his father the short end of the project's stick, and Barton Deal had smiled and demanded his due. In the end, both men had profited handsomely, with most of the Colombians dead or imprisoned by the time the job was finished.

Franklin Stone was notorious then, but Deal had seen him work from the inside and believed he knew enough to back away if this was one of Stone's more suspect propositions. And he'd already done some checking of his own. The day he'd gotten the summons from Stone, he'd called Rusty Malloy, an old college friend and Key West attorney who kept his ear attuned to the local goings-on.

What the coconut telegraph had assured him, Rusty reported, was that the city was determined to see the parcel developed, if not by Stone, then by someone else. The so-called wildlife refuge was blighted by petrochemical runoff from the nearby airport, nothing more than a muddy slough that probably contributed more harm to the ecosystem than good. If Deal could grab a piece of the action and keep Stone from taking a piece of his backside in the bargain, Rusty assured him, then by all means he should.

Deal might have passed along some truncated version of all this to his jogging partner, but as he turned, something caught his eye. A hundred yards or so up the lonely road, a police cruiser had pulled someone off to the shoulder. Deal hadn't heard any siren, but a bank of cumulus clouds had dimmed the early sun again, and the whirl of blue and red flashers was clear, even at this distance. The door to the cruiser had opened, though the patrolman was not in sight. Down the windswept beach, Deal heard what might have been a command being barked through a grill-mounted speaker to the driver of the car.

A few more strides brought the scene into sharper focus, and Deal felt himself groan inwardly. "Guess who?" he said to Russell.

Russell squinted down the beach road until he recognized the unmistakable silhouette of the Pinto as well. "Sonofabitch," Russell said, his jaw clenching in reflex.

And Deal knew he wasn't referring to the annoying kid who'd been shadowing them, either. Russell had spent a dozen years in a Georgia penitentiary on a charge that in all likelihood would not have merited a white man a slap on the wrist. Understandably, he was no fan of the American justice system, even at its most mundane levels.

"That boy can't stay away from trouble," Russell said, glaring at the sight before them.

They were close enough now to be sure: It was the kid all right, him in his out-of-date Afro climbing out of his car, turning as the patrolman, a big man in blue uniform shirt and black trousers bloused at his boot tops, advanced. The patrolman—who would be a Monroe County sheriff's deputy, Deal realized—was capless, carrying what looked like a nightstick with a pistol grip crooked in his arm. He called out something and the kid turned and put his hands atop the rusted-out Pinto that Deal could now see had probably been yellow in one of its former lives.

"If they're black, then brace 'em," Russell muttered at Deal's side.

"Take it easy . . ." Deal began, then caught sight of something out of the corner of his eye.

The deputy had shouted another command and now was running toward the Pinto where the kid still leaned, unmoving. The deputy shouted again, then kicked the legs out from under the kid, bouncing off the car himself with the force of his charge. The kid hit the ground and rolled across the shoulder of the road, trying to scramble to his feet.

The deputy, apparently unaware of the approach of Deal and Rus- 57 sell, swung his riot stick in a backhanded arc, and Deal heard the crack echo in the still air. The kid caught the blow across his cheek and flipped over onto his back.

"Motherfucker," Deal heard at his side, and then Russell Straight was pounding past him, his legs pistoning, gravel flying backward from the treads of his running shoes.

"Russell . . ." Deal called, kicking into high gear after him.

They were both bearing down on the Pinto now. The kid was still on his back, his arms crossed in front of his face to ward off the repeated blows of the deputy's nightstick. At the same time the kid was using his feet, trying to shove himself backward through the loose gravel. It looked like he was trying to drive himself under the Pinto, where he'd be safe from the rain of blows, Deal thought, but the car was slung too close to the ground for that.

"Hey!" Deal cried as he raced toward the scene, his mind whirling.

Could the kid have pulled a weapon they couldn't see? Is that what had set the deputy off? But if that were so, then why would he be trying so hard to get away? And if the kid had lost his gun or knife—if he'd had one—why was the deputy *still* slamming his riot stick down on the kid's arms and legs? Every blow was murderous, accompanied by the sharp crack of wood on bone, along with grunts and the cries of pain.

The kid had scrunched himself into the crease between the ground and the rocker panel of the Pinto now, his arms pulled tight atop his bushy head. Deal heard a thud as the deputy saw his opening and drove his stick hard against the kid's unprotected ribs. The kid groaned as his breath left him and clutched his gut in pain. It was exactly what the deputy had in mind, Deal saw, as the beefy man steadied himself for a mighty swing at the kid's unprotected head.

It was a blow that might have killed him, but at the last instant the kid managed to duck away, and the tip of the heavy club slammed into sheet metal instead of bone. There was a splintering sound and the business end of the riot stick sheared from its handle. It rebounded across the asphalt, an ebony fragment spinning across Deal's path like some angry creature from a dream.

If the deputy was aware of their approach, he was far past caring, Deal saw. The big man, his neck glowing red now, tossed the useless stem of the riot stick aside and, with his hands braced at the Pinto's roof, began to kick the kid, who was wedged up against the car at his feet, each blow measured, each brutal enough to be deadly. Whatever the kid had said, done, held, snorted, or sold, it didn't matter, Deal thought. A few minutes ago, all the kid had wanted to do was sell him some phony gold. Now, there was a sheriff's deputy who'd come along to kill him, here at the side of the road.

Meantime, the kid had gone limp. Maybe he was unconscious, or maybe he'd simply given up, Deal thought as he ran. The deputy had zeroed in on the kid's head again, his heavy boot drawn back for the *coup de grâce.*

"Stop," Deal cried, but the deputy seemed not to have heard. He was about to drive the toe of his boot into the kid's temple when Russell Straight arrived, just ahead of Deal, driving his shoulder squarely into the deputy's kidneys.

The deputy's breath left him in a gasp, and he went down face forward against the rear passenger glass of the Pinto. He bounced backward like he was made of rubber, a white star blossomed now on the shattered glass.

Russell, too enraged to hold anything back during his charge, glanced off the deputy's backside and hit the rear quarter panel of the Pinto headfirst, right behind the gas tank door. The sheet metal buckled inward with a pop, and Russell staggered backward, his eyes as glassy as a bull popped in the skull at a slaughterhouse. He tottered for

59

a moment, then sank to the ground in a sitting position, a trickle of blood draining from one nostril. He was perched on the safety line at the verge of the asphalt road, his legs splayed, his hands dangling at his lap, his eyes sightless, and for a moment Deal wondered if he might have snapped his neck.

The deputy was bleary-eyed himself, but still functioning. He was on his hands and knees, the top of his close-cut scalp glowing pink as he scrabbled for his holstered firearm.

He'd managed to pull his weapon free and was swinging it toward Russell when Deal reached him, kicking with everything he had toward the deputy's outstretched hand. Deal felt small bones give as the toe of his running shoe met the back of the deputy's hand. There was a blast from the pistol as it flew free, and a cry that Deal realized came from the deputy's throat.

He felt arms encircle his legs, and in the next instant he was going down, his breath leaving him as he bounced heavily off the asphalt. He lay motionless for a second or two, his nose an inch from the bottoms of Russell's running shoes. He heard sirens wailing from somewhere and realized that the deputy had probably called for backup before he'd confronted the Pinto's driver.

Deal wanted to believe it was the cavalry on the way to a rescue, but reminded himself that he was one of the Indians right now. He smelled a mixture of oil and tar and dust, and sensed an acrid taste in his mouth that was probably blood. For an instant he wondered if he'd been shot, but as breath began to pulse back into him, he discounted the thought. He'd bitten his tongue as he fell, that was all.

He felt a hand slam against his back, snatching a wad of his T-shirt into a ball. A powerful punch landed at his kidneys, another at his ribs. The deputy was on his knees now, pulling Deal up to get a clear shot at his jaw with one of his boulder-sized fists.

It might have been all over if the deputy had managed to land that punch, but in the next moment Deal saw a pair of skinny arms fold around the deputy's neck from behind. The deputy reared back, then bellowed in pain as the kid clamped his teeth down on the flesh of his ear.

The deputy thrashed in pain, swinging with his free hand to try to dislodge the kid on his back without giving up his hold on Deal. One of the deputy's blind punches finally landed, and the kid went sprawling backward, his hand thrown to his nose.

For a moment, the deputy was arched backward, his hand clamped over his ear, his hold on Deal loosened enough for Deal to get his knees beneath him, his palms braced against the ground. He glanced backward beneath his arm, saw blood trickling down the side of the deputy's rage-swollen neck, and saw as well what would be his own target. He was still gasping for breath, and operating at about three-quarters steam, but for what he had in mind the blow would be plenty.

Deal drove his fist back, hammering it between the deputy's legs with all the force he could muster. The deputy went rigid, groaning like he'd been stuck with a cattle prod. He lost his grip on Deal's shirt at last and went over on his side, gasping, clutching at his groin, his face gone pasty white.

Deal struggled to his feet, ignoring the fire in his ribs and the small of his back. Russell Straight glanced woozily up at him from where he still sat at the shoulder of the road, and Deal stuck out a hand to help him up.

A few minutes ago, he thought, the two of them had been enjoying a jog alongside a beach in paradise. Now there was a sheriff's deputy writhing in the gravel at his feet, and, judging by the growing clamor of sirens, plenty more of his kind on the way. Maybe they could simply jog away, pretend that none of this had happened.

At that same moment, a pair of Monroe County cruisers rounded a curve down the beach road, both locked in a power slide that might have been choreographed for film, their flashers popping, their engines gathering strength as they hurtled down the straightaway toward the scene.

Russell gazed down at the still-gasping deputy. "Looks like he fell on his nightstick," he observed, a smile playing at his lips.

"We are in deep shit," Deal said, glancing at the onrushing cruisers.

"Shots fired, officer down, couple of black dudes on the scene, I'd say so," Russell replied mildly.

Deal glanced down at the kid, who was pulling himself up by the Pinto's door handle. The kid glanced at the groaning deputy, then back at Deal, speechless with fright. His face was dust-covered, there was a knot on his forehead, and one of his shirtsleeves was ripped clean at the shoulder. On the other hand, Deal didn't see any blood.

Deal glanced at the onrushing squad cars, then back at Russell. "You're experienced with this sort of thing," Deal said, calling above the sound of the sirens. "You have any ideas?"

Russell gave him a silent look, then turned to lean against the Pinto, spreading his legs wide. He glanced at the kid in the Afro. "Assume the position, fuckhead," he said. When the kid opened his mouth to say something, Russell cut him off. "And shut the fuck up."

The kid did as he was told. Russell glanced over his shoulder at Deal, then. "You're the boss," he said. "*You* do the talking."

And then the wailing cruisers were upon them.

# 5

**"WHAT HAPPENED THERE?"** Rusty Malloy asked, pointing at the bruise above Deal's right eye.

Deal stared back for a moment. He was alone with the attorney in an interrogation area in the sheriff's substation, a sterile room with one high, barred window, a battered table fastened firmly to the linoleum-tiled floor by steel L-brackets, and a couple of metal chairs that looked like they could withstand nuclear attack. A deputy had locked the door behind Malloy, but was probably at the watch just outside, Deal thought.

"If you asked the arresting officers," he said to Rusty finally, "they'd probably tell you I bumped my head getting into the back of the cruiser."

"Is that what happened?" Rusty persisted.

Deal wondered which shrug of Driscoll's to use. "In a manner of speaking," he said. He could have added that one of the deputies was holding him by the hair at the time, and that he'd somehow "bumped" into the top of the door frame two or three times while being ushered into the cruiser, but he didn't see the point. Russell Straight and the poor kid they'd tried to help had fared far worse, that much Deal was sure of.

"Assault on a police officer, interference with an officer during the performance of his duty, resisting arrest . . ." Malloy shook his head. "They've got a pretty long laundry list, Johnny."

"What were we supposed to do, let him kill that poor kid?"

Malloy shrugged. "Officer Conrad says that 'poor kid' came after him with a knife—"

"Bullshit," Deal said. Still, a little worm of doubt had crept into his brain. *Had* there been a knife? What if he and Russell had just been too far away to see it? Still, there hadn't been any knife in the kid's hand by the time he and Russell had made it to the scene. The deputy had been about to kick the kid to death, he was certain of that much.

"The kid's a known offender—drug dealing, petty theft, public intoxication . . ." Malloy ticked the charges off as if they were simply the tip of a large iceberg. "He was driving without a license, with expired plates, maybe the car was stolen, too. The cops are still trying to run the VIN down."

"Expired plates? That a capital offense down here?"

"Forget that little grifter," Malloy said, waving his hand impatiently. "You've got plenty of problems of your own."

"How's Russell?" Deal said sullenly. "I expect he bumped his head a few times, too."

"Russell's fine," Malloy said, nodding over his shoulder. "They've got him in a holding cell down the hall. I spoke to him briefly, told him to keep his mouth shut until we had a chance to talk."

"Russell's done time," Deal said. "You don't need to tell him how to behave."

"He's a convicted felon?" Malloy said, staring in disbelief. "What else do I need to know?"

"That we did exactly what anybody else would have done," Deal said. "That asshole cop was ready to kill that kid. All we did was stop him."

"That's not the way Deputy Conrad puts it," Malloy said.

"He was ready to blow Russell away, too," Deal said. "I kicked his gun away just in time."

"Conrad says he drew his gun and ordered Russell to cease and desist. That's when you blindsided him."

"Like hell," Deal said. "Did he tell you I had a knife, too? Or maybe it was a two-headed axe I came after him with."

"They did find a knife on your person, John."

Deal stared at Malloy in disbelief. "My Swiss Army knife?" he asked, incredulous. "The one with the two inch blade, the tweezers, and the nail file?"

Malloy shrugged. "No one's making a big thing about your Swiss Army knife," he said. "I'm just trying to make a point."

"Look," Deal said, "I appreciate your coming down here, Rusty, but maybe I need to talk to somebody who's on my side."

"I *am* on your side," Malloy said testily. "I just want to be sure I understand exactly what happened out there. If you expect me to help, I need the facts."

Deal took a deep breath. "Maybe Russell got a little excited," he told Malloy, "but if you'd been there, you'd have probably done the same."

"I doubt it," Malloy said. "I might have *said* something, but assault is hardly my style—"

"It wasn't the time for conversation," Deal said. "Russell tackled him just as he was about to put the kid's lights out. The cop went ass over teakettle, then came up with his pistol in his hand, ready to blow Russell away. No cease, no desist. Just *sayonara*."

"And that's when you kicked the gun out of his hand?"

Deal nodded. "Whereupon Deputy Conrad came after me and made it clear that it was his intention to clean my clock."

"Which is when you kicked him in the balls?"

"*Punched* him in the balls," Deal said. He decided to leave out the part about the kid sinking his teeth into Conrad's ear. Besides, he could still hear the groan the surprised deputy had made. The memory cheered him slightly. Maybe it would keep him going during his time on the chain gang, he thought.

"Whatever," Malloy said, making a note on a pad he'd produced from his coat pocket.

"I'd have kicked him if I could have," Deal added, "but the sonofabitch was sitting on my back."

Malloy seemed to stifle a smile. "Conrad considers himself a major badass, that's what I picked up in the squad room. I get the feeling a few of his peers are kind of enjoying the way he's walking right now."

"He's not going horseback riding anytime soon."

"Nor you either," Malloy said. "Conrad may be a dirtbag, John, but he is also a cop."

"It's the word of three people against one," Deal said. "Doesn't that count for anything?"

Malloy did smile at that one. "It counts for something. But alas and alack, one of you is a habitual offender and another is a felon, as I have just been informed. Not to mention that two of your party also happen to be other than white—you will forgive any imputation of racism, of course. And then there's the fact that both you and Russell hail from outside the Conch Republic and are accused of committing mayhem upon one of the officers deputized to protect that entity from attack by foreign parties." Malloy stopped and gave him a baleful look. "You're an intelligent person, John. How's all that stack up in your eyes?"

"It's the twenty-first century," Deal said. "You're talking like we're in Bull Connor, Alabama."

"It's not Alabama," Malloy said. "But it *is* Key West."

There was a commotion in the hallway outside then, and the sound of a key turning in the lock. The two of them looked up as the door swung open and a dapper-looking man hurried in with a look of concern on his tanned and handsome face. He was wearing linen slacks, a dark T-shirt, and a raw silk jacket that draped him like he'd been born to the garment. His swept-back hair was silver, but his features suggested that was an anomaly. Franklin Stone was in his sixties, Deal knew, but he exuded a certain agelessness.

"Counselor," Stone said when he saw Malloy.

"Mr. Stone," Malloy replied, giving Stone a respectful nod.

Stone, meantime, had turned to Deal. "Johnny-boy," he said, extending his hand as though they were meeting unawares. "What the hell's happened to your face?"

Deal glanced at the sullen deputy who'd followed Stone into the room. "My hammer slipped," he told Stone.

Stone shot the deputy a look of his own, then turned back to Deal, managing something of a laugh. "Well, let's get you out of here, shall we? I'm sure you'd like to get cleaned up."

Deal stared at Stone for a moment, then glanced at Rusty Malloy. "I'm not sure it's that simple, Mr. Stone," Malloy began.

"What on earth are you talking about?" Stone said. "It's all taken care of. A regrettable misunderstanding. Isn't that right, Deputy?"

The deputy behind Stone looked as if a furry animal had slipped suddenly into his shorts. "That's right," the deputy said to Malloy, his tone carefully measured. "He's free to go."

67

Deal stared suspiciously at Stone. "How about Russell?"

"Your sidekick?" Stone said. "He's already outside in my car, waiting."

Malloy rolled his eyes. "Well, you heard what the man said. Let's take our leave."

Stone nodded and put his hand on Deal's shoulder. Malloy snatched up the pad he'd been jotting notes on and started for the door. Deal put his own hand on the lawyer's sleeve. "How about the kid? The one we tried to keep from getting killed."

Malloy turned in astonishment. "John . . ."

"Dequarius Noyes." Franklin Stone shook his distinguished head patiently. "That boy's nothing but trouble."

Deal shot a glance at the silent deputy. "I don't want him left here, Mr. Stone. Not after what I saw this morning."

Stone's eyes flashed, and he seemed about to say something. Then he swallowed whatever it was and turned to the deputy. "What's he charged with, Peters?"

Peters looked as if the animal burrowing around in his shorts had clamped its teeth down hard on something tender. "Driving with an expired license," he said grudgingly. "His plates had lapsed and he couldn't produce a vehicle registration."

"No assault, no resisting arrest?" Stone's nostrils flared.

Peters shrugged. "We could talk to Conrad again."

"That's not what I asked you," Stone thundered.

Peters threw up his hands in surrender.

"Let him go," Stone said.

"Well, the sheriff might—"

"I said to let him go. I'll take personal responsibility." Stone's eyes were daggerlike now.

"If you say so," the deputy said.

"I'll speak to the sheriff," Stone said. "Noyes isn't running off anywhere."

Deputy Peters gave Deal a last murderous glance, then turned and went off down the hall. "Get that dickhead out of his cell," Deal heard him call to someone. "He's skatin' again."

"I appreciate it," Deal said, turning to Stone.

"All in the interest of justice, Johnny-boy," Stone said. He moved to put an arm around Deal's shoulders, guiding him out of the interrogation room. "Now come on, we've got more important matters to attend to."

**6**

"**WHAT DID HAPPEN** to your face, anyway?" Russell Straight asked Deal. They were standing on a shaded deck at the back of Stone's home, which had turned out to be one of the imposing antebellum mansions the two of them had jogged past a few hours earlier, practically across the street from the Hemingway home.

"Cut myself shaving," Deal said, putting a hand to a lump on his forehead. At least he'd been able to wash the grit out of the scrapes and scratches, he thought. Stone's driver, Balart, a tall, wiry-looking Hispanic in his fifties, had taken them by limousine to the hotel and waited while they'd changed and showered, then delivered them back to the house.

"Funny," Russell said. "Happened to me, too." His knuckle absently traced a welt on one of his cheekbones.

Deal found himself musing that it had been a while since he'd been in a limo. He wondered if Russell ever had. He glanced at his watch, noting that it was nearly three o'clock. Time flies when you're having fun, as his father might have said. So much for making it up to Miami in time to check on the progress of the port job.

A houseboy in shorts and a flowered shirt similar to those of the Pier House staff approached, a tray of drinks in his hand. Deal took the Myers's and Coke, Russell the beer. The houseboy took what looked like a glass of seltzer off to the other end of the deck, where Stone had excused himself to take a phone call.

"What about your wine diet?" Russell asked.

"It's Friday," Deal said. "You get to do whatever the hell you want on Fridays."

Russell stared at him for a minute. "You okay?"

Deal gave him a look, then turned his gaze out to sea. "I'm fine," he said. Nothing a little ocean-gazing couldn't cure, anyway.

And it was a fine view from the deck Stone had built out over the shallows here, one hundred and eighty degrees of seascape, over waters that were a patchwork of blue and turquoise and cobalt and steel, depending on whether the bottom was hip-deep or full-fathom five, or something in between.

One of the features that made the Keys special, he thought. The whole chain of islands that stretched down from the mainland a hundred miles or so to where he stood now weren't really islands—the type that poke up in the middle of a nowhere ocean, anyway—but a series of reefs jutting barely out of the sea, and surrounded by neighboring formations that fell away gradually toward the deeps. The varying bottom depths close to shore were what made for that interesting array of colors out there, one of the many things that distinguished the place.

Another feature, Deal thought, was the calm that usually descended upon him in the Keys, just about the time he crossed Jewfish Creek and reached Key Largo, the northernmost in the chain. He'd always assumed it was a psychological phenomenon, simple hooky-playing relief that anyone might feel upon crossing the boundary between the regular world and the gateway to Margaritaville. But not long ago he'd heard a scientist being interviewed on a Miami radio talk show, the guy explaining that when people went to the beach they found themselves bombarded by gazillions of ions sweeping in on the ocean breezes, these ions carrying along with them some kind of charge of zone-out juice they'd picked up from bounding over the wave tops.

Deal didn't really care whether the sensation was physiological or psychological . . . right now, all he wanted was for that calm to descend. He had a healthy sip of the Myers's and Coke, hoping to help things along.

"I guess your Mr. Stone swings a pretty heavy stick down here," Russell said at his shoulder.

"So it would seem." Deal nodded.

"I could have used him up in Georgia a while back," Russell said. "Might have saved me a few years of my life."

Russell glanced over at Stone, suspecting that what the man said was true. Russell had been a boxer once, and had killed a man in the ring. It might have been ruled an accident, except for the fact that it had happened in a cracker-ass town in rural Georgia, and that Russell had thrown off his gloves at one point and used his bare fists to continue the process. They'd had to drag him off his opponent, a white boy who'd made the mistake of growling racial epithets at Russell at the same time he was head-butting, low-blowing, thumb-gouging, and otherwise fouling him in the ring. The white boy's head had struck a ring post at some point during the riot that erupted after Russell finally tackled him and dragged him down to the canvas, there to pummel the ever-loving crap out of him.

The next day, the white kid—a local—had died from a freakish blood clot that broke loose and lodged in his brain. Nineteen-year-old Russell Straight had ended up serving eight years on a manslaughter charge. And he was probably right, Deal thought. It was the sort of thing that a Franklin Stone—had one existed in the town where Russell had been so unfortunate, and had he cared a whit about the plight of an ill-educated and angry young black man—might have been able to smooth over.

"I'm so sorry," Stone was saying, hurrying toward them now. He snapped the tiny cell phone he'd been using shut and slipped it into his coat pocket. "It's been a hell of a week, but that's no excuse, I know. I trust they've been treating you well at the hotel."

Russell nodded his assent and Deal tilted his glass at Stone. "The hotel was great," he said. "Though we never did get around to checking out."

"Don't give it a thought," Stone said. "I had Balart call over." Stone gestured off toward the front of the place. Deal noted that the house-boy had reemerged and was busy arranging what looked like hors d'oeuvres on a nearby table. "Everything's been taken care of."

Deal shrugged. "We were planning on going back today."

Stone looked somewhat crestfallen. "But we haven't even gotten down to business yet."

Deal started to say something, but Stone pressed on. "And I've been such a terrible host. I was hoping—" he broke off for a moment "—assuming you could put this morning's unfortunate business out of your mind—that is, that you and Mr. Russell would be my guests through the weekend."

Deal glanced at Russell, who maintained his usual impassive expression . . . no matter what images of he and their cocktail waitress might be cavorting through his mind, Deal thought. "I'm not sure . . . ," he began, but Stone cut him off.

"I'm terribly sorry for what happened today," Stone said, turning a meaningful gaze upon Russell in turn. "The officer involved has been reprimanded. He'll have a week's desk duty during which he can calm himself down."

Deal stared. A couple of hours ago, he was facing the prospect of a weekend in the Monroe County jail. Now, Stone seemed ready to hand him the keys to the city.

"Was his word against ours, when it came down to it, Mr. Stone," Russell was saying. "How come you took ours?"

Stone smiled and put his hand on Deal's shoulder. "Because I've known your employer here for more than thirty years," he said. "And his father, too, God rest his soul. If Barton Deal had told me the sun was going to come up in the west tomorrow, I'd have taken him at his word. The same thing holds for this man right here."

Russell pursed his lips, apparently satisfied. Stone seemed about to go on, when Deal cut in. "Say you hadn't known me, Franklin," he said. "What if we'd just been a couple of guys from out of town who jumped into that mess?"

Stone paused. "It's hard to say, isn't it? But I've been made aware that Officer Conrad can be a bit, shall we say, *overzealous* in carrying out his duties. The two of you performed a public service this morning, that much I am convinced of."

"Well, I'm convinced you did us a service," Russell Straight offered. "I appreciate it." He lifted his glass to Stone, who returned the salute.

Deal nodded and joined in with the toast, although something was still troubling him. Maybe he needed a heavier breeze, one carrying a major ion transfusion, he thought, or maybe it was just the throbbing from his sore head.

He was relieved that he and Russell had been sprung from jail, sure, but still, none of it should have happened in the first place . . . and something about the ease with which Stone had engineered their release bothered him as well. Franklin Stone was a pillar of the business community to be certain, but he was no elected official, not by a long shot.

"How'd you find out we'd been picked up, anyway?" Deal asked.

Stone turned back to him. "Why, Rusty Malloy called to tell me what had happened, of course."

Deal nodded. He needed to stop looking this gift horse in the mouth, he told himself. An old acquaintance of his father's wanted to do business with him and had used his clout in a small town to get him and Russell Straight out of a jam. End of story.

He had another sip of his drink and walked to join Stone and Russell, who had made their way to the hors d'oeuvre table. Don't Worry, Be Happy, he recited to himself. The Caribbean Credo.

**7**

**"Now *here*,"** Franklin Stone was saying, moving a mouse pointer over the image on the screen before them, "is the centerpiece of Villas Cayo Hueso."

A few minutes before, they had moved in from the deck through a set of French doors leading to a nautical-themed study that Stone used for a presentation room. Deal and Russell, fresh drinks in hand, sat in leather easy chairs while Stone manipulated the controls of a notebook computer at his desk, a suitably massive rosewood affair that took up one corner of the airy room. The computer had been hooked up to a huge flat-panel monitor recessed in a bookcase wall, a setup that must have cost thousands, Deal thought. At DealCo, he was still sketching out preliminary plans for clients on lunchtime napkins.

"The tower was one of the original gun emplacements commissioned by the commander of Fort Taylor, back in 1858," Stone said, running his pointer around the image of a tall, red-brick structure that looked like a wing of the Smithsonian snapped off and dropped down in the Tropics.

"It was a star-crossed undertaking from the beginning," Stone continued. "The bricks had to be imported, of course, and an outbreak of yellow fever, likely carried by mosquitoes from the neighboring salt ponds, decimated the work force. Before they'd finished, the development of rifled cannon shells made such fortifications obsolete. The tower was never completed by the military, in fact. There wasn't even a roof until the local historical society stepped in, in the middle of the last century."

"Wait a minute," Deal said. "You're talking about the East Martello Tower? That's a museum."

"Until recently," Stone said, looking decidedly agreeable.

"You *bought* the East Martello Tower?"

"A white elephant, really," Stone said. "As you know, there is a West Tower as well, a counterpart structure that sits a short distance away, but never developed due to a lack of funds. We agreed to make a donation that would allow the historical society to renovate the West Tower in its entirety." Stone smiled. "We also conveyed ownership to a neighboring tract with little development potential which the society could use for parking or whatever else. In exchange, we took over a ninety-nine-year lease on the East Tower, where we'll install a restaurant, club rooms, and the like."

"The city council went for that?" Deal said, feeling slightly foolish as the words left his mouth.

"Why wouldn't they?" Stone asked, his expression bland.

"I could think of about a dozen reasons," Deal said. "It's a historical site, for one thing."

77

"And that's one reason why I want you on this project, Johnny-boy. I'm well aware of what you've been doing on the Terrell property up in Miami. You've got an appreciation for history. You'll see that things are done right."

Deal shook his head in wonder. The "Terrell property" that Stone referred to was an antiquated bayside home in Coconut Grove, rescued from ruin by computer magnate Terrence Terrell, designer of the machine that had successfully competed with the IBM prototype for years. Taken by the elaborate fancy of the Italian Renaissance architecture and the beauty of the secluded grounds, Terrell had hired Deal to renovate the twenty-seven-room coral-rock structure, a sizable commission that had kept him afloat through the some of the leanest years of struggle to bring DealCo back from the dead. Work on the Terrell compound still continued, for that matter. Like painting the Golden Gate Bridge, it was a job that threatened never to be finished. The only difference was that Terrell's compound was private property, and always had been.

"What about the wildlife refuge?" Deal said, pointing toward the screen.

Stone gave him another smile and pushed a button on his controls. The image of the tower disappeared, replaced by an aerial view of the southeast corner of the one-mile-by-four-mile island. Along the bottom of the screen ran the beach road where he and Russell had been jogging. Just to the north of the beachside road lay the undeveloped marshland that Stone planned to transform into a community of million-dollar townhomes. At the upper right-hand corner of the plot, a section of airport runway was visible. In the lower corner was the top of the tower they'd been looking at a moment ago. Not far from the tower was an area carved out of the marsh by a dotted white line, marking the boundaries of the wildlife refuge, Deal supposed.

Stone clicked his mouse and the image shifted, transforming itself into a tightly packed network of barrel-tiled condominiums springing up where there had been only salt marsh an instant before. The area outlined in white remained pristine, however, though it was now criss-crossed by what looked like wooden walkways elevated over the bog. What he'd just witnessed was not only a developer's dream, but a tax-assessor's as well, Deal thought.

"We've been putting the finishing touches on the plans to incorporate the refuge," Stone said. "We'll present to the commission next week, but I'm sanguine about the prospects."

As well he might be, Deal nodded. Maybe after he was finished with Key West, Stone could work things out in the Middle East.

"What's that say, anyhow?" Russell Straight asked. He was pointing at the inscription at the top of the screen: "Villas Cayo Hueso," went the bold inscription above the image, flanked by what looked like coats of arms.

"It's Spanish," Stone told him. "Cayo Hueso means 'Key of Bone.' It's the name the original explorers gave Key West."

"Why would they do that?" Russell persisted.

Stone shrugged. "Some say it's because of the look of the coral rock, or because of all the fossilized remains therein. Others say there might have been some terrible massacre here."

Russell grunted. "Well, it's America now," he said. "Why not call your houses something in English?"

Stone smiled. "I understand your sentiments, Russell. But the marketing people know what they're doing."

"Uh-huh," Russell replied. "The boss and I had us a bottle of wine last night. They put this French label on it so they could charge whatever they wanted. If you call it Mad Dog 20/20, it's only a dollar twenty-five."

"Something like that," Stone said, though he seemed a bit uncertain.

The image on screen had shifted again, becoming now a ground-level virtual tour of the planned complex, replete with splashing fountains, tanned couples lounging on balconies, even a virtual crocodile basking contentedly on the shores of the refuge pond, indifferent—in this made-up world—to a great blue heron wading nearby. Deal wanted to point out that in the actual universe, the bird might last all of a second or two before it disappeared inside a pair of snapping crocodile jaws, but he didn't see the point.

He'd had a couple of drinks now, and either they, or the ions, were having their effect. The mention of the wine had in fact rekindled memories of his stint at the Pier House lounge the night before, especially those of Annie Dodds and the dress she'd been wearing, and Deal found himself stealing a look at his watch, wondering if he might still make happy hour back at the hotel.

"I've had my people put together some figures, John," Stone was saying as the images flickered across the screen. "There's a package in your room at the hotel."

Deal nodded absently, his attention on the screen. Various elevations of the condos. A family strolling at a sunset-streaked beachside, the Martello Tower looming in the background. A couple in tennis whites, cavorting on a red-clay court. "I think you'll find the terms more than agreeable," Stone continued, "but if you've the slightest reservation, just let me know. I need someone with know-how, someone I can trust, someone who hasn't been corrupted by too many seasons down here in Mañanaville, Johnny-boy."

Deal found himself wondering why, if Stone was so anxious to get him signed on to the project, it had taken him two days to manage this meeting. But there was no need to be confrontational. It was Key West, after all.

On the screen was the image—so vivid as to seem three-dimensional—of a sun-bronzed woman in a scanty two-piece bathing suit, poised for a plunge into a crystalline pool. Something familiar about *her*, Deal was thinking, wondering if it was some luminary Stone had inveigled into the pose, or simply a model he might have seen in another ad. He had turned with a question on his lips for Stone, in fact, when he heard a familiar voice behind him.

"Oh God, Franklin," she said. "I've asked you a dozen times to get that picture out of there."

# 8

"ANITA," FRANKLIN STONE SAID, a smile lighting his handsome features.

Deal swiveled in his seat to find Annie Dodds standing in a hall doorway, clad in a lime-green version of the previous night's floor-length gown. She'd been attractive enough then, but here, in such disparate surroundings, she looked positively stunning.

When she saw him, her gaze barely flickered. Deal couldn't be sure, but he assumed his jaw was somewhere near his chest.

"I'm sorry to interrupt," she said to Deal, then turned coolly back to Stone. "Really, Franklin. It's embarrassing." She gestured at the screen, where the image had shifted to a dreamy couple watching a raging sunset from the balcony of their virtual condo.

Stone gave her a conciliatory nod and snapped the monitor into darkness. "An oversight, I assure you. But on the other hand, why cloak such beauty?" He sent what was supposed to be a good-natured grin toward Deal and Russell Straight, then turned back to her. "This is John Deal and his associate, Russell Straight," he said. "Mr. Deal's is the most highly regarded building firm in South Florida. I'm hoping to convince him to take on the Villas project."

"Actually, Mr. Deal and I have met," she said, moving to extend her hand Deal's way. When she bent toward him, Deal swore he could feel heat rising from the plane of her tanned chest. He willed himself to look away from the front of her low-cut gown, fumbling for something to say. Should he invoke the Miami High fight song, mention all the good times in the National Honor Society?

He managed to get to his feet, realizing Annie's fingers still clasped his. "You were the one at the bar who complimented me on 'When Sunny Gets Blue,'" she continued.

Deal felt himself nodding. "I liked that," he managed, turning to Stone, whose eyes remained fixed on Annie. "She was awesome."

Stone nodded. "So I keep telling her, but she's a tough one to convince."

"He means I'm a perfectionist," she told Deal. "He thinks I'm too hard on myself."

"I met Anita when she was performing in a play in New York. When she started to sing, it was as if the rest of the cast had vanished," Stone said. "I managed to convince her that her future lay in music."

Annie gave Deal a tolerant smile. "Anita Dobbins is a stage name," she said. "My real name is Annie Dodds. I went to school in Miami, did I mention that?"

Deal stared back at her, then found himself shaking his head. "I guess not," he said.

83

"It was a long time ago." She shrugged. "And, speaking of time . . ." she added, with what must have been an apologetic glance at Stone, "duty calls."

"Balart will bring the car around," Stone said, moving to give her a peck on the cheek. "Break a leg," he told her.

"You are going to get rid of that photograph, aren't you?" she said, pulling away from him.

"I promise," Stone said.

She turned and gave Deal her smile. "It was good seeing you again," she said.

"Likewise," Deal answered. He had to pry his gaze away from her departing form.

"She is something, isn't she?" Stone was saying at his shoulder.

"You could say that," Deal managed, his mind an utter whirl. Annie Dodds was living with Franklin Stone? That was enough to chew on all by itself. No wonder she'd turned down his offer to buy her a drink last night.

But as to why she wanted to keep their high-school romance a secret from Stone, he couldn't fathom. And the way she'd looked at him moments ago . . . it was as if she'd never laid eyes on him before. Either he had dreamed up the whole encounter, he thought, or Annie Dodds was as accomplished an actor as she was a singer.

"You've heard her sing, then," Stone was saying. "Do you think I'm mistaken about her talent?"

Deal turned to Stone, who seemed beside himself with pride. "Not even a little bit," he said.

Stone nodded, his gaze still on the hallway where she'd disappeared. They heard the sound of a motor starting outside, and Stone's smile turned wistful. "She could take that ability anywhere," he said, then lifted his shoulders in a gesture of helplessness. "But she seems content

84

just fooling around." He waved his hand, as if appearing in the Pier House lounge meant nothing.

Deal nodded, his gaze taking in their surroundings. It seemed a place where contentment might come easily, when you thought about it. Outside, it was dusk, and a series of discreetly placed lamps had snapped on to illuminate the palms that waved above the jutting deck. He heard the distant sounds of a steel band drifting through the open French doors, probably the ragtag group of Bahamians who drifted around Key West setting up impromptu performances anywhere a crowd might gather.

Stone's house sat very near to Southernmost Point, a spot where a giant buoy poked up from the rocky shoals, marking the end of the American continent. It was a place at the end of Duval Street where tourists liked to congregate at the close of day, if they didn't want to join the throngs at the Malory Docks on the west side of the island to watch the sun sink into the sea, that is.

Though you couldn't see the sunset at Southernmost Point, you stood a much slimmer chance of having your hair singed by the fire swallowers or your pocket picked, Deal thought. You didn't have to dodge the knife jugglers or shoo away the face painters or the caricature artists.

You simply took your drink in hand and walked out of your room or away from the bar, down to the literal end of the American road, and stood and stared out past the buoy in the direction of Havana, which was less than a hundred miles away, closer by half to the island than Miami. And, almost always, you found yourself standing at the end of the line, marveling where life had taken you. He could recall being there with Janice, not so many years ago, gazing out to sea and congratulating himself on how far he had come.

Now he turned back to Stone, suddenly feeling as if he were carrying a lead-filled safe on his shoulders.

85

"You look tired," Stone said.

"It's been a day," Deal agreed, still trying to come to terms with the feelings that roiled within him.

"Balart will be back shortly. I can have him run you to the hotel."

"It's all right," Deal told him. He put his half-finished drink down on a table. "I could stand the walk."

He cut his gaze to Russell Straight, who gave him a shrug worthy of Vernon Driscoll.

"You'll have a look at that proposal, then?" Stone asked.

"I will," Deal said.

"Take your time," Stone said. "Get a good night's sleep, maybe spend some time on the beach tomorrow. Your man here might enjoy a look at what goes on over by Louie's." He gave something of a leer as he clapped a hand on Russell Straight's brawny shoulder.

"I'll pick you up at the hotel about seven tomorrow evening," he continued. "We'll have a drink and you'll let me know then if there's anything I've left out of the package."

"I'll have a look," Deal said, "but it's only fair to tell you, Franklin—"

"Not now," Stone said, putting a finger to his lips. "Don't say a thing until you see what I've got in mind. Whatever you decide, you can let me know tomorrow, fair enough?"

Deal felt himself give an inward sigh. What the hell, he thought. One more day on the cuff in paradise. With work on the Port project closed down for the weekend, there was no point in hurrying back to Miami, was there? His daughter, Isabel, was in good hands, Janice was off on her own holiday. And he owed it to himself to study Franklin Stone's proposal with a careful eye, didn't he?

Even if Stone's style was abrasive, even if he had more than a few doubts about the wisdom of the venture the man proposed, there was a great likelihood that the project would go forward. If all the obstacles

86

had indeed been overcome, someone would build Franklin Stone's Villas of Cayo Hueso and would probably make a healthy return in the process.

And as for a healthy return, it had been all too long since Deal had enjoyed one of those. He'd been under the gun for years now, ever since his father had died with DealCo business in the crapper. He'd been supporting Janice ever since she'd decided to move out "for a while," and not only had "a while" turned out to be significantly longer than he expected, but there were also significant bills for Isabel's private schooling, Janice's continuing therapy, and the like.

So why shouldn't it be Deal to take on Stone's project? He was not a corner-cutter nor a builder who would perpetrate some environmental outrage and worry about the fallout later. He'd known others to clear-cut vast swathes of protected coastline mangroves, for instance, and simply shrug when inspectors tried to shut their projects down. "The subcontractors did it," was a favorite response. Sure. Blame it on some traveling tree-trimming outfit that existed nowhere but on paper, vanished like smoke, and was just as impossible to prosecute. Meantime, the mangroves were gone, and even the condos on the first floor had gained their unobstructed view of the sea. In a few days, business would be back to normal.

In that way, he could be the best part about Stone's project, Deal told himself. Wouldn't it be nice to think so, at the very least?

"Tomorrow evening, then," Stone said, clasping Deal's hand in both of his.

"At seven," Deal agreed.

"Thanks for the drinks," Russell Straight added, and then Stone was showing them down a cool, high-ceilinged hallway to the front door.

# 9

"**WHAT'S BETWEEN YOU** and Stone's squeeze?" Russell Straight asked, as the two of them ambled past the smallish crowd gathered near Southernmost Point.

"What are you talking about?" Deal said, his eyes on the gathering. It was the ragtag steel drummers holding the crowd past sundown, he saw, a couple of breakdancing kids added to the act. With the sun down and the breeze off the water picking up, it had become a near-perfect summer's night. Except for the hubbub, these narrow streets had the feel of a genteel Southern town, he thought. Just one more pleasant anomaly of the place as far as he was concerned.

"Don't try to con a con," Russell said. "Was sparks flying all over that room."

"She's attractive, if that's what you mean."

"I'm surprised Stone still wants to do business with you, way you looked at his old lady."

Deal turned to Russell. "I'm sure he's used to it."

"It would take some getting used to," Russell replied.

"I think we may have exhausted this topic," Deal said. "Don't you?"

"Whatever you say," Russell told him. He paused to check a street sign. "I think this is where I leave you, anyway."

Deal glanced at him quickly, about to say something. Then he saw the expression on Russell's face and it sunk in. "Lady from the cocktail lounge told me this was her night off," Russell offered.

"But you and I aren't even supposed to be here," Deal protested. "If you hadn't . . ." He broke off, then began again. "If *we* hadn't gotten involved in that mess this morning, we'd be back in Miami right now." There was a dull clang from above as some unseen hard-shelled bug collided with the old-fashioned metal shade of the street lamp.

Russell looked at Deal blankly. "Maybe *you* would be. I was planning on a day off, myself. I kind of like this town. Reminds me of Georgia, except with spunk."

"And how were you planning on getting home?" Deal asked, his voice rising.

Something like a smile crossed Russell's features. "You sound like my momma."

Deal opened his mouth, then closed it again. What *was* he giving Russell such a hard time about, anyway? "You're right, Russell," he said. "Have a good time. I'll see you in the morning."

Russell nodded. "One thing I meant to tell you," he said, hesitating.

"What is it, Russell?" There was a louder clang at the street lamp shade, the bug getting worked up, it sounded like, maybe ready to kamikaze itself right into the glowing bulb.

"That kid we saved from an ass-kicking," Russell said.

"Dequarius? What about him?" Deal glanced up at the street lamp, saw nothing but a couple of soft-looking moths fluttering about.

Russell was working his tongue around in his mouth as if he were stirring a potful of possible words. "While we were cooling our heels, he told me he worked for your man Stone," he said finally. "Grunt work. Clearing brush. Hauling junk. Stuff like that."

Deal thought about it for a moment. "Well, maybe he does."

"Kind of strange Stone didn't say anything about it," Russell persisted.

"Why should he?" Deal said. "That's probably why the sheriff let him go without a fuss."

Russell looked dubious.

"What are you getting at, Russell?"

There was another clang at the street lamp, then a sizzling sound, and something fell to the street with a crack. Deal saw a roundish dark knot the size of a jawbreaker rolling across the pavement. So much for that, he was thinking . . . but in the next moment the fallen insect had unfolded itself and was buzzing angrily up into the night air once again.

"Now that is a serious bug," Russell offered.

"What about Dequarius?" Deal said.

Russell looked ready to forget the whole thing. He turned away, then back, then seemed to make a decision. "He said he *knew* something important, that's all."

Deal felt the beginnings of a headache coming on. "Something about *what*, Russell?"

Russell shrugged. "Wouldn't say. Said that's what he wants to talk to you about."

"Maybe he's looking for a new job," Deal said.

90

Russell glanced at him. "Does Dequarius strike you as the worker type?"

Deal didn't say anything.

"Besides," Russell continued, "he was being pretty skittish about it. Like he didn't want anyone else to hear. He wrote his number down, asked me to give it to you." Russell had his wallet out now, was fishing around for something in its folds.

Deal sighed. So Dequarius Noyes had some dirt to dish him on Franklin Stone, that was what it was all about? Only trouble was, that would be like warning him to pack snowshoes for the Antarctic. "Thanks for the tip, Russell," Deal said, holding up his hand, "but don't worry about the number. I'm sure Dequarius will find me if he has to."

Russell glanced up, then shrugged and put his wallet away. "By the way," he said, as Deal started off, "what was Stone talking about anyway, 'show your *man*' some beach or whatever?"

Deal shook his head. "Nothing," he said. "It's topless where he's talking about."

Russell stared at him for a moment, then rolled his eyes. "Man oh man," he said, waving his hand as if Deal was the lamest prospect he could imagine. "I'll catch *you* later."

Deal watched after Russell as he disappeared down the tree-shrouded side street, then finally turned and got his bearings. Actually, he wasn't far from Louie's Backyard, he realized. And, as he had finally managed to remember, he'd had an outstanding piece of yellowtail snapper there the night before. The dish seemed so good in his memory, in fact, that he considered the possibility of another go-around, especially now that he was sober. But, much as he hated to admit it to himself, something else was nudging at him.

91

He glanced down at his watch. Not half an hour had passed since Annie had left Stone's house. It would take him maybe fifteen minutes to get across the island to the Pier House, less if he managed to snag a taxi on the way. With any luck at all, he could be there by the time she took her first break. The hell with Louie's, he thought. There would always be time to eat.

"Yo, Magnum," he wanted to call to the bartender, realizing he still had not learned the man's name. Deal had to wait until the guy had loaded a server's tray with what seemed like an impossible number of drinks to wave and finally catch his attention.

"What's with this?" he said, pointing at the stage as the mustachioed guy finally leaned across the counter.

"With what?" the bartender called. There were half a dozen dreadlocked Jamaicans on the lounge's platform, all of them decked out in electric blue slacks and patchwork shirts, belting out a version of a Bob Marley song while most of the packed room joined in. The white-shoes-and-jacket crowd from the night before had been replaced by a decidedly younger, more casually dressed crowd, many of them with the deep tans and bleached locks that suggested they were locals.

"Where's Annie?" Deal asked, gesturing at the stage. The bartender looked at him blankly.

"Anita Dobbins," Deal said, raising his voice a notch. "The singer who was here last night."

The bartender finally raised his chin in acknowledgment. "She's off tonight," he said. He was clapping his hand to the bar in time to the reggae beat.

Deal glanced aside, summoning his patience. There was a harried-looking waitress bearing down on the service station, a second on her heels. If he lost the guy's attention now, he'd be doomed. "I'm sure she told me she was working. Maybe at another club?"

The bartender seemed to be thinking. Suddenly he pointed at Deal. "You must mean the play."

Deal shook his head, the echo of Stone's "break a leg" replaying in the recesses of his mind. "What play?"

The bartender noted the waitresses fuming at the station. "I'm a little busy here," he said, giving Deal a meaningful look. Deal dug in his pocket, found a bill, slapped it on the bar.

The bartender palmed the bill smoothly. "The Malory Docks Theater," he said, pointing out a bank of windows. "Right across the street. That's what she does on the weekends."

"Thanks," Deal said.

The bartended clapped Deal on the shoulder. "Good luck," he said. He was gone too quickly for Deal to ask just what he meant.


As Deal discovered after plopping down twenty dollars and being told to wait until a scene change to enter the small theater, *Buccaneers of Biscayne* turned out to be a musical of sorts, a song-and-dance revue that featured plenty of mediocre talent along with a house orchestra led by the piano player who'd accompanied Annie on the previous night. What passed for a plot had to do with the early days of Key West, when the principal economy relied upon the "salvage" of ships driven onto the treacherous outer reefs by hurricanes and other, less catastrophic storms.

Annie played the role of Preacher Egan's devoted wife, whose lot was, apparently, to wring her hands and lament this man of God's weekday enterprise: the setting up of fake lighthouses meant to lure unsuspecting ships to disaster on the rocks, then plundering their remains under the operative law of the seas. If the role was a thankless one, Annie nonetheless gave it her all, and on the occasions when she broke into song—a bluesy "What's Wrong With My Man" being Deal's favorite—even the distracted gaggle of tourists among whom he sat were galvanized to pay attention.

The show closed with the good squire's conversion back to righteousness, his reward a soulful embrace from Annie. As the lights came up and the curtain call concluded, Deal hesitated, then peeled away from the departing crowd making its way out.

He turned and walked back down a side aisle, passing a pimply kid who was gathering trash from the seats. Deal half-expected the kid to ask what he was up to, but he never so much as glanced up from his task.

Deal pushed through a curtained entryway at the side of the stage, a musty odor washing over him as he entered a dimly lit hallway. As he stood for a moment to allow his eyes to adjust, two young men whom he recognized from the performance ducked out of a room ahead on his right, arm in arm. One of them, his eyes still heavy with makeup, glanced at Deal.

"Looking for someone?" he asked, in a lilting voice.

"As a matter of fact . . ." Deal began.

The man's partner rolled his own mascara-ed eyes. "Don't mind my friend," he said. "The women's dressing room is down the hall on your left."

The second man gave Deal a weary smile and pulled his friend away. Deal shook his head and moved on down the hallway. Annie had called him guileless, hadn't she? Now he could add something to his growing self-image: guileless and straight.

He found a door marked LADIES, and hesitated. What was he doing here, anyway? He was curious about her behavior earlier that evening, but she was clearly involved with Franklin Stone, for God's sake, and he was a married man.

That was the word from his logical half. The other part of him was undeterred. Deal felt his hand go up, about to knock on the door, when it suddenly flew open and he found himself staring at a young woman sporting a punk hairdo, a series of stiff pink spikes scattered randomly about her scalp. It took him a moment to remember her as the demure-looking blond girl who'd had the ingenue's role in the play.

"Is there something wrong?" she asked.

"No," Deal said, glancing over his shoulder. "I'm looking for Annie . . . Anita Dobbins, I mean."

The girl peered more closely at him and Deal attempted to adopt his most guileless pose. After a moment she turned, letting the door swing shut.

"Some guy wants to see you," Deal heard, followed by a muffled reply. The way the girl said *guy* did not connote either guileless or straight, Deal was thinking. More like dorkus or asswipe.

In the next moment the door opened again. "Are you Balart?" the girl asked.

Deal shook his head. "It's John Deal."

The girl nodded as if she'd heard many more exciting things. "He says his name is Deal," she called, holding the door open this time.

"It's okay, Chelsea," Deal heard.

The girl shrugged and pulled the door open for him, rolling her eyes as she went past him into the hallway. Deal entered the dressing room, blinking at the sudden brightness.

Annie sat at a dressing table that looked like it had been built in the Jolson era, changed now into a pair of jeans and a sleeveless cotton top. If she had looked like a diva in the green satin gown, she'd now been

95

transformed into a college girl. Whatever she was, Deal found himself feeling light-headed.

She glanced up, giving him a smile as she finished brushing out her hair. "Welcome to Fifty-second Street," she said. A couple of the bulbs circling the long mirror were out, he noted, and the backing had begun to flake around the corners as well. The floor of the room was bare concrete. Costumes dangled from a length of galvanized pipe fixed to the opposite wall. The air held a curious combination of dusting powder, perfume, and sweat. About as erotic a blend of scents as he could imagine.

"You were great," he said.

"Thanks," she said. "If I'd known you were interested, I'd have had you comped."

Why on earth *wouldn't* he be interested? Deal thought, but decided it wasn't the right thing to say. "It's okay," he said. "It was a bargain at twice the price." Another of his old man's cornball sayings, he thought. What a conversationalist. Then again, she'd always liked Barton, hadn't she? Maybe between him and his father, he could get through this.

She wrinkled her nose. "The show sucks, in fact, but I still get a kick out of it."

"It's apparent," he said.

"So," she said, smiling again. "You've sent Balart home and have come for me yourself."

"That's a great idea," he heard himself saying. "I wish I'd thought of it."

She glanced at her watch. "So he's still out there waiting?"

Deal shrugged. "He wasn't in the audience."

She gave him a patient stare. "Give me a second, okay?"

He nodded as she checked her appearance one last time, then stood and disappeared through an inner doorway. After a moment, he heard a toilet flush, followed by the sound of water running. Then she was back, to take him by the arm. "Ready?" she asked.

"I think so," he said. And let her guide him out the door.

"This way," she said when they were back in the hallway, and Deal realized they were turned away from the direction he'd come earlier. After they'd taken a few steps through the darkness, he felt her hand leave his arm, then the unmistakable sound of a breaker bar clanging against an exit door.

"Damn thing," he heard her say. "Give me a hand, will you?"

"Sure," Deal said, moving toward the sound of her voice. He put his hands out in the darkness, brushing an arm, then a hip.

He'd encircled her, he realized, one hand grasping the breaker bar on either side of her. He felt her move backward, into him, felt the heat of her all the way down his body.

He felt himself stir, felt her shift ever so slightly against him. Twenty years shed as easily as that, he thought. He wasn't sure that he could still breathe.

"Push hard now," he heard her say, a certain huskiness in her voice.

She didn't have to ask him twice.

The two of them nearly collided with a group of Japanese tourists as they tumbled out onto the sidewalk flanking Whitehead Street. Two men with cameras held their companions back as if they might be fearing attack.

"Sorry," Annie called to them, stifling laughter.

Deal glanced down at himself, automatically tugging at his khakis. He saw that the Japanese were staring at him uncertainly.

"The door," he offered, gesturing at it. "Stuck."

The Japanese murmured, backing away as one, like a school of nervous fish.

"There he is," Deal heard at his shoulder. He turned to find Annie pointing across the street to where the black limo idled at the curb. "He's always there," she added.

Deal started to follow her, but she put her hand to his chest. "I'll be right back," she said.

Deal watched her cross the street, noting that she looked every bit as alluring in a pair of jeans as in a clinging dress. She'd been attractive enough, all those years ago, but now . . . He shook his head, marveling at his ability to miss what must have been there all along. A pity to waste youth upon the young, he thought. Another canard come from nowhere, or maybe it was his old man's ghost whispering in his ear.

Annie bent to rap on the driver's window and the dark panel slid quietly down. Deal heard the sound of metal wrenching behind him and turned to see the kid who'd been mucking out the seats in the theater struggling to pull the bulky back door closed. He heard the sound of a motor then, and glanced back to find Annie walking toward him, the limo gliding away toward the intersection of Duval Street, where the nighttime crowds were swelling.

"I think you offered to buy me a drink," she said, taking his arm again.

"Seems like a long time ago," he said.

"You've changed your mind?" she asked.

"Not a chance," he said, and they were off.

**10**

THEY SAT IN a secluded dockside bar at the Pier House, a spot he'd noted on the way out to jog earlier that same morning. Not much more than a dozen hours ago, but now it seemed forever. "I was thinking about that part you had in the play," Deal said as the waiter put down their drinks and left.

"What about it?" she said. She lifted her glass to his and sipped.

"You were miscast," he told her. He could hear the faint slap of waves on the pilings beneath them. A few degrees cooler here, right by the water. A faint tinge of ammonia drifted in, from exposed flats somewhere out there. Tide going out, he thought.

"You think I should have played the ingenue," she said, no question in her voice. She had another sip of her drink, staring at him over her martini glass.

He laughed. "No. It's just that I had a hard time believing the Good Squire Egan wouldn't have done anything you asked him to."

She raised her eyebrows. "That's all I have to do, huh, just ask?"

Deal felt his ears burning.

"You *are* something else," she said.

Deal had a sip of his own martini, which he had asked for after hearing her order. He couldn't remember the last time he'd ordered such a drink.

"See-throughs," he said, holding up his glass. "That's what my old man used to call these."

She nodded and held her glass up to a string of tiny lights that bordered the railing at their side. "You can't hide anything in a martini," she agreed.

He turned to face her then. "What I've really been wondering is this: How come you didn't tell Stone we knew each other?"

"That's a good question," she said. "I meant to, of course. But when I opened my mouth . . . well, you heard what came out."

"You're not married to him . . ."

She laughed, a sound so sudden and sharp that it startled him. "Of course not," she said. She tossed her hair back and glanced out at the dark water for a moment, then turned back to him.

"I've been with Franklin on and off for three years now, but it's not quite what you're thinking."

"What am I thinking?" Deal asked.

"That he keeps me." Her eyes were steady on his.

"He doesn't?"

She shrugged. "In a manner of speaking," she said.

Deal had a healthy swallow of his own drink. "Franklin Stone wants to make me a rich man," he said. "Maybe we shouldn't be doing this."

"Doing what?" she asked coolly. "We're old friends. We're having a drink together."

"You should come have a talk with my daughter," he told her. "I've been having trouble convincing her that there really is a Santa Claus."

She gave him a humorless stare in return. "You seem pretty sure of yourself."

It stopped him, as surely as if he were a high school kid cut dead by the prom queen. Of course she was right. Just because he'd tied himself up in knots didn't mean she saw things the same way at all.

He tipped his glass at her. "I'm sorry if I sounded presumptuous," he said, glancing around. After a moment, he turned back to meet her gaze. "I guess I'm just happy to see you."

It got a smile from her. "I think that's supposed to be my line." She turned and signaled toward the idling bartender for another drink.

"I met Franklin through a man he conducted some business with, a man named Grosjean," she said when she turned back. She stared at Deal for a moment before continuing. "Grosjean was the one who showed up backstage down in the Village one night, a few years ago." She gave Deal a smile that was more like a grimace. "He claimed to be a businessman, but I came to realize it wasn't the sort of business that traded on the stock exchange." She shrugged, toying with her glass. "Over time, things got complicated between Grosjean and me, and Franklin stepped in to help me out of a jam." She stared at Deal neutrally.

"There's more to it, of course, but that's enough for now." She lifted her glass and drank deeply, then stared off. "Let's just say that I'm grateful for everything that Franklin has done for me."

Deal stared. He'd always imagined his own past—including his tortured relationship with Janice—as one for the books, but the things

that Annie hinted at—French gangsters, fleeing to Florida for safety—
made his history seem downright ordinary.

"Besides." She turned back. "You mentioned a wife, if I'm not mistaken. Maybe we should be talking about her."

"We're separated," he said. "I already told you."

"Right," she said. "She's in Colorado, you're in Key West. I meet guys
in the lounge every night: 'I'm separated,' they say. 'My wife's up in the
room asleep, I'm down here.' Who can argue with them?"

"It's not that way with us," Deal said, trying to avoid her gaze. "I told
you it was a long story."

"Do you have somewhere to go?" she persisted.

The bartender was there with their drinks, then. The guy picked up
Annie's empty and waited while Deal slugged what was left in his. As
the bartender walked off, Deal noted that Annie had been rummaging
in her bag and now appeared to be lighting a cigarette. There was a
flash of flame and she took a deep drag, then exhaled.

Not a cigarette, Deal realized, as the smoke rolled over him. "Jesus,
Annie." He turned in alarm to the bartender—a short guy with a
Sonny Bono haircut and mustache—who was back at his post inspect-
ing his nails. The blue cloud of smoke drifted over the guy's head, then
out to sea.

"Don't worry about him," she said as Deal turned back. "Who do
you think I bought this stuff from?"

She was leaning forward, offering him the smoldering joint. Deal
stared at it for a moment. The last time he'd smoked marijuana had
been with Janice, three years or more ago. They had still been together
then, but barely. She'd come home from a session with her acupunc-
turist with a couple of joints and a series of very specific notes on how
to restore the bliss to their union. Deal had given it a shot, but he had
fallen asleep somewhere around Step Fourteen.

Annie was about to stub out the joint when he put his hand atop hers. What the hell.

He tweezered it out of her fingers with his own and held it up to his lips, dragging until sparks flew into the dark before his eyes. He exhaled and handed what was left back to her. "It usually doesn't do anything to me," he said.

She gave him a skeptical look, then flicked the roach over the rail into the water. "I think you were about to tell me a story," she said.

"I was indeed," Deal said. He had picked up his drink, to chase the bitter taste from his tongue, when he saw the bartender rounding the service counter and heading their way, a no-nonsense expression on his face. So much for disregarding the guy, Deal was thinking, as the bartender bore down on them.

What was next? he wondered. A scolding? Ejection from the premises? A phone call to Deputy Conrad?

He was about to say something to Annie, when the guy reached for something at his belt. *Were they about to be shot?* Deal wondered.

"You're John Deal?" the guy asked, staring at him intently.

"That's me," Deal said, his mind a jumble of possibilities. It had begun to occur to him that his thoughts were leaping in strange ways.

"It's for you," the guy said, thrusting his hand forward. Deal found himself gazing down at a portable phone, a little green light pulsing on its face.

"A phone," he said.

The bartender nodded wisely. "Just press the button that says talk."

Deal thought the bartender was rolling his eyes as he turned away.

11

DEAL GAVE ANNIE a look as he raised the phone to his ear, but she raised her expressive eyebrows in a "who knows?" fashion.

"It's John Deal," he said into the receiver. After a moment, he remembered to press "Talk." Annie turned away, either giving him a measure of privacy or trying not to laugh.

"This is Deal, right?" Deal heard the familiar voice. Still, it took him a moment.

"Dequarius?" Deal said finally. "Dequarius Noyes?"

Annie heard something in his voice and turned in her seat, her smile fading.

"Same one," the kid's voice came back. He sounded subdued, not at all the bullshit artist Deal had become accustomed to. "I been trying to find the brother that was with you."

"You mean Russell," Deal said.

"Whatever," Dequarius said. "I need to talk to him, right quick." His voice was urgent but guarded, as if he were worried someone might overhear.

Deal gave a humorless laugh. "Well, I'm afraid you're out of luck, Dequarius." He glanced at Annie. What was he supposed to say? *Your man is shacked up with our former cocktail waitress.* "Why don't you give me your number and I'll have Russell call you in the morning."

"Fuck a bunch of morning, man," Dequarius said, his voice rising. "We got a *situation* here."

Deal shook his head, trying to shake off the wooziness. Two martinis with a marijuana chaser, he thought. Not exactly the Bruce Jenner diet.

"Russell said you had something to tell me," Deal said wearily, "but this really isn't the time—"

"You don't have to tell me what time it is, motherfucker," the kid cut in. "I wasted too much time on you already. I'm on my way out of Dodge, right now. I called to tell Russell you two better do the same, unless . . ." He broke off for a moment, then Deal heard him curse, "Aw, shit . . ."

There was a crashing noise in the background, followed by a clattering that suggested the phone had been dropped. There was the sound of a door slamming, then a muffled explosion, followed by another and another. Gunshots, Deal realized. Shotgun blasts, he guessed.

"Dequarius?" Deal called into the mouthpiece. Annie was looking at him strangely now.

". . . phone," Deal heard a voice call out on the other end of the connection. There was a curse, the sound of approaching footsteps. "Who is this?" a voice growled. Whoever was speaking, it was decidedly not Dequarius.

"Who is *this?*" Deal countered. And then the line went dead.

105

Deal pulled the phone away from his ear, staring dumbly at it for a moment. No Caller ID, of course, it being a business phone.

"What is it?" Annie asked, her face a mask of concern.

Deal willed away the haze that seemed to lap at his consciousness. A part of his mind willed him to do the automatic thing. Dial 911, tell the sheriff's dispatcher what he'd heard. Then again, he had no idea where the call had come from, nor could he be sure what had happened—not really.

And there was something else holding him back, though he couldn't pinpoint it at first. *Who is this?* He heard the voice echo in his mind, and along with it came the vision of Deputy Conrad with the tip of his heavy black oxford aimed at the temple of Dequarius Noyes.

Deal felt a chill run through him. He'd only heard the deputy utter a few strangled curses—no way he could be certain it was the same voice on the phone—but even the thought had momentarily frozen him with fear.

"Russell," he said, his eyes focused at a point somewhere in the distance.

"Something's happened to Russell?"

Annie's worried voice brought him back. He glanced at her, shaking his head. "I need to find Russell," he told her. He gripped the edge of the table, ready to leap up, though he had nowhere to go.

"He's with a woman who waited on us in the lounge last night," he blurted. "Tall, blonde, attractive . . ."

Annie was nodding. "Denise," she said.

"Where does Denise live?" Deal said, impatient.

She looked at him blankly. "I don't even know her last name."

Deal rolled his eyes in exasperation. What next? he wondered. Hurry back to that street corner where he'd parted ways with Russell, start knocking door-to-door?

Annie was staring at him uncertainly. "This is important, right?"

Deal gave her a look. Annie nodded and took the phone from him, then stood and strode purposefully to the bar. She beckoned to the bartender, who nodded at whatever she said. Annie handed the phone over and the guy punched in some numbers, said something to someone, then jotted down a note on a pad. In a moment Annie was back, notepad in hand.

"Home phone, cell phone, address," Deal said, glancing at the information, then up at her. "Your guy wired into the phone company or something?"

Annie shrugged and handed over the phone. "She's one of his customers," she said.

Deal gave her a look as he punched in the home number. The phone rang three times without an answer, and Deal was about to try the cellular number when he heard a voice. "No way am I coming in. I don't care who quit, how crazy it is, I am off tonight, and that is that—"

"Denise," Deal cut in. "It's not your boss. I need to speak to Russell."

There was a pause. "Russell *who?*"

"Cut the shit," Deal said. "Tell him it's Deal on the phone."

Another pause, then some murmured conversation. In a few moments Russell was on. "How'd you get this number?" he asked, his voice edged with annoyance.

Deal glanced at the bartender, who was propped on his elbows staring out toward the dark sea. Probably thinking about where to buy his retirement home, Deal thought. "Just listen to me," Deal said into the phone.

"I'm here," Russell said patiently.

"I need that number Dequarius Noyes gave you."

"You're kidding, right?"

"I need it *now,*" Deal said.

107

Russell's sigh was profound, but he must have heard something in Deal's voice. "What's up?" he said, grunting as if he might be dragging himself out of bed. Deal heard what sounded like chair legs dragging across a wooden floor.

"The kid called me in a sweat a minute ago," Deal said.

"So what? I told you he wanted to talk. "

"So, I think that someone shot him in the middle of our conversation," Deal said, replaying the scenario in his head.

During the pause that followed, Deal watched Annie Dodds's eyes widen at the news. "You call the cops?" Russell asked.

"Not yet," Deal said. He wasn't going to bother with an explanation. Not yet, anyway.

"Good," Russell said.

"Do you have that number or not?"

"I got it," Russell grumbled. "Stuck right here to the back of my license all along. Got a number *and* an address."

Deal picked up the pen Annie had brought back with the notepad and scribbled down the information. "Thanks, Russell," Deal said, about to hang up.

"What are you gonna do?" Russell's voice came.

Deal brought the phone back to his ear. "Call back," he told Russell, gazing down at the address. "If nobody answers, go over to this address, see what's what."

"I'll meet you over there," Russell said.

Deal tried to imagine just what scene he might have interrupted. "You don't have to do that," he said.

"You go to that part of town at this time of night, you want me with you," Russell said.

Deal glanced at the address again, then shrugged. "It's probably nothing." Indeed, it probably was, he thought. He'd misheard everything somehow, imagined any connection between Conrad and the voice on the phone.

Just as likely it was some disgruntled customer Dequarius had ripped off. People probably shot at guys like Dequarius all the time. He'd seen this assailant coming and had simply ducked out without bothering to say goodbye.

On the other hand, Dequarius had saved him from a beating at Conrad's hands. Maybe even worse.

"You don't hear from me in the next minute," Deal heard himself say into the phone, "I'll meet you there."

"Was a nice night up until now," Russell said. Deal hung up, then dialed.

**12**

"**WHAT KIND OF** car is this, anyway?" Annie asked as they rumbled southward down Whitehead Street.

"It's a Cadillac," Deal said.

"I didn't realize they made pickups," she said, glancing through the windowed partition that separated the driver's compartment from the Hog's customized cargo bed.

"A client of mine who owned a dealership fixed it up this way," Deal said, glancing at her. "He kept race horses and liked to run out to the stables with the occasional bale of alfalfa. He just wanted to do it in a gentlemanly way."

Annie nodded dubiously. "So why do you have it?"

Deal paused, thinking of Cal Saltz, one of his father's fondest friends, yet another ally long since dead. "The guy couldn't come up with what he owed me on a project," Deal said. "I took the Hog instead."

"The Hog?"

"Janice named it."

Annie glanced around the rumbling passenger compartment. "Seems appropriate," she said.

Deal nodded. Everything about the vehicle—its weight, its throbbing engine, its throaty exhaust—suggested bulk and power. He'd never have gone looking for such a car, but now that it was his and his doting Miami mechanics had fallen in love with the machine, continually refining its suspension, steering, and engine—even its coachwork—Deal had developed something of an appreciation for its singularity.

They passed a bar called the Green Parrot, an open-air place where the late-night crowd had spilled out onto the sidewalk. A sheriff's cruiser was pulled up in front, facing the opposite direction, two wheels on the curb, its blue and red flashers popping silently. A pair of deputies—neither of them Conrad, Deal noticed—flanked a big man wearing nothing but a bathing suit and a pair of rubber flip-flops. The guy's skin glowed lobster-bright, no doubt from the combined effects of vast quantities of sun and alcohol. His eyes were glassy, seeming to stare off at nothing while the deputies spoke earnestly up at him. Most of the other patrons milled about, seemingly indifferent to the confrontation.

"Why don't I drop you off at home?" Deal said, glancing at Annie as they rolled past the scene.

"I don't feel like going home," she said. "Besides, you need a navigator." She held up the pad with the address Deal had jotted down.

Deal gave her a skeptical look. "I'm not sure what we're getting into," he said.

"All the more reason," she said. "I have friends in high places." **111**

"Suit yourself," he said.

"I generally do," she told him, then pointed out the windshield. "You want to turn right up there. Try not to hit the chickens."

Deal glanced ahead. Sure enough, there were half a dozen roosters scratching in the sand where a narrow street branched off from White-head. The birds took their time getting out of the way—one of them stretched up on his toes and flapped his wings as if he might be ready to take on the bothersome automobile—but finally Deal was able to ease the Hog past and down the narrow lane.

The houses were small here, even by Key West bungalow standards, most of them wooden shotgun cottages with flaking paint, sagging eaves, and cluttered porches, though here and there a few stood out, bright with paint and flowers planted in the dusty yards. It was the old service quarter of the city, an area of several square blocks populated largely by blacks ever since there had been a town.

His old man had brought him in here once during a family vacation to the Rock, as he called it, the ever-flamboyant Barton hot on the trail of a cock-fighting match he'd heard about in Captain Tony's Bar. They'd never found the match that day, much to Deal's relief, but it had surely been there somewhere. Those birds they'd driven through were probably the survivors' descendants, in fact.

No one on the streets at this hour, no lights burning in the houses they passed. "There," Annie called, pointing out her window at one of the bungalows.

Deal slowed as the headlights of the Hog washed over one of the tidier cottages. The house was built facing them, at a point where the roadway jogged and burrowed deeper into the quarter. A set of reflective house numbers had been nailed into the gatepost of a white-washed picket fence. Beside the gate was an iron jockey, its face painted

112

white. No car in the driveway, no lights burning inside, no welcoming bulb glowing on the porch.

Deal pulled the Hog over to the curb, its snout still facing the cottage, and cut the engine. After a moment the headlights snapped off automatically. There was a faint glow in the sky, the reflection of the downtown lights just a few blocks away, along with a vague buzz of party-time Friday night. Here all was quiet and dark.

"You heard shots?" Annie asked him, staring out toward the neat, still house.

"A shotgun, I'd guess," Deal said.

"Don't you think other people would have heard?"

He nodded.

"Then why aren't people out in the streets?"

"Maybe they don't want to get shot, too," he said.

"But surely someone would call the police."

"Depending on where you lived," Deal said agreeably.

In the rearview mirror, he had noticed a set of headlights coming down the narrow street behind them. He leaned into the door of the Hog and swung his legs out, then turned to Annie. "Sit still," he told her. "The keys are in the ignition. Something happens, you slide behind the wheel and get out."

"Oh sure," she said.

He shook his head and got out of the Hog, moving in the direction of the headlights, ready to dive for cover if he had to. The headlights of the approaching car flicked to bright, blinding him for a moment, and Deal threw up a hand to shield his eyes, the other tensed on the rail of a chain-link fence beside him.

"That's him," he heard a familiar voice say over the whine of a small car's engine. "Kill your lights."

Abruptly there was darkness and the sounds of the motor died away. Deal lowered his hand, felt the muscles in his upper back relax as Russell Straight unfolded his bulk from the passenger seat of a compact car. Deal caught a glimpse of Denise behind the wheel—he registered tousled hair, a brief tank top, a pair of boxers maybe, before the door slammed shut and the dome lamp winked out.

Russell leaned back through the window and said something Deal couldn't catch. In a moment, the small car started and began backing away slowly, its headlights still doused. "Like to break my back," Russell said, his hands held to his kidneys.

Deal glanced at him.

"I'm talking about her car, man."

"I didn't say anything, Russell."

Russell rolled his eyes. "That the place?" he said, nodding at the tidy cottage down the lane.

Deal shrugged. "That's the address you gave me."

"Pretty quiet around here," Russell said, checking their surroundings. As if in answer, a cock crow split the night. Probably the rooster who didn't like cars, Deal thought, happy to see Denise passing by.

"We were just saying so," Deal said.

"We?" Russell asked. He bent down and peered through the Hog's back window, then glanced up at Deal. "Who is that in there?"

"Annie Dodds," Deal told him.

"Stone's woman?"

"She's the one you met," Deal said.

"What's she doing here?"

"We were having a drink when Dequarius called," he said. "She didn't want to go home."

Russell nodded, considering things. "You called the number, I guess?" he asked, his eyes on the house.

114

Deal nodded. "A couple of times. A busy signal, that's all."

"You go up there yet?" He was still staring at the house.

"I was just about to," Deal said.

"Let's go then," Russell said.

They had just started forward when the explosion came.

**13**

DEAL HEARD ANNIE'S cry as he dove for the pavement behind the Hog, then felt Russell's bulk slamming down beside him. There was another deafening explosion, and, after that, the rattle of buckshot raining down on the roof of the Hog.

Deal glanced at Russell, who was pressed to the pavement like a boot-camp recruit ready to count out push-ups. "You okay?" he asked.

He saw Russell's head dip in affirmation. "How about you?"

"So far," Deal said.

"Come on out," a man's voice called from the darkness. "Both of you. With your hands up."

Deal glanced at Russell, who gave him an uncertain look in return. A powerful flashlight beam snapped on suddenly, illuminating both of them in a bright pool of light.

"Get up, I say," the voice commanded. "I'm through fooling around, now."

Deal slowly raised one hand to the tailgate of the Hog, then brought his other hand to join it. "Just like that," the voice crooned. "Pull yourself on up. Your buddy, too."

Deal did as he was told, trying to catch sight of Annie through the rear glass of the passenger compartment. Why had he let her come along? he wondered, cursing himself as Russell rose carefully to his feet beside him. It was one thing to stupidly put himself in danger, but what had he been thinking of, allowing her to join in?

"Now turn around so I can see you," the voice said. "Slow."

Deal did as he was told, wincing as the beam of the torch washed over his face. He couldn't see Russell for the glare, but the scrape of shoes on pavement suggested he had done the same.

"You mind getting that light out of my eyes," Deal heard Russell say at his side.

"Never mind that," the man said. "Now, you boys start walking, nice and easy, right over this way . . ." the voice began, then broke off suddenly, with a sharp intake of breath.

"I'll take the gun," Deal heard a familiar woman's voice. "Turn it loose this instant, or I'll blow you away."

It was Annie's voice, Deal realized, somewhere out there, past the blinding orb of light.

"Get the light out of their faces. Now!"

The torch beam wavered, then slid down to puddle in the street. "John," he heard from the darkness. "I've got his gun."

"Annie?" Deal said, staring in amazement toward the sound of her voice. His eyes were still adjusting from the glare, but he could make out two vague silhouettes standing close together, just down the sidewalk. A tall man, pointing his flashlight at the ground now. And a     117 woman behind him, one hand raised high, pointing something at him, what looked like a shotgun under one crooked arm.

"Don't move," she said, beginning to edge away. "It's okay, John," she said, turning toward him for a moment. He sensed what might happen at the very instant that it did.

The man's arm swung suddenly upward, the arc of the flashlight beam cutting through the night sky before him. He heard Annie cry out, saw something shiny fly from her upraised hand. There was a distant clattering and the sound of scuttling feet as the man began to run down the sidewalk toward him.

"Don't shoot!" Deal heard Russell cry, even as he left his feet. His shoulder hit the man just below hip level, driving them both through the spindly picket fence that bordered the house.

Not a bad tackle, Deal found himself thinking, as the two of them rolled through the dewy grass. Especially not for someone as long out of the game as himself.

The guy he'd hit was tall and light but wiry, seeming to move in several different directions at once. Deal struggled to get his weight atop him, catching one of the man's flailing hands that pounded at his chest, snatching the other as a feeble punch glanced off his ear. He had managed to pull himself astride the man, a knee pinning each of his thin arms, when he saw the glint of the shotgun move in front of his nose, its dual barrels pointed in the general direction of Deal's knees.

"Just lay still," he heard Russell's voice above him. Deal felt the struggling figure beneath him go lax. In the next moment the flashlight beam had snapped on once more, illuminating their prey.

"What the hell?" Deal said, staring down at the person who lay pinned beneath him. A snowy-haired black man, eighty if he was a day, glared up defiantly into the flashlight's glare.

"You think I'm scared?" the old guy said.

118

"You'd better be," Russell said, waving the shotgun in a tiny circle above the guy's face.

"Be careful with that thing," Deal said. His groin was inches from the old guy's chin.

"He don't have to be," the old guy said. "It's empty." He tried to buck out from under Deal at that moment, a surprisingly strong move for someone his age and build.

"He's right," Deal heard Russell say over the sound of the shotgun breaking open. A pair of spent casings fell to the grass at his side. "What the hell are you doing, old man?"

"Better question for you people," the old guy said sullenly.

"Are you all right?" Deal heard Annie's voice from behind him. He wasn't about to turn. Keeping his balance atop the squirming old man was like trying to ride an eel.

"I'm fine," he called. "How's your arm?"

"It's okay," she said.

"What is *that?*" Deal heard Russell's voice. It seemed to be a question for Annie.

"You'd better take this," Deal heard her say. "My hand's a little sore."

"Is it loaded?" Russell's voice came.

"Why would I carry a pistol that wasn't loaded?" Deal heard her answer. It was only beginning to sink in. A moment ago, he'd been feeling guilty for dragging her into danger. Now, he realized, she had saved their skin.

"Just asking," he heard Russell say.

In the next minute, the big man was crouching beside Deal, a tiny, pearl-handled derringer in one of his big hands. "See this?" he asked the old guy.

The old guy stared up sullenly. "You couldn't get your fat finger through the guard," he said, writhing violently in Deal's grasp.

"You're right about that," Russell said, and brought the heel of the pistol down smartly on the old guy's forehead.

Deal stared down at the suddenly limp form beneath him. "Jesus, Russell. What if that thing had gone off?"

Russell gave him a baleful look, holding up what looked like a .22 shell between two of his fingers. "Give me some credit, will you?"

"What is going on here, anyway?" Annie asked.

"I was going to ask you the same thing," Deal said, glancing up at her. At the same moment, he felt a stirring beneath him.

"You tried to kill Dequarius," Deal heard the old man's voice. No more snarling now, more like a sob. "Now you're gonna kill me."

For a moment, the three of them stared at one another in surprise. And then Deal was helping the old man to his feet.

# 14

"**You're John Deal?**" the old man asked doubtfully. "The one going to work for Stone?"

They'd helped him inside his house and propped him in a chair at the kitchen table, where he sat now, holding a towel full of ice cubes to the knot on his forehead.

"Have a look," Deal said. He pulled out his wallet and flipped it open to display his driver's license.

The old guy checked the license, then peered into Deal's face. "Not much of a picture," he said.

Deal wasn't going to argue that point. He glanced at Annie, who'd been on her cell phone, checking admissions at the emergency room at the only hospital on the island. She broke off the connection and shook her head dismissively at Deal. "No luck," she said. "One drunk who was in a car accident, one woman in labor. That's it."

Deal turned to glance at the old man. "You think we ought to have you looked at?" he asked.

"For this?" the old man said, pulling the ice pack from his head. He glared at Russell. "I been hit harder by small children."

"Take it easy," Russell Straight said. He was standing in front of the sink, shaking his head. "You already caused enough trouble for one evening."

The old man's eyes flashed. "I didn't cause trouble for nobody," he said.

"You could have killed *us*," Russell countered, gesturing at the ancient double-barreled shotgun that he'd propped in a far corner.

The old man snorted. "I fired straight up in the air, sonny-boy. I wanted you dead, you'd *be* dead."

Deal gave Russell a warning glance, then turned back to the old man. "I just want to be sure I've got it straight. You're Dequarius's grandfather—"

"*Great*-grandfather," the old man corrected.

"Great-grandfather," Deal repeated. "How about telling me your name?"

The guy took a last look at Deal's license, then folded the wallet and handed it back across the table. "Spencer is my name," he said. "Ainsley Spencer. And don't ask me for any driver's license because I don't have one." He glared up at Russell. "Never have, never will."

"Take it easy," Russell said.

The old man ignored him, turning back to Deal. "I was asleep when they come for Dequarius," he said. "If I hadn't been, maybe I could of helped." Despite the jut of his jaw, his eyes had reddened as he spoke, and Annie put a soothing hand on his shoulder.

The phone still lay in a corner of the kitchen where someone had tossed it, its cord ending in a multi-hued snarl where it had snapped. One of the shotgun blasts had peppered the front of an old Kelvinator refrigerator, and another had torn out a gouge of plaster beside the back door. There was a smear of blood at the doorjamb and other spatters on the back stoop, which the old man had pointed out to them a few moments before.

"I don't understand why the police aren't here," Annie said, staring at Deal, who thought of that growling voice he'd heard on the telephone. *Perhaps they've been and gone,* he might have told her, but it was only a fleeting thought.

"That's just the way it is here in the quarter," Ainsley Spencer said. "We don't bother the *police,* and they don't bother with us."

"Even if someone gets shot?" she said in disbelief.

"Specially if someone gets shot," he said, fixing his red-rimmed gaze upon her.

"What about Dequarius?" she persisted. "He could have been hurt."

The old man glanced at the scarred wall across from him. "He's someplace he don't want to be found," the old man said. "Not till the ones who came after him get taken care of. What do you think I was doing out there?"

"But the police could help—"

"Give it a rest, Annie," Deal broke in. She glared at him, about to protest, then clamped her lips shut and turned away, her arms folded tightly to her chest.

Deal turned back to Ainsley Spencer. "Do you have any idea where Dequarius might have gone?"

The old man stared at him for a moment, then turned away.

Deal followed his gaze to the smear of blood by the doorjamb. "How about the people who were here, Mr. Spencer?"

"That was my father's name," the old man said quietly, still staring at the blasted doorway. "Mine is Ainsley."

Deal nodded assent. "Ainsley it is, then," he said, still waiting for an answer.

The old man turned back to him. "Dequarius had him a few run-ins, of course . . ."

"A *few?*" It was Russell, still shaking his head.

"As I can tell you have," the old man countered, nodding at one of the jailhouse tattoos curling from beneath Russell's shirtsleeve. It stopped Russell, and the old man turned back to Deal. "They was white, that's about all I can say, because I heard them talking while I was getting my gun out from under the bed. By the time I made it into the kitchen, they was gone, all of them."

"You think Dequarius got away?"

The old man glanced at the smear of blood on the doorjamb. "I think he'd still be lying out there if they got him good," he said.

Deal glanced at Russell, then back at the old man. "Your grandson called me just before this happened—" Deal began.

"Great-grandson," the old man interjected.

"Right," Deal said.

"I only got one great-grandson," the old man continued.

"We were still on the phone when the shooting started."

The old man simply shook his head.

"I'm wondering what it was he wanted," Deal said.

The old man gave Deal a neutral look. "He wouldn't have told me, that's for sure."

"He usually tell you when he's got some scheme cooked up?" Russell asked.

The old man glanced coolly at Russell. "The boy sells a little weed

124

sometimes, but that's mostly in the neighborhood, and this man here don't seem the type." He finished with a nod at Deal.

Deal cut a glance at Annie, but her gaze stayed on Ainsley Spencer. "Sometimes he peddles some trinkets to the tourists, too," he added, this time to Deal. "But you don't strike me as stupid, either." He shrugged then, as if that ended the matter.

Deal sat back in his chair, wondering just what he should do next. Comb the island for Dequarius Noyes? Without some clue as to his whereabouts, he doubted he could find the boy if he had a cordon holding hands and marching from one end of the town to the other.

Sleep was a prime consideration, another part of his mind suggested. His head was hollow with fatigue, his body drained. There was an acrid taste in his mouth, still lingering from the dope he'd smoked, he supposed, and a soreness in the small of his back, courtesy of Deputy Conrad's fists.

There was the undeniable upside of Annie Dodds's presence at his side, but even that was leavened by the knowledge that she was involved in some as-yet-undetermined way with Franklin Stone. Add to all that the events of the past hour, and he was more than ready to put this day into rewind. Go to sleep, wake up, and discover that some of this mess had been a dream.

He rubbed his face with his hands and glanced around the kitchen, trying to bring some focus to his thoughts. Save for the blood and the buckshot scars, it was a tidy place, which somehow seemed at odds with his impression of Dequarius Noyes. "It's just you and Dequarius who live here?"

The old man nodded.

"How about his parents?" Deal asked.

The old man lifted his shoulders in a barely perceptible motion.

125

"His momma passed a few years back. I couldn't tell you where his daddy might be."

Deal took it in with a nod. "You mind if I look at his room?" he asked the old man. Maybe there was something there that would give him a hint of what the kid had been up to, or where he might have gone.

The old man gave him a sharp glance, then seemed to relent. He gestured down a hallway that led away from the kitchen. "Help yourself. The one on the right is mine. Across the hall is Dequarius's."

Deal stood and walked out of the brightly lit room into the dim recess of the hall. A few paces along, he caught a glimpse of the old man's neatly arranged room through an open doorway—single bed, oak dresser, padded rocker—then turned to the facing door and nudged it open. He found the light just inside the jamb and snapped it on.

Dequarius's was a small room as well, with its own chenille-covered single bed, a painted chest of drawers, and a small desk with a wooden straight chair drawn up in its knee-hole. Nearly as tidy as the old man's digs, Deal thought with renewed surprise. Either Dequarius had learned a few things or the old man kept house for the both of them.

He crossed to the closet and pulled it open to loosen a faint smell of marijuana as well as expose a few pairs of slacks and an array of basketball jerseys on hangers. There was a stack of shoe boxes on the shelf, one of which he suspected held something other than the advertised brand of sneakers. On the floor below the clothing was a pair of scuffed black work boots and a wooden tennis racket with its strings exploded. He was about to close the closet door, taken with the image of Dequarius Noyes loping around a tennis court in Afro, baggy shorts, and Heat jersey, when he noticed something else and paused.

He swung the closet door open wide, to be sure it wasn't just a trick of the light. But the image remained: In the corner opposite the boots

126

and the blasted racket was a perfect rectangle outlined by dust. Dequarius's housekeeping skills had certain limits, Deal saw, squatting down to run his finger through the thin film of dust covering the opposite half of the closet floor. There'd been a box or carton here until recently, he realized, though just how long ago it had been removed was open to conjecture.

He sniffed at the pungent odor emanating from the closet again, wondering if that, in fact, was what had prompted the invasion and shooting. Someone after Dequarius's stash.

Deal stood and began going through the boxes on the top shelf. The first box, in fact, held a pair of sneakers—an outlandish zebra-striped pattern, their soles worn smooth—as did the second, in this case a black leather pair with red lights that still raced about the perimeter of one heel when Deal jiggled the container. Not the thing to wear when fleeing the scene of a crime, Deal thought. Maybe that's why they seemed scarcely used.

The third box was so heavy it nearly plunged to the floor when he pulled it from the shelf. Inside he found a glittering array of treasure—treasure of a sort, anyway. Golden coins stamped from a press, shiny silver bracelets, pendants bearing bits of colored glass; it wouldn't take a genius to spot it for carnival loot, Deal thought, replacing the lid. If Dequarius Noyes had made a living selling crap like this, he deserved every penny of it.

He slid the heavy shoe box back in its place and brought down the next, as feathery light as the last had been brick heavy. He glanced at the label skeptically. If there was indeed a pair of Reebok running shoes inside, then he was going to scour *Runner's World* for a matching set the moment he got back to Miami.

The odor that struck him the instant he loosened the top told him his suspicions had been correct, however. He removed the top and    127 glanced at the contents—the dark green buds obscured beneath what looked like doubled Ziploc bags—already discounting his earlier theories about the invasion. He put the top back on and replaced the Reebok box, then found three more on the shelf very nearly like it: Nike, Adidas, and Tommy Hilfiger.

Deal stared at the line of boxes, had a sudden vision of Dequarius out on the street, offering his wares by brand. "Now your Adidas ain't bad, but your Tommy, that's some bad shit, my man. And your Nike is one-hit city. . . ." He shook his head and swung the closet door shut, wondering what had been so intriguing inside that carton missing from its spot on the floor.

He crossed to the desk, scanning its bare top, then slid the chair back to get at the single drawer. Inside, he found a scattering of pens and pencils, and a pad with the telephone number for the Pier House scrawled on the top page, beneath it some random doodlings and scribblings. "Vino, vidi, vici," Deal read in one corner, the familiar phrase misspelled but triple underlined, as if Dequarius—street corner scholar—had been planning some major campaign of his own. He tore off the page and folded it into his pocket, then went to join the others, snapping off the light as he went.

When he walked back into the kitchen, he noted that Russell Straight was staring at him with a defiant look, as if Deal might be somehow responsible for Dequarius's hard road. Deal turned back to the old man. "You sure you don't want to talk to the police?"

The old man stared at him tolerantly. "Mr. Deal, I appreciate you coming over here on account of Dequarius and all . . ." He trailed off, his gaze traveling to the shotgun propped in the corner. ". . . And I feel bad if I scared you all." He put the bunched towel down on the table-top between them and gave his earnest gaze to Annie. "But it's like I say, there's just no point to getting the police involved."

128

"But if Dequarius is hurt—" Annie cut in.

"The police don't care about Dequarius, ma'am," Spencer said gently. "That's one thing we know for sure. When he wants us to hear from him, that's when we'll hear."

She stared back at him, ready to jump out of her skin with frustration, or so it seemed. "Look at that bump on your head," she said after a moment. "We ought to have *that* looked at, at least."

The old man mustered a weary smile for her. "A couple of aspirin and a good night's sleep, I'll be just fine."

"Where do you keep your aspirin?" she said. She stood, glancing at Deal and Russell as if daring them to interfere with these small ministrations.

Spencer pointed over Russell's shoulder. "In the cabinet there," he said.

Deal watched as Annie brushed by Russell and pulled open a tall cabinet door above the sink. As she rummaged about, he caught a glimpse of a box of Kix—his daughter Isabel's favorite cereal—a bag of rice, and what looked like a bottle of wine. In a moment Annie was back with the aspirin and a glass of water she'd drawn from the tap.

She shook a couple of aspirins into her palm and handed them to the old man, along with the water. As he dutifully swallowed the pills, Deal opened his wallet and found a card. He copied the number of his room at the Pier House on the back and handed it to Spencer. "If you hear from Dequarius, would you let me know?"

The old man took the card and glanced at it before putting it in the pocket of his grass-stained white shirt. "I'll do it," he said to Deal, who turned then and urged the others out.

129

**15**

"I can't believe we're just going to leave here like nothing's happened," Annie fumed as Deal worked at turning the Hog around on the narrow street.

His rear wheels were already up over the curb. Maybe once you got yourself in this neighborhood, he mused, you weren't supposed to get out.

"Not much else we *can* do," Russell offered, his head out the window to help with the maneuvering.

"I'm afraid he's right," Deal said, glancing at her as he stopped backing and cut his wheels.

"We can check the hospital again later, but if we called in the sheriff, they'd be all over that old man's house," he continued, mindful of what he'd found inside Dequarius's closet. "Who knows what they might turn up. And if they did come across something, it'd be Spencer who'd pay the price." And never mind his suspicions about Conrad, Deal thought as he wrestled with the Hog's wheel. Those he'd keep to himself for now.

And what *had* happened, when it came right down to it? A well-known scam artist had been bird-dogging him since his arrival in Key West, anxious to unload some unknown swag—gold, jewelry, shoe boxes of marijuana—for reasons Deal couldn't begin to fathom. There'd been a phone call, a shooting, some smears of blood left behind.

For all he knew, there'd been a turf battle between a couple of drug dealers, and one of them had been winged in the process. If it weren't for the fact he'd been sure it was Conrad's voice he'd heard, and that Dequarius had been so eager to contact *him,* even warn him to get out of town, Deal would be ready to forget the whole thing.

"You think the police would harass an old man like that?" Annie's reply to Russell broke into his thoughts.

"Old *black* man," Russell shot back.

It stopped her. Deal had the Hog pointed back the way they'd come by now and had begun to pilot them slowly up the dark street. For all he knew there were dozens of pairs of eyes upon them up and down this gauntlet of dark houses, watching through all those blank windows and ghostly curtains. Waiting for the invaders to leave, he thought, waiting to close ranks, begin the healing of the wounds.

"Look out!" Annie cried suddenly, and Deal turned to find something flying out of the darkness at the windshield. He hit the brakes and turned loose of the wheel at the same time, throwing one arm up in front of his face and using the other to shield her. The Hog skidded to a halt, rocking them forward, then back.

"Goddamn rooster," Russell Straight said as the thing fluttered over the roof of the Hog like the world's largest, angriest moth.

131

Deal released his breath and glanced at Annie, who stared up at the sound of scratching on the roof above. In the next instant, he realized that his hand was resting on her breast. The jolt that ran through his body was electric, almost painful.

"Sorry," he said, removing his hand.

"For what?" she asked, staring at him neutrally.

He opened his mouth to say something, then realized he had no words. His heart seemed to be hammering from a run that had begun about twenty years before.

"We better get out of here before the chickens get their shit together," Russell said, giving him a baleful glance.

Deal nodded, then gripped the wheel and drove.

"Right here is good," Russell said as the Hog came to a stop at a signal perhaps a quarter mile from where they'd started out. Trees shrouded the streets into leafy tunnels and the smell of gardenia drifted on the balmy air. They seemed to have traveled halfway around the world.

Deal glanced aside at Russell, then noted the silhouette of a compact car parked in the shadows catercorner from where the Hog idled. The signal turned green, but at this hour there was no one behind them.

"I'll catch you first thing," Russell said, levering the door handle at his side.

Deal nodded. What was it Russell had said what seemed like aeons ago? There's women everywhere? He stared at the porch of a gingerbreaded bungalow where a yellow light still burned, then stole a glance at Annie. Well, apparently not, he thought.

"We'll get some sleep," Deal said. "Figure out what to do in the morning."

132

He'd added the last as much for Annie's benefit as anything. What was there to do but wait and see if Dequarius turned up like the bad penny he seemed to be? Track down Deputy Conrad and ask for a sniff of his riot gun's barrels? Whatever had taken place this night, he thought Conrad might be all too eager to go along with that request.

Russell lifted one of his big hands to wave acknowledgment, then nodded a goodnight to Annie. In the next moment he was gone, slipping through the shadows down the block.

"It's green," Annie said after a moment.

He looked up at the signal, then prodded the Hog forward with a touch of the accelerator. There was plenty of room on the broad bench seat now that Russell had gone, and she had taken advantage of it. She sat in the corner of the compartment, her knees drawn up to her chest, her arms locked around her shins. Deal was nearly loony with exhaustion, thoughts bouncing in his head like electrons popping in a skillet. Only one thing burned clear: the feeling of his hand on her breast.

"You're upset?" he tried, turning onto Whitehead Street. The moon was behind them now, outlining the big houses down near the water's edge.

She started to say something, then stopped and began again. "Men and women think differently about things," she said. "Why don't we leave it at that?"

*Forever?* Deal wondered. The question was unutterable, of course. His mind raced, some voices raising questions about Dequarius, others demanding some account of his intentions. Why had he had his hand on Annie's breast to begin with? Why had he taken it away?

He employed desperate measures to counteract the fierce feelings that seemed to have constricted his throat to the size of a pinhole. *What if your daughter were here?* But that was no good. He saw Isabel

133

perched on the Hog's broad leather seat grinning and bouncing in place, Annie with an answering smile.

*Your wife, for God's sake!* Same story, he discovered, willing Janice onto the scene. But she only patted him on the shoulder and wished him well, vanishing into the night as deftly as Russell had. My oh my.

"We're here," Annie said softly as the Hog swung past the shadow of the Hemingway house.

No help from the ghosts in that quarter, Deal thought. Four wives and who knows what all, before he'd swallowed his own shotgun. Ye Gods.

"So we are," Deal said, turning into the drive of Stone's mansion. No porch light here, he noticed. Some discreet landscape lighting, but no lamp in the window. He left the Hog's engine running as he turned to her.

"I'll check the hospital when I get back to the hotel," he told her. "If I hear anything . . ."

She nodded and put her hand up to stop him. "It's all right," she said. "I know you'll do the right thing."

Would that he were as certain, Deal thought. "By the way," he said, "neither one of us said thanks for what you did tonight."

"Getting the drop on Spencer?" she asked, the hint of a smile on her lips. "I'm glad it wasn't a real badass."

"Do you always carry a gun?" he asked.

She gave him the look he was getting familiar with, the "*I'm not sure I know you well enough*" stare. "I lived in a pretty rough neighborhood there for a while," she said finally. "I got a permit and learned how to use it, in case you're wondering."

He gave her an all-purpose Driscoll shrug. "Anyways, it was a pretty gutsy move. You didn't know who was out there. Anything might have happened."

She thought about it for a moment. "Yes," she agreed, "anything might."

In a movement so quick that it startled him, she leaned forward, brushing her lips against his cheek. In the next moment, she was out of the Hog and gone.

**16**

DEAL PARKED THE Hog in what seemed to be the last space available in the Pier House lot, and stood with his hand on the dew-streaked car's roof, waiting for his head to clear before he moved toward his room. It was an unaccustomed quiet at this hour, the moon a yellow disk on the far horizon, about to sink into the sea.

He could hear the tick of the Hog's cooling engine, the flurry of a bird deep inside the branches of a nearby banyan. Was there anything as sorry as a tourist limping back to his Key West room late and alone? he found himself thinking, and shook his head at the pathetic quality of the thought. A few hours before he'd been sitting at dockside, having a cocktail with a woman so lovely she could steal his breath with a simple glance—and how long had it been since he'd experienced that feeling, anyway?

How could things have gone so awry? he wondered. What bad karma, what past sins? Why had he ever answered that phone?

He checked the discreetly placed numbers on the building before him, made a jog left, then right, crossing a lawn that seemed smooth enough to be a putting green. Golf, he found himself thinking blearily. Maybe he should rise early, return to Miami just as Dequarius had suggested, and throw himself into the sport.

He knew more than one builder who conducted business on the golf course. Crack one down the middle, strike a deal—he could pardon the expression—then turn his attention to something important: the upcoming chip and putt. His old man had had a handicap hovering near scratch until the booze had finally gotten him, in fact, so he surely had the genes. Golf, booze, cards, and dice, a little business on the side. If there had been other women involved in his old man's life, Deal had never known about it. Maybe there *was* an answer to this feeling of uncertainty that now gripped him, if he just searched hard enough.

He found the right staircase and made his way slowly up to the second floor, the memory of the last time he'd visited a golf course burning brightly in his mind.

Things had been crazy then, too. Janice had gone missing and was presumed dead, and Deal himself was surely at fault. He'd found his way somehow to the club where his old man's founding membership still stood. He'd charged a set of clubs and a lunatic golfer's outfit to a tab that hadn't seen action in a decade, then dressed and hauled himself out to a practice tee, where he'd smashed every ball in the enormous bucket the pro had provided until his tears were too thick to continue.

He'd tossed the clubs aside, peeled off the ridiculous clothes, right there on the tee, right down to his skivvies . . . which is when a solicitous attendant who'd been fond of his high-rolling father had come to escort him inside.

No, he told himself ruefully as he ticked off the numbers toward his room, golf might not be the answer. He couldn't find the key card at first and found himself struck with despair at the thought of a walk all the way back to the office for a duplicate. There would have to be conversation, perhaps some providing of identification, not to mention the actual walking all the way there and back. There were lawn chairs and chaises down at poolside, he thought. He'd sleep in one of those first.

He remembered that he'd slipped the card into his wallet then, right behind the license that Ainsley Spencer had eyeballed a bit earlier. Blessed relief, he thought, reaching into his pocket. He pulled out his wallet and opened it and stopped, staring at the glassine window where his license—lousy head shot and all—was normally kept.

No license there now, he noted with a stupid stare. Someone had slipped a card in there instead. *Come back alone.* The words were scrawled in pencil, below his own room number.

Deal flipped the card over and saw that it was indeed the same card he'd given to Ainsley Spencer, along with the request for the old man to call if Dequarius should return. How on earth? he wondered, turning first the card and then his wallet over in his hands.

The old man would have to be a sleight-of-hand artist, he thought, or some kind of pickpocket . . . And then he stopped, a rueful smile coming over his features. Of course. What better way to explain certain of Dequarius's talents? The old coot, Deal thought, fishing his key card out from behind his sorry-assed license.

He shoved the thing into the slot, then stared at the blinking red lights that danced around the face of the lock. Like the lights on Dequarius's dumbass tennis shoes, he thought. He withdrew the card, turned it around, and tried the other way. This time the lights flashed green and he reached confidently for the lock.

LES STANDIFORD

He needn't have bothered with all the folderol of the key, he realized, as the door swung inward at the brush of his hand. The latch had been open all the time.

Maybe he hadn't closed the door carefully on his way out, he thought. Or maybe the mechanism was faulty. Hadn't Russell Straight told him his door had been ajar earlier that morning?

If he hadn't been so tired, the warning signals would have been flashing inside his mind, of course. But he was exhausted, dazed with the twists and turns of the night's experiences, and still not certain he'd done the right thing where Dequarius was concerned.

He'd get some rest, though, then go see the old man first thing. He was inside the room now and had flipped the light switch in the foyer, kicking the door shut behind him.

Odd smell, he was thinking, must be his night for them. But this was the unmistakable aroma of trouble and danger, something in his weary brain urged.

The smell of blood, and something else darker and more sinister, and a clumsy smear like finger-painting on the bright wall before him . . . *Someone in here,* an inner voice was screaming now, his mind scrambling at last toward full alert.

He spun around, every nerve ending snapping fire, his hands raised to ward off the hounds of hell themselves.

It was then that he saw that Dequarius Noyes had turned up, after all. Sitting in the easy chair beside Deal's ocean-view windows, his comb cocked jauntily in his thick Afro, his hand extended and clutching what looked like a card or a note or a ticket unavailable from any other source. His eyes were sightless, his shirtfront a mass of blood, and the other smells told Deal everything. He staggered quickly into the bathroom and vomited, then splashed water on his face.

139

Deal willed the apparition to be gone when he came back out, but there was no such luck. None for him this night, and decidedly none for Dequarius Noyes.

He walked toward Dequarius then, and reached out his hand to close his sightless stare, then take the offering that Dequarius had brought for him, slipping it out of the corpse's cool, stiff grasp.

It was a brittle slip of paper, about the size of a note card, its edges nicked and crumbling. He turned it over and blinked, bringing it closer to the desk lamp to be sure of what he was looking at. A wine label, he realized, soaked or scraped from its bottle, or so it appeared. Faded with age, the French script dulled, the outlines of an imposing château a dimly visible outline beneath the print.

He glanced briefly at this item that Dequarius had thought so important, then slipped it into his pocket, along with the note from Ainsley Spencer and the sheet of paper he'd taken from the pad in Dequarius's room. Finally, he sagged down on his bed and made the inevitable call.

**17**

"THIS IS JUST the way you found him?" A plainclothes officer stood beside Deal, who was watching numbly as the medical examiner finished his work with the body that had once been Dequarius.

"I closed his eyes," Deal said.

The detective made a note on the screen of a handheld organizer, then glanced up. "You didn't touch anything else?"

Deal shrugged. Before the sheriff's men arrived, he'd taken the faded label and the notes from his pocket and slipped them under the cover of the ironing board stowed in his closet. He was long past the point of trusting anyone from the sheriff's office.

"The phone," he said to the detective. "The toilet where I threw up. The sink handles."

The detective touched the tip of the stylus to his tongue and made more notes. When he noticed Deal watching him, he gave a smile that was more like a grimace. "They handed these things out first of the year," he said, meaning the handheld. "I tried to lose mine a couple of times, but the hammer came down from up top." The detective gave Deal his screw-the-brass look. "Now I learned how to use it, you'd be surprised how much time it saves."

Deal nodded. He supposed it did save time. Reduce a life to a few strokes on a liquid crystal screen, from there on, everything's done by machine.

"The ME says he bled out right there," the detective said, nodding at the chair. There was a photographer at work now, using a digital camera to record various angles of the scene. Those images could go straight to the computer as well, Deal thought, untouched by human hands.

"But since it was a shotgun took him out and your windows are still intact, I'd say it was a safe bet he was shot elsewhere."

Deal nodded again, trying to imagine a shotgun blast taking out those big windows, scattering glass over the putting-green grass below. Hardly the sort of thing the Pier House would be happy about. What had taken place so far was surely troubling enough for the public relations team.

The detective replaced his organizer in his coat pocket and reached for something on the nearby dresser. He turned back, holding up a plastic bag. Inside was an oblong card that might have seemed a duplicate of Deal's room key, except for an inch-thick wedge of plastic affixed to one end. "This belong to you?" the detective asked.

Deal looked again, then shook his head.

"I didn't think so," the detective said, gesturing over Deal's shoulder. "It's a universal master for locks like these, something only a thief would have. I found it lying on your hallway floor."

142     Deal turned to glance at the door, then back at the detective. There

could have been a dozen of the things lying there, he would never have noticed.

The detective replaced the bag on the dresser. "Our boy over there could have gotten into any room in the Pier House. The big question is, Mr. Deal, why did he pick yours to come die in?" The expression on the detective's face was not unsympathetic. "Must have been a hell of a thing to come home to," he added.

The big question for Deal was somewhat different, however. His major consideration was with just where to begin. "He called me earlier," Deal said finally.

"Called you?" Deal waited for the detective to go for his handheld, but it didn't happen. "This is a friend of yours?"

"No," Deal said. "I met him in the bar downstairs, on Thursday evening, right about the end of happy hour."

The cop's expression was neutral. Deal suspected it would remain that way no matter what he said next. *We were lovers and I shot him in a jealous rage. He sold me phony gold coins and I killed him for it. If I'd given him the time of day he might still be alive.*

"He wanted to sell me some jewelry he said had come up from a sunken treasure ship," Deal continued. "I told him I wasn't interested. The bartender noticed him then and chased him out." Deal stopped, hating something about the way he was talking. "His name is Dequarius Noyes, by the way."

He was also wondering how Ainsley Spencer would receive this news. Deal had consoled himself with the knowledge that the phone was inoperable at the old man's house, but that was really just a cop-out. Now, the thought that someone like Deputy Conrad might deliver the news to the old man seemed a double blow.

The detective nodded. "We got that," he said. "Kid's got a history a yard long, dealing dope off that houseboat of his—"

143

"Houseboat?" Deal heard himself blurt.

"Yeah," the detective said. "He's got a place out on houseboat row, the worst of a pretty bad lot."

He gave Deal a speculative look, then recovered his train of thought. "So if I got this right, the next thing you know, Dequarius is back on the phone with you earlier this evening, wanting to see if you're still interested in this treasure."

"I was never interested," Deal said, his mind racing along. So Dequarius kept a place apart from his great-grandfather's home in the quarter, then. It would make sense, he supposed, given the young man's proclivities—a place to hide a stash in a pinch, that was the cynical take on it. But there was an upside as well. For all Deal knew, the police would make no connection between Dequarius and his great-grandfather. So long as Deal didn't tell them of it, that is.

Deal forced his attention back to the moment then, wondering if the detective knew what had happened yesterday morning or was simply testing him. "And the fact is, I saw him again the next morning, while we were out jogging."

"Who's this 'we'?" the detective asked.

"I was with Russell Straight, a man who works for me."

"He staying here at the hotel?"

Deal nodded, deciding to leave out the "more or less" part.

"He approached you again about this jewelry while you were out jogging?"

"He was persistent," Deal said.

"He must have been," the detective said. "What time of the morning was this?"

Deal calculated. "Probably about six-fifteen."

"That seems a little early for Dequarius to be on the hustle," the detective observed. "Wouldn't you say?"

Deal shrugged. "It could have been a little later. I'm sure you could look it up in the police report."

The detective's eyes narrowed. "I think you're a step ahead of me, Mr. Deal. What report would that be, exactly?"

"The one you're free to consult anytime, Dickerson," someone behind them said, and Deal turned to see Rusty Malloy coming through the doorway, clad in a T-shirt, a pair of khaki shorts, and sandals. As far as Deal could tell, he hadn't bothered to comb his hair since taking his phone call.

"My client intervened in an assault by one of your deputies upon Mr. Noyes yesterday morning," Malloy continued, wincing as his gaze fell upon the bloody corpse. "The matter was disposed of, no charges filed."

The detective took all this in with remarkable calm, Deal thought. "This was after Dequarius had approached you for the second time?" he asked.

"It was." Deal nodded.

"So when Dequarius called you earlier this evening, that was the third time you'd spoken to him about this jewelry," Dickerson said.

"We never really talked in any detail," Deal said. *Three times thou hast forsaken me,* came the line swimming up out of his past. But surely that hardly applied in this case, he thought, stealing a glance at Dequarius's body.

"Is there something funny, Mr. Deal?"

Deal turned back to Dickerson, feeling a tide of unreasoning fury swelling up inside him. He'd seen Driscoll pull the same stunt with suspects, lulling them along with innocuous questions before turning suddenly hostile. But he was no suspect and he wasn't about to put up with an iota of bullshit from Dickerson, or anyone else.

"Was I laughing?" he said, careful to control his tone.

145

The two stared evenly at each other until Malloy cut in. "My client's a bit tired, Detective. If it's all the same to you, why don't we continue this in the morning?"

Dickerson lifted his eyebrows and glanced toward the windows, where a couple of uniformed deputies were wrestling Dequarius's body into a zippered bag. His expression didn't indicate there was any great haste in the matter.

"Sure," Dickerson said. "We can finish up in the morning." He gave Deal what passed for a smile, then dug into his wallet for a card.

"Just give me a call in the morning, Mr. Deal, whenever you're feeling up to it." He glanced blandly at Malloy. "Couple more questions, that's all," he added.

Deal had heard that one before as well. He might as well have said, "We'll get down to business the next time around."

Malloy nodded. "I gotta go to the can. You guys doing anything in there?" He pointed at the bathroom, and Dickerson shook his head.

"Help yourself," the detective said, and Malloy went off, closing the door behind him. "Careful," he added to Deal, pointing as a couple of technicians came through the door of Deal's room with a folded gurney.

Deal stepped aside as the men passed. In seconds they had the thing unclipped and raised and had secured the bag with Dequarius's body atop it. The ME said something to the pair and in the next moment they were wrestling their burden away.

The toilet flushed and Malloy reappeared just as the gurney was disappearing out the door. He was mopping his pale face with a towel, and Deal realized then what had sent him to the bathroom in the first place.

"You all right?"

Malloy nodded, looking decidedly un–all right. There was a soft tapping at the door then, and the three of them turned to find a young

146

man in a tropical shirt smiling brightly at them. "I'm here for the bags," the kid said.

Deal turned to Malloy, who raised his finger in acknowledgment. "I stopped by the desk on the way in," he said. "The hotel's full, but they managed to find something."

Deal nodded and turned back to the kid, who'd spotted the gore-drenched chair and pool of blood near the window. "Jesus," he said. "What happened?"

Malloy gave him a scowl, then turned to Dickerson. "We can have his things moved out of here, can't we?"

Dickerson glanced around the room. "Why not?"

"You want to pack up, John?"

Deal realized he'd been staring at the closet where he'd stashed the papers. He'd barely bothered to unpack his suitcase, which still sat atop the dresser at his side. He had nothing hanging in the closet, no reason to go there, even if he was willing to try to extricate the papers with Dickerson staring over his shoulder.

He turned to Malloy with what he hoped was a grateful nod. What was he going to say, "I'm sorry, but I can't leave without my ironing board"?

"Just take a second," he managed. He thought Dickerson was look-ing at him strangely, but it was probably just his imagination.

He'd already stuffed most of his dirty clothes in an outer pocket of his soft-sided bag, so it wasn't much of a process. He went into the bathroom, which smelled like the head of a tourist boat in a typhoon, swept his toiletries into his travel kit, then came back out and dropped it into the main compartment of his suitcase. The kid, who'd turned as pale as Malloy by now, snatched up the bag quickly and hurried out the door.

"I think we're ready then," Malloy said, pointing after the kid.

147

"I guess we are," Deal said, careful to keep his gaze away from the closet.

Dickerson gave him a two-fingered salute. "Get some rest," he said. "I'll see you in the morning."

Deal gave a last glance at the chair where Dequarius Noyes had spent his final minutes waiting for him, then followed Malloy out.

**18**

"**NOT BAD, EH?**" Malloy said, gazing around the living area of the suite the bellhop kid had led them to.

Deal stared up at his attorney from the soft leather couch where he'd collapsed. Malloy had pulled the cork on a bottle of red wine and was swirling a glassful in his hand as he surveyed the bank of floor-to-ceiling windows comprising two walls of the room. There was a view of a pool down below, for the sole use of the "suites residents," the kid had assured them.

"Anything else I can do, gentlemen?" the kid called from the bar, where he'd been arranging liquor bottles and ice. "Anything at all?" He'd regained some of his color, Deal noticed, along with a bit of his programmed solicitousness.

"We're fine," Malloy said, handing him a bill. The kid seemed to find the tip more than generous, practically salaaming his way out.

"Can I get you something?" Malloy asked, hoisting his glass, as the door closed behind the kid.

Deal held up a hand. "Jack up the day and slide a new one under it," he said.

"You do have a way with words," Malloy said.

"That was one of my old man's," Deal said. "He had a million of them."

Rusty nodded. "Barton would have liked this place," he mused.

"He was always partial to the high-roller's suite," Deal agreed. He had another look at the glass in Malloy's hand. "Maybe I"ll try some wine," he added.

Malloy glanced over at him. "I thought you were a beer drinker. There's a six-pack of Red Stripe in the fridge."

Deal suppressed a sigh. The thought of explaining a diet right now seemed ludicrous. "As the president of a major development firm, I'm trying to refine my tastes," he said.

If he caught the irony, Malloy chose to ignore it. He nodded, going behind the bar for a glass. "I know what you mean. Everybody's getting into wine these days. Half my clients are drug dealers or worse, but I swear they all subscribe to *The Wine Spectator*."

He checked the bottle, then poured a glass for Deal and brought it to him. "A Chilean Malbec." He shrugged. "Tastes pretty good to me."

"So you're into wine now, too?" Deal asked.

Malloy shrugged. "In the old days it was the three-margarita lunch down here. Nowadays I have to bone up on my reds just to take somebody out to dinner."

"Sounds like a tough life," Deal said, raising his glass to Malloy.

"We're a long way from Miami, John," Malloy said, returning the

150

gesture. He smiled and used his glass to point over Deal's shoulder. "Did you catch the mirrored ceiling in the bedroom?"

"I didn't," Deal said without turning. "But I'm going to go watch myself fall asleep, any second now."

"Yeah, I'll bet," Malloy said, taking a healthy sip. "With any luck I'll be able to get back to sleep myself."

"Sorry," Deal said, reminding himself that Malloy was doing him a favor. He rubbed his face with one hand and glanced out at the soft blue nimbus of the pool. Like a glowing, happy cloud, he thought. He could dive in and sink straight to the bottom. Unfortunately, he still had business to attend to before the night was over.

"I'm glad you came over, Rusty," he said. "I was getting a little fried down there with our buddy Dickerson."

"No apologies necessary," Malloy said, lifting his glass. "'Tis the barrister's lot."

"You're going to send me a bill for all this," Deal added.

Malloy waved his hand in dismissal. "We'll take care of that part once you get under way with Stone. I'll take enough out of his hide to make me *and* my heirs happy."

Deal glanced up. "There's nothing certain between me and Stone, you realize that, don't you?"

"Oh sure," Malloy said. "He's a pain in the ass, but don't worry. I've been down here long enough to know how to handle him."

"I'm just saying—"

"Forget it, John. We're pals, all right? Whatever happens."

Deal shrugged. He was way too tired for looking gift horses in the mouth.

"So what were you holding back from Dickerson?" Malloy asked abruptly.

Deal managed a humorless laugh. "Was I being that obvious?"  151

"Not at all." Malloy grinned back. "But now my curiosity's up." He raised his glass in a salute.

"Pretty good the way you just did that," Deal said.

"You're just tired," Malloy said. "And besides, as your attorney, I need to know what my client's interests truly are."

"If I was charged with killing somebody, you'd want to know whether I really did it?"

Malloy held up his hand. "If you shot Dequarius Noyes, I do not want to know about it."

Deal shook his head. "That's not it," he said, then gave Rusty a quick version of what had transpired during and after the phone call he'd taken from Dequarius at the Dockside, leaving out any mention of the voice he'd heard after the shooting and of the papers he'd stashed.

No need for his attorney to be aware that he might have in fact concealed evidence, he told himself. But the truth was more complicated than that.

By the time he'd gone through it all, Malloy had finished his wine and was headed back to the bar for a refill. "Dequarius Noyes is like a bad penny," he said, shaking his head as he poured.

"*Was*," Deal corrected, and Malloy raised his brows in acknowledgment.

Malloy finished filling his glass, seeming to consider all that Deal had told him. "So what are you asking me, John?" Malloy said as he came back around the bar.

Deal turned his palms up in a gesture of uncertainty. "I just didn't want that old man to have to take it for some of Dequarius's bullshit, that's all. That's why I didn't call the cops earlier. Then, after I found Dequarius and realized Dickerson didn't know about the old man—"

"You're telling me you want to go back over there and help the old guy clean out Dequarius's stash before the storm troopers kick the door down?"

"Something like that," Deal said. "Also, I ought to be the one to tell him about his grandson. Or great-grandson."

Malloy laughed, but there wasn't much humor in it. "Legally speaking, I think you'd be nuts to do it—you'd be open to charges of interference, concealment, I'm not sure what all."

He broke off and took a slug of his wine. "But, I can understand why you'd want to," he added.

"How I see it," Deal said, leaning forward, "I go over there now, break the news to the old man, flush the dope down the toilet . . . then I go see Dickerson in the morning and tell him the rest of the story. That way Ainsley Spencer's in the clear. It seems the least I can do."

Malloy stared at him, shaking his head. "What are you talking about, 'the least you can do'? You sound like a man who's guilty of something. Whyever Dequarius Noyes got himself shot, it wasn't your fault," Malloy said.

Deal sighed inwardly. Part of him wanted to lay out everything in front of Malloy, but he worried that would simply confuse the issue.

His own suspicions about who might have killed Dequarius, not to mention the imponderables concerning why, were far too nebulous to discuss. What was on his mind right now was far more practical.

"You're right," Deal said to Malloy at last. He finished his glass and set it down on the bar. "But at least I can keep someone else from getting hurt."

Malloy closed his eyes, nodding his weary assent. He finished up his own glass, then started toward the door. "Do what you have to do, John," he said. "And be sure and call me when they pick your ass up."

153

# 19

THE GREEN PARROT was shuttered when Deal passed the bar for the second time that night—the crowd and the patrol car and the big, par-boiled man in the bathing suit and flip-flops had long since disap-peared, all of them gone to gather strength for the Saturday about to come, he supposed. The guardian roosters had deserted their post as well, he noted as he turned the Hog back down the narrow lane that led to Ainsley Spencer's bungalow. Where did roosters go to sleep it off? he wondered.

The narrow street itself was as dark and quiet as the first time he'd been there, he noted, though the air that drifted through the open win-dows of the Hog had turned a bit cooler. Not more than an hour or two until dawn, he thought, glancing up at the sky.

A hell of a time to roust an old man out of bed to tell him that his great-grandson was dead. But what was the alternative? Deal reminded himself. Deputy Conrad pounding on the jamb with the stock of his riot gun?

He pulled the Hog to the curb in front of the gap in the picket fence, vowing to send someone over to make the necessary repairs. If it came down to it, he thought, he'd swing by a hardware store for the tools and fix the damned thing himself. The least he could do, he told himself, and never mind if he was beginning to repeat himself.

He pulled himself out of the Hog and walked slowly toward the porch of the bungalow, too exhausted to rehearse what to say. To hell with it, he thought. He'd handle matters on the fly.

He raised his hand to knock, then pulled the flimsy screen door open to use the brass clapper that was mounted on the solid inner door. He let the echoes of the sturdy knocker die away, then tried again. No sound of footsteps. He tried a third time, but still with no success.

He was considering trying the doorknob, maybe stick his head inside and call if it was unlocked, when he heard footsteps behind him and turned. At the gate that opened off the sidewalk stood a heavyset woman in a blouse and ankle skirt.

"He's gone, mister."

Deal eased the screen door shut behind him. "You mean Dequarius?"

"Is that who you're looking for?" She rested one hand on a cane, he saw. Something in her voice suggested she didn't use it just to get around.

"I was looking for Mr. Spencer," he said.

"Again?" she said, a note of skepticism there. She had a broad face and her hair was done up in some kind of bandanna, but this was no jolly grandmother. He glanced up the dark street, wondering which of the quiet houses she'd been watching from. He wondered how many others were watching now.

He nodded. "I wanted to talk to him," he began. "It's about Dequarius." **155**

"He knows," she said, cutting in. The tone of her voice left little doubt just what.

"You mean . . . ?"

"Dequarius passed," she said. "We know."

With the last, Deal felt a chill run through him. He glanced back at the house, then up the deserted street. How on earth had word arrived?

He took a breath, trying to sort the thoughts banging inside his weary head. "Did Mr. Spencer say where he was going? When he was coming back?"

"He had to leave," the woman told him, her voice flat but final.

So much for being the bearer of bad news, he thought, glancing again at the stolid door behind him. "This was another reason I came," he told her. He wondered about the propriety of divulging a confidence, then reconsidered. If word of Dequarius's death was already common knowledge here, then what was he worrying about?

"The sheriff might be coming here—" he began.

"Maybe you left something inside, when you was here earlier," she said, cutting in.

He stared down at her moon-shadowed face. He couldn't see her eyes. He wasn't sure he wanted to.

"Why don't you go have yourself a look?" she said. "Spencer isn't going to mind." She lifted her cane and pointed. It seemed aimed at his breastbone. "Door's open," she added.

Deal gave her an uncertain glance, but she nodded encouragement. He turned and pulled the screen door, then tried the knob. The door opened easily in his hand. He gave a last look toward the woman who stood by the gate, then slipped inside.

A different odor greeted him this time—the tropical mustiness characteristic of any un–air-conditioned house in such a climate, of course, but changed somehow. This was the scent of a house that had

156

been closed, unlived in, for weeks, or even months. Its silence was equally profound.

He fumbled for the light switch, then flipped it on, bracing for the sudden glare, but nothing happened. Moonlight streamed into the tiny living room from a lace-shrouded window, enough for him to get his bearings. He crossed to the hallway where the bedrooms were and felt about for another light switch, but found nothing.

The doorway to the old man's room was a dark shadow on his right, the opening to Dequarius's a matching stripe of darkness on his left. Deal hesitated, feeling the skin prickle on his arms, the back of his neck. He had the feeling he was entering a place he'd never been before, which was crazy, he told himself. He'd walked down this very hallway not two hours before.

He put his hand into his pocket for his keys and pulled the ring out with a jingle that sounded like a dropped garbage can lid in the confined space. He kept a tiny penlight clipped there, a Christmas stocking gift from his daughter. The thing was supposed to be used for locating keyholes in the dark, though he couldn't remember the last time he'd used it. If his current run of luck held, the batteries would be long dead, he was thinking, then pressed the button with his thumb to find a wavering pool of light on the hallway wall in front of him.

He wouldn't want to explore any caverns with the light, but it was enough to cast a dim glow on his surroundings. He saw the foot of Dequarius's single bed jutting out from the wall and the dark lines of the wooden desk and chair across the room.

No bogeyman in sight, he thought, though he did check quickly behind the open door. The tiny light seemed to be weakening though, and he eased up on the thumb button to give the batteries a rest. A bit of light reflected in from the single window, but the house was close up against its neighbor here, and the angle of the moon was wrong. He

157

crossed quickly to the closet and reached for the door, pressing the button for the light.

The slick plastic button slipped in his fingers and his keys fell to the floor with a resounding clatter. He looked downward after them, but the corner of the room was in full shadow. He glanced over his shoulder and saw nothing but the vague shadow of the hallway door and the glowing nimbus that was Dequarius's bed. He thought briefly of going to check beneath it, then dismissed the notion out of hand. He was behaving like a child, he told himself. Driscoll would be beside himself with scorn.

He turned and eased himself down on his hands and knees and began to grope in the darkness for his fallen keys, ignoring the lunatic thoughts in his head—*This is when it happens, son. Someone coming through that door!*

He wouldn't have turned if he'd heard the thud of combat boots, he was telling himself . . . then stopped when his hands encountered something cool and hard on the floor in front of him. A floor grate, he realized, a source of ventilation or even heat, if such a thing was ever necessary in Key West. That would explain all the noise when his keys fell, he was thinking . . . and in the next instant, his fingers were probing the interstices of the grating, praying the clutch of keys was too big to fit through the openings.

He'd covered the entirety of the grate and gone over it a second time with his flattened palms, was about to pound his head against the wall in frustration when he caught a glint of metal out of the corner of his eye. He scurried on his hands and knees halfway across the room, where he found the keys bunched against the floorboard. He tried the penlight, relieved that it still worked, then pushed himself off the floor, intending to head for the closet at last.

158     He felt a stunning blow at his head, accompanied by a crashing

sound—furniture being flung to a wooden floor—then he was staggering sideways across the room, his legs as rubbery as a day sailor's in
a storm. He threw his hand up to protect himself from what was coming next, then felt his legs hit the side of the bed. He went down in a sitting position, dazed, one hand held to the back of his head, the other
pointing his penlight as if it were a weapon.

Some weapon, he was thinking, wondering what he'd been hit with
and why he hadn't been nailed again. He had to move, his brain told
him, duck and cover, do something or he'd be toast.

Then he stopped, realizing he was staring at an empty room. He
blinked, then tilted the penlight downward, as if an assailant might be
wriggling toward him like a snake . . . but there was nothing.

Someone had clubbed him, then run away, he thought. But why
hadn't he heard footsteps? What kind of house was he in, anyway?

Then, as the weak beam of light swept over the room, he began to
realize what had happened. The desk now sat askew, jolted out from its
place at the wall a foot or so, the chair tumbled onto its back. But there
was no killer hulking in the shadows, no club-wielding ghost about to
beat his brains out.

In fact, no one had hit him. He'd nearly knocked himself out. As
he'd searched for his keys, he'd lost track of where he'd been in the
darkness. When he straightened up, he drove his head squarely into the
corner of the oak desk. He felt the lump that was already rising and
would have shaken his head if it weren't so sore. What would Driscoll
have to say about this? he was wondering, when the voice burst from
the darkness and his eyes went blind with light.

# 20

"FREEZE!" DEAL HEARD one man cry.

"Move a muscle and you're dead," a more familiar voice added.

The light in his eyes was blinding. A handheld torch, he realized, trying to shield his face from the beam.

"Police officers," someone else cried. "Get your hands up."

Deal did as he was told, turning his face to escape the glare. "Well, look who it is," he heard as the whole room was bathed in light.

Deal glanced up at the illuminated ceiling fixture, now glowing brightly, then turned back to the doorway, where Conrad and two other deputies stood, pistols trained on him. One of the deputies stood with his hand still at the light switch he'd thrown.

"What the hell are you doing sitting in here in the dark?" Conrad

asked.

Deal shook his head. Had he been that stupid? he wondered. Hadn't even tried the switch in Dequarius's room? Driscoll would have a field day with that one.

"Aren't you supposed to read me my rights?" Deal said to Conrad, who glared back at him.

"Fuck you," Conrad said. He turned to the deputy who had his hand on the light switch. "Put the cuffs on him, Stroud."

"You're making a mistake," Deal said as Stroud holstered his weapon and came forward.

"You're the one made a mistake, buddy," Conrad said. "Keep him covered," he said to the third deputy, who nodded uncertainly.

Conrad gave Deal the look he probably reserved for perpetrators being dragged from a courtroom after sentencing, then strode across the room to throw open the closet door. Deal was already imagining how he'd begin his next phone call to Rusty Malloy when he saw Conrad stop short, as if he'd taken a punch to the solar plexus.

"Sonofabitch," the big deputy said, staring into the closet in disbelief.

"What is it, Marcus?" The cop who was supposed to be cuffing Deal glanced up.

"Sonofa*bitch*," Conrad repeated, swiping his arm across a row of empty hangers.

Deal stared over Conrad's shoulder into the closet. No slacks, no jerseys, no boots, no rows of stacked boxes on the shelf that ran above the length of galvanized pipe where the hangers danced. Deal couldn't tell whether the odor of marijuana might still be lingering there, but even if it was, that was the only thing the closet held.

"I don't see anything," the third deputy said.

Conrad turned a murderous gaze upon his partner, then strode to the painted dresser and began yanking open the drawers. He'd gotten to the last of them when a commotion sounded from the hallway.  161

"Get your hands off me," Deal heard a woman's voice cry, followed by a whacking sound and a yelp of pain.

"Put the club down, ma'am," Deal heard a man call. Then came a louder thwack.

"Goddamn!" the man cried. "Somebody help!"

Conrad stared up from the empty drawers at his two companions, his face glowing with rage. "Why doesn't he have cuffs on?" Conrad said, pointing at Deal. But Stroud was already on his way into the hall-way, and the third deputy seemed paralyzed with indecision.

Seconds later, Stroud was backpedaling furiously into the room, followed by the woman from the sidewalk who now brandished her cane like a rapier. There was a fourth deputy lurking in the hallway, but he seemed in no hurry to join the group inside the bedroom.

Conrad reached out and snatched the woman's cane away, an eye-blink move Deal would not have thought the man capable of. "Just simmer down," the big man said, holding up his free hand as if he were directing traffic to halt.

"You give me my cane," the woman demanded, uncowed by Con-rad's looming presence.

"I'll arrest you for assault, Auntie," Conrad said. "Just cool your jets, right now."

The woman hesitated, her cheeks glowing with fury. Conrad pointed to Stroud. "Get the cuffs on this man, *now*."

Stroud, who had a circular red welt rising in the middle of his fore-head like an outsized Buddhist's beauty mark, nodded, then began to fumble at his belt, where a pair of handcuffs dangled.

"What are you arresting him for?" the woman demanded.

"How about breaking and entering?" Conrad countered. "Burglary in the night season. Possession of . . ."

He stopped, glancing back at the empty closet. Deal thought he could hear gears grinding beneath the dome of the man's sheared skull. "Check his pockets," he called to Stroud. "See what he's got."

Stroud paused, the cuffs finally unclipped from his belt. "You want me to cuff him or search him?" Deal thought he detected a bit of impatience in the deputy's voice.

"Get out of my way," Conrad said, snatching the cuffs from Stroud and advancing on Deal.

"I invited this man into my home," the woman thundered. "How dare you be arresting him."

Conrad stopped short, blinking up at her. "Your home?" He glanced around the room. "This is *your* house?"

"Of course it's my house," she said, "just like it says down at the courthouse. I'm Minerva Betts and it's been my house for twenty-seven years now, bought and paid for by Mr. Marcus Betts himself, God rest his soul."

"But, Ainsley Spencer lives here."

Ms. Betts drew herself up, uncowed by Conrad. "Ainsley Spencer may spend time here, sir, but I don't know that it's any of your business. I demand to know what you and these—" she broke off to sweep a withering gaze over the three deputies "—these *men* are doing here."

Conrad's mouth opened and closed, then opened again. "We got a call there'd been a shooting," he said, trying a new tack.

"And what time was that?" she demanded.

Conrad seemed to be calculating. "Midnight, or thereabouts," he said, trying to regain his composure.

Her eyes widened. "And you show up five and a half hours later to investigate this so-called shooting?"

There was a tapping sound at the window of Dequarius's room, and everyone turned to stare. "Miz Betts? You all right?" came a muffled voice from outside.

163

"What the hell is that?" Conrad said.

Stroud went to the window to peer out. When he turned back to Conrad, there was a concerned expression on his face. "There's three or four people out there—"

"Tell them to go home," Conrad said. "This is police business."

He might have said something else, but the clapper on the front door was pounding now. "Miz Betts?" A woman's voice this time. Deal heard the sound of footsteps, as if a crowd might be gathering on the front porch.

"Burt, maybe you ought to take a look at this," the fourth deputy called from somewhere in the living room.

"I want you out of here this instant." Minerva Betts had her jaw pointed at Conrad now. "There's been no shooting in this house, and no one has called the sheriff. If you don't get out of my house, I'll see that harassment charges are filed on the lot of you."

Conrad started to stay something, then broke off when a new pounding began at the back door. "You want me to call for backup?" Stroud asked, his expression one of woe. Sweat beaded on the forehead of the other deputy.

"With what?" Conrad demanded. "The goddamned phone's tore out."

Conrad sent Deal a glance intended to be withering. "You are getting to be a bad penny," he said, then turned back to his men.

"Put that gun away before you hurt yourself," he growled to the deputy cowering by the bedroom door. He tossed the handcuffs to Stroud, who managed to catch them as they bounced off his chest.

"You heard the lady," Conrad said to the others, starting for the door. "Waste of time even coming down here."

"She stabbed me with her cane," Stroud grumbled, touching the welt between his eyes gingerly.

Conrad didn't even pause. "Why don't you put that down in your log, Stroud. 'Old woman cleaned my clock.'"

Stroud gave him a wounded look but said nothing. The other deputy stumbled out of Conrad's way.

"I'd like my cane back," the woman called before Conrad had cleared the bedroom door. The big deputy stiffened as though he'd been hit in the back with a cattle prod. By the time he turned around, however, his face bore what passed for a smile. "Sorry," he said, extending the knurled staff Minerva Betts's way.

As she took it, he pointed a thick finger at her. "Better be careful how you use that thing," he told her. Then he turned on his heel and led his party out.

"I'm sorry about all that," Minerva Betts told Deal as the front door slammed behind Conrad and his men.

"Sorry?" Deal said. "You saved my skin." The second time a woman had done so this night, he thought.

She waved a hand to dismiss such talk and went to the window where the tapping had come moments before. "It's all right now, Jonsey. They'll be going."

Deal heard mumbled conversation outside, followed by the sound of receding footsteps. Minerva Betts gave him a contemplative look. "Did you find what you were looking for?" she asked.

Deal might have smiled, save for the serious expression on her face. "I must have left it somewhere else, Ms. Betts," he said.

"That happens," she said, then added, "My name is Minnie to my friends."

"Minnie," he said. "I'm John Deal."

"I know," she said. She took a closer look at him then and her expression shifted. "What happened to your head?"

165

Deal thought she was talking about the injury the desktop had inflicted on him a few minutes before, then realized she couldn't even see that knot. He raised a hand to his forehead and felt about gingerly. Still sore, but the lump seemed smaller. Not even twenty-four hours, and that skirmish seemed like old news. "I ran into Sergeant Conrad earlier," he told her. "We just can't seem to get along."

"Uh-huh," she said. It wasn't a sound of agreement. "You got to be more careful down here, you understand what I mean, Mr. Deal?"

Sage advice, Deal thought. He gave her a nod as he pushed himself up from the bed. He felt himself reeling suddenly and had to steady himself with a hand at the doorjamb until his head settled back on its base.

"You sure you're okay?" Minerva Betts asked.

He nodded, but carefully. "I need some rest, that's all," he told her. "Maybe a glass of water."

She took his arm and helped him into the kitchen, flicking on the wall switch for the overhead light with an expert jab of her cane. While she went to the cupboard for a glass, Deal leaned a hip against the table where he'd sat earlier with Russell and Annie, talking with Ainsley Spencer about where Dequarius Noyes might be. Not six hours had passed, but it seemed like ages ago.

Minerva Betts opened the same cupboard where Annie had gone for the aspirin earlier and shook her head disapprovingly at something she found. "Might as well eat sugar right from the jar," she said, pulling a box of candied cereal down from the cupboard.

She stepped over the tossed and tumbled telephone as if it weren't there and tossed the cereal into a trash can, then went back to the cupboard to bring out a glass and the aspirin container. Deal saw that the bag of rice was still there, but the bottle of wine seemed to have disappeared. Gone to ground along with Ainsley Spencer, he supposed.

He shook four of the aspirins into his hand and downed them with the water she'd brought. "That's Miamah water, you know," she told him, as she watched him chug. She used the pronunciation characteristic of many old-timers when referring to the city. His own mother had grown up knowing better, but maintained the practice to her dying day. "If it wasn't for that water, wouldn't be a soul alive on this island," Minerva Betts added.

True enough, he thought. There was no source of fresh water in the entire Florida Keys, for that matter. Early settlers survived on rainwater trapped in cisterns or depended on water brought by boat. Now a two-foot pipe ran down the archipelago all the way from Miami, keeping paradise from going dry. How many more mouths would Franklin Stone's new project add to all those already sucking at the tap? he wondered idly. He could also imagine Stone's rejoinder: "Hell, it's Key West. Let 'em drink rum." Or words to that effect.

"Do you mind if I ask you a question?" he asked when he'd drained the glass.

"You can ask."

It got a smile out of him. "Is this really your house?"

She gave him a look that might have seemed disapproving if he hadn't seen what she'd laid on Conrad. "You don't think I would lie to the sheriff's men, now, do you?"

"I guess what I mean is, do you *live* here?"

She fixed him with a stare, though it was still nothing to that megawatt glare she'd used on the deputies. "Just how much of my business do you need to know?" she asked.

Deal held up his hands in surrender. "Only idle curiosity," he said, though it didn't stop him from trying another question he didn't expect an answer to. "You sure you don't have any idea where Ainsley Spencer might be?"

167

"He'll turn up when he needs to, that much I know," she told him. Her glance turned more solicitous then. "You want me to have one of the boys drive you back to your hotel?"

He shook his head, happy to find that the movement didn't turn his legs rubbery. "I'm fine," he assured her. "Really. And thanks."

He put his glass down on the counter, then turned and headed down the narrow hallway toward the front of the house.

"You remember what I said, Mr. Deal," she called as he pulled open the front door and moved out into the soft gray light. "Man from Miamah needs to be careful down here."

Indeed, Deal thought. He glanced around the porch, then checked the surrounding yards and streets, as empty now as they had been when he'd first arrived. If there had been crowds surrounding this bungalow just moments before, they had become invisible spirits now.

And, Deal couldn't help thinking, had Dequarius Noyes stayed here in the quarter among them, he might have found a way to survive. He was at the sidewalk's gate now, and turned to find Minerva Betts at the door of the bungalow with her hand held high in a gesture of goodwill. He gave her what he hoped was a suitable wave in response, then turned and moved blearily toward the dew-shrouded Hog.

**21**

WHEN DEAL WOKE, he found himself blinking stupidly at the numbers on the bedside clock: *100,* he thought. *What does that mean?*

By the time he had managed to swing his feet to the side of the bed, reason had begun to return. He had slept into Saturday afternoon, he managed to understand, and at the same time also began to process the avalanche of recollection concerning the preceding thirty-six hours or so. There seemed to be enough experience there to make up a fairly eventful lifetime, though he suspected there was plenty more on the way.

His forehead was still sore from where Conrad had pounded it into the side of the squad car the morning before, and a low-grade ache oozed up from his kidneys. Nothing a few dozen Advil couldn't handle, he thought, pushing himself up from the bed.

The suite they'd given him hummed with quietude—no shouts **169** from any rummy poolside crew, no sounds of housekeepers banging down the hallways. Somewhere in this vast, somnolent space, he thought, there would surely be a bathroom. Somewhere.

He stayed in the shower until the hot water gave out, a not inconsiderable time, then pulled on a T-shirt and a pair of running shorts and made his way out through the living area to the bar, where Malloy had been pouring drinks the night before. He rummaged around in the tiny refrigerator beneath the counter until he found a can of Bloody Mary mix and hauled it out, along with a tray of ice cubes. He had filled the glass halfway before his gaze strayed to the bottle of Ketel One that some thoughtful minion of Stone's had provided. It wasn't like him to drink until the sun had cleared the yardarm, but what the hell, somewhere in the world it was well past five o'clock.

Besides, this was more like the practice of medicine than drinking. He added a generous splash of the vodka and stirred the drink with his index finger. He had a tentative sip and then another. By the third, the pain in the small of his back was already beginning to fade.

It took him a moment to locate the pull cord for the long bank of drapes, and another minute or two until his eyes could stand the afternoon glare, but finally he could see well enough to unclasp the locks on the sliding glass doors and make his way out into the sultry afternoon. He'd stumbled out onto a portion of the balcony that faced the water, he realized, gazing out at a glassy-calm expanse reflecting a sky so blue it was painful to look at.

A sailboat was making its way out through the channel between the mainland and a mangrove island where an open fisherman puttered in the shallows, searching for snapper that had taken refuge from the midday sun. An admirable strategy, Deal thought, carrying his drink around the corner of the balcony into the shadows overlooking the pool.

170      There was only one woman lounging elegantly in a poolside chaise,

he noted, but she had presence enough to stand in for a crowd. She wore a broad-brimmed straw hat wrapped with a colorful band, the same patterned fabric as that which made up her suit, though there might have been more fabric circling the crown of the hat than there was on her tanned body.

Deal realized he was staring, but she seemed engrossed in a magazine she was holding, and besides, he thought, taking a sip from his drink, this was a body that deserved to be stared at. It was not until she crossed one bronzed ankle atop another and put her magazine down to gaze up at him from behind a pair of oversized sunglasses that he realized it was Annie. The realization made his knees weaken.

"Are you just going to stand up there and look?" she called to him.

"Just for another hour or so," he said. He thought his voice had a strangled quality.

"Too bad," she said. "I was hoping you'd bring me one of those." Deal glanced down at the drink in his hand. He supposed that was what she was pointing at; surely she couldn't mean the swelling that he felt in his blousy shorts.

"Don't go anywhere," he said. He saluted her with his glass, then turned deftly, to bounce his forehead off the closed glass door behind him. He steadied himself as smoothly as he could, then made his way around the corner of the balcony and through the doorway where he'd come out. He freshened his own drink and made another for her and was about to head for the door when he remembered he'd need his key to get back in.

He took a deep breath, put the drinks on the bar, and walked into the bedroom to find his key. "She is not going anywhere," he said to the sleep-puffed image he saw in the mirror above the enormous dresser where he'd tossed his pants the night before. "You can walk. She will be right there when you get outside."

171

He found his key card and gave himself a nod of agreement, but the image of Annie in her two-handkerchief bathing suit still had him stepping smartly as he made his way out.

The logical half of him had been right, he saw, as he pushed his way through the breezeway doors that opened onto the pool area. She'd donned a light cotton wrap and was sitting sideways on the lounge chair now, smiling as he approached.

"You staying here?" he said, handing her the glass.

She glanced around the lushly landscaped pool area. "It seems like a nice place," she said.

"You should see the rooms," he told her.

She stared at him from behind her dark sunglasses. "I have," she said.

It stopped him for a moment. "I was hoping for something more like, 'maybe I will,'" he said.

She shrugged, and a trace of her smile came back. "You should stick with guileless, John. It suits you better."

He gave her a rueful nod and raised his glass as he sat on the chaise next to hers. They toasted, then sat in silence for a moment.

"That was quite some night," she said after a moment, her gaze fixed out on the water. The sailboat had vanished, he noted, as had the open fisherman. Nothing but the dark smudge of the mangrove island out there pasted against a cloudless sky and a sea that were almost indistinguishable.

"You haven't heard the half of it," he told her.

She turned to him, her expression mild. "Perhaps I have," she said.

He stared at her for a moment. "You know about Dequarius . . . ?"

"How do you think I knew where you were staying?" she said, waving her hand around the pool compound. "Franklin keeps this wing for himself and his friends. It's empty most of the off-season," she said.

172

Deal nodded, his mind traveling back to his lame come-on. He didn't want to think about her draped on Stone's arm at some poolside bash, or worse, curled beside him in one of those monster beds.

"It must have been awful," Annie was saying, cutting into his thoughts.

He nodded and took a sip of his drink. "Yeah, well, after they moved me, I decided to go break the news to the old man—"

"Who had disappeared himself," she said, finishing his sentence.

He stared back at her. "I knew it was a small town," he said. "I guess I didn't realize how small."

"Franklin keeps in pretty close touch with the sheriff's office," she said. "Especially when he's concerned about his friends."

"Would that include me?"

She gave him a tolerant smile. "As much as anyone is a friend of Franklin's," she said.

Deal nodded. "Maybe he could put in a word on my behalf with Sergeant Conrad," he said. "One of us is about to stub our toe."

She shook her head. "I don't know any Conrad," she said. "But if there's a problem, I'm sure Franklin can take care of it."

Deal had begun to think so, too, but he didn't say anything to Annie. So Franklin Stone had been given a full account of the previous night's proceedings, he thought. He supposed it made sense, given what had happened with him and Russell yesterday morning, but still it bothered him to be the subject of such scrutiny. He'd been leery enough of getting involved with someone like Stone to begin with. Now he understood why.

It was the kind of relationship that had never seemed to pose a problem for his old man, of course. *If they have money, then take it,* was Barton Deal's motto. He'd managed to do it successfully for the biggest part of his life, Deal thought, and wished his father were here to advise him now.

"I don't suppose Stone has any ideas about what Dequarius was doing over here," Deal said to her.

She shook her head in puzzlement. "Why on earth would he?"

"I'm not certain," Deal said. "The kid worked for him, that much I know."

"For that matter, so do I." She shrugged.

He glanced at her. "What are you talking about?"

"Do you think I appear in that lounge for free? I'm a professional, John."

"Hey," he said, holding up a hand. "I was just asking."

"Forget it," she said. "We were talking about Dequarius."

"Right," he said.

"And you were trying to connect what's happened to Franklin."

"I didn't say that."

"You didn't have to."

"Jesus, Annie . . ." he began.

"It's all right," she said, "why wouldn't you?"

Deal shrugged. "I keep telling myself that the kid was just a small-time grifter and I was the doofus mark."

"You wouldn't strike anyone as a doofus," she said.

"You said I was guileless," he told her.

"As an ear of corn," she said. "But that's different. Dequarius wasn't seeing you the way I do at all."

"And how is that?" he heard himself say.

"Whatever he wanted from you, it was serious," she said, ignoring the question.

"Given what happened, I'd say you are right."

"He never told you what he wanted?"

"He said he'd found something. That's as far as we got."

174

"He didn't say what?"

Deal shook his head.

"Or where?"

He shrugged and took a sip of his drink. "I thought he was talking about buried treasure. Our pal Magnum the bartender tells me that was one of Dequarius's favorite scams."

"Like I said, it doesn't make sense that he'd take you for a sucker."

He gave her a smile. "I'm heartened by your confidence."

"You should be," she said. "But why was Dequarius so set on you as his target?"

Deal threw his hands up. "That's what I've been asking myself. He knew I was in town to talk to Stone about his project. I thought he might want to sell me some inside information, some dirt on Stone, but he told me he'd *found* something . . ." He broke off, shaking his head.

At about the same moment, Deal noticed that her wrap had fallen open. He tried to keep his eyes from the view of her scantily covered breasts, but it was like telling himself not to breathe. If Franklin Stone knew the thoughts that were racing through his mind, perhaps he'd end up like Dequarius.

"Does Stone have a big interest in wine?" he asked her abruptly.

She looked at him. "He keeps a wine cellar, if that's what you mean. I wouldn't call him a collector. What's that have to do with anything?"

Deal hesitated, wondering if he ought to continue. Annie Dodds was living with Stone, after all. What would keep her from sharing anything he told her with the man? On the other hand, why should he care? he told himself. He was simply trying to make sense of all that had happened.

"I found some things, that's all," he told her.

"Where?" she said, shaking her head. "What things?"

"It's probably nothing," he told her. "Just a series of coincidences, but still . . ." He waved his hand in the air as if he were trying to bring shape to something.

"You're being pretty mysterious," she said.

"It is a mystery, isn't it?"

She held up her glass. "Maybe we could have another one of these?"

"Sure," he said. He stood and held out his hand for the empty. "I'll be back in a flash."

"I'll go with you," she said, taking his hand to pull herself up.

"Sure," he heard himself saying. "Why not?"

She stood behind him in the long and silent hallway as he pulled his key card from the pocket of his running shorts and inserted it in the slot. He jiggled the door handle but the tiny electronic dots blinked obstinately red.

"I think it goes the other way," she said, pointing at the card slot.

He nodded and withdrew the card, then turned the thing around. This time the tiny lights turned green and a click sounded somewhere inside the mechanism. "I knew that," he said, ushering her in ahead of him. "I was just testing you." As she passed, he smelled a hint of lemon blossom mixed with the tang of perspiration. Oh my, he thought. Oh my.

"I'll be right out," he heard her call as the door to the foyer bathroom closed.

He went to the bar and found another can of mixer in the fridge, then pulled out the last of the tiny trays of ice. Ice in the glass, he told himself. Vodka. A little mixer after that. Why did his fingers seem numb?

"Quite a place they've given you," he heard.

He glanced up to see her coming around the corner of the bar. She'd taken off the cotton wrap, he noticed, and had hung it over the back of one of the stools. As he handed her the drink, she removed the broad-brimmed hat and tossed it onto the granite bar top.

"That's good," she said after she'd taken a long sip of the drink. She gave a toss of her hair, then gathered it in one hand, twisting it back from her shoulders. "It was getting hot out there."

"I thought so," Deal said, taking a sip of his own drink. His voice seemed to echo in his ears.

She put her drink down on the countertop and moved quickly against him. He felt her arms go around his waist and back, felt her pull herself hard against him.

What he felt inside seemed tidal in its power. He managed to get his glass down somehow and then his arms were around her, pulling her even closer, if that was possible. She yanked her sunglasses off and buried her mouth at his neck. He felt exquisite jabs of pain where her teeth nipped at him, and thought he might go down in a swoon.

His hips were backed into the bar sink now, and hers were writhing against his. If he'd ever been more breathless, he couldn't remember when.

"You're okay with this, aren't you?" she said, her breath coming in gasps, the words scorching at his ear. "Tell me you're okay."

"Way okay," he managed, and forced his lips toward hers.


He tried to get them to the bedroom, but they made it only as far as the couch, where, in another life and time, he had sat while Rusty Malloy read him the riot act. This time, however, it was Annie Dodds who was with him, and the riot was of a markedly different character.

She'd lost the minuscule bottom half of her suit somewhere behind the bar, about the same time that Deal felt his T-shirt go over his head with what sounded like a ripping sound. He was tumbled back against the plush white cushions, his hands on her breasts, which had tumbled 177 free from her top. She was astride him, her hand under the hem of his running shorts, caressing him through the thin fabric liner.

"If you keep that up . . ." he managed.

"Then what?" she said, wiggling herself higher up his lap.

In the next moment, her hand was all the way under the fabric, squeezing him, pulling him toward her writhing hips. He thrust himself up to meet her, felt a moment's resistance as they met, then the exquisite slipperiness as she rode down hard upon him with a groan.

Their movements became galvanic then, a coupling that seemed intent upon restoring every pleasure denied over the course of twenty years. Deal felt his consciousness recede to some Pleistocene level, all ooze and scrapes and nips and scratches, all nuances of equilibrium gone. Up, down, and sideways became synonymous.

Everything was wetness, pink and black and bone on bone. At some point, he realized he was atop her, that she lay atop the spine of the couch's back, her legs straddling the sides. He had one foot sunk in the cushions, the other struggling for purchase on the shell-stone floor as he drove himself deep inside her and she pounded herself back against him with every beat.

When he came, it seemed as painful as it did glorious, as if he might not ever reach such heights again. She was off the couch entirely, her arms wound around his neck, her legs clamped to his back.

"I'm going to stay just like this," she told him. "I'm not going to move, ever."

"You don't have to," he told her. Then managed to carry them, locked together like that, all the way into the bed.

The second time was far more measured, almost stately in its pace, and ended with her astride him, collapsing onto his chest as she came. She lay panting for a bit before she finally glanced up at him. "I didn't mean to take so long," she said.

"You're apologizing for that," he said.

"I didn't want to take more than my share," she said.

"You can have my share anytime," he assured her.

"That was something," she said.

"Keep it pent up for twenty years, something's going to happen," Deal said. "What's that on your cheek?"

She turned and lay her head back on his chest. "Nothing," she said, her voice muffled.

"Did I do that?" he asked, tucking his finger under her chin for a better look.

"Don't," she said, pushing his hand away. She rose to a sitting position, her back to him.

"Hey," he said, an awful premonition sweeping over him as he recalled the dark glasses. He started to reach for her, then stopped, his hand inches from the flesh of her upper arm.

Three dim finger-sized bruises were striped horizontally there, just above her elbow. He shifted his hand to her shoulder and drew himself up at her side.

"What happened?" he said, struggling to keep his voice under control.

She gave him a neutral glance. There was a mouse under her left eye, a pale yellow bruise rising in a half-moon above it. He felt light-headed suddenly, a queasiness growing in his stomach, along with a rise of anger at himself for having missed it earlier. "I walked into a door," she told him.

He felt his hands clench into fists. "Stone did this . . . ?"

"Get a grip," she said, her voice almost angry. She stopped and drew

179

a breath. She put a hand to his chest, forcing a smile. "You should see the other guy."

Deal was shaking his head. "No," he managed. "No way he can do this—"

"John," she said, her voice rising again. "You weren't there. You don't know what happened."

"I don't care what happened," he said. "He can't hit you."

"I hit *him*, all right?" she said, her eyes flashing. "He grabbed my arm to stop me from nailing him again and I jerked away, right into the edge of the door."

He stopped, trying to digest it. "You hit him?"

She nodded.

"Why?"

"I'm not sure how much of this I need to get into with you," she said.

He blinked at the words, feeling as if he'd been punched himself. "I'm sorry," he said. "I didn't mean to get so personal."

She glanced at his damp chest, then down at her own sweat-glazed body. "That's pretty good," she said, then gave him a rueful smile. "Imagine what it would feel like if we really let ourselves go."

He nodded, then glanced back at her eye. "You sure you're okay?"

She nodded. "I didn't mean to sound so hostile," she said. "Franklin was waiting up when I came in. He was worried, that's all. I told him to go to bed and he said something. That's when I lost it," she said. "I just wanted him out of my way." She gave him a contrite look. "It was more like swinging my purse at him than a punch."

"I'm glad you kept your gun put away."

She nodded, then gave him a smile. "I'm glad you *didn't*," she said. She leaned into him, sliding her hand between his legs. "Look who's still awake, would you?"

Deal glanced down, surprised at himself. There might have been a time in his distant, hormone-filled youth when he'd made love three times in an afternoon, but he couldn't really be sure. All he knew for certain, watching her head descend to his lap, was that he was surely going to do so this day.

**22**

DEAL WOKE TO a pounding that seemed like it was coming from some-where near the base of his skull. But by the time he managed to pull himself out of the tangled sheets, he realized that it was someone at the door of his suite. He also realized, with a certain hollow feeling in his gut, that he was alone in the bed.

The knocking came again, accompanied by a muffled voice that sounded familiar. He forced himself to his feet and moved groggily into the bathroom to wrap one of the oversized towels around his waist, then padded through the living room, noting glumly that An-nie's things had disappeared as well.

"Yo, Deal," he heard the familiar voice outside his thundering door.

"I'm here," he called, moving to open up.

"Whoo-eee," Russell Straight said when he opened the door and gave Deal's bare chest the once-over. "You look like a flesh-and-blood cat post, my man. What you been doing in here anyway? "

"None of your business," Deal said, retreating into the living room. He collapsed on the couch while Russell paused to take in the new surroundings.

"I heard what happened to Dequarius," he said finally. "How come you didn't call?"

Deal gave him a look that sent Russell's hands up in surrender. "Forget I asked," the big man said. He glanced at his watch. "You remember we had a dinner engagement?"

Deal considered the concept of "dinner engagement" for a few moments until it finally sank in. Though it seemed a vestige of another existence, he could not deny the memory of Stone's invitation. In another dimension, or so it seemed, there lived a building contractor named Deal who had come to Key West to discuss a business proposition with a high-rolling developer his father had known.

Undeniable facts, indeed. But they seemed to have so little to do with life as he now knew it.

"What time is it?" Deal asked Russell finally.

"Limo o'clock," Russell answered. "The man's ride is sitting out front, waiting on us."

Deal nodded slowly. Somewhere there was a proposal he'd been asked to study. Perhaps a packet waiting for him at the front desk. Or perhaps Dequarius Noyes had bled out on it, and it was now bagged up in the Monroe County sheriff's evidence room.

No sooner had he thought it, than he remembered what he'd left beneath the ironing-board cover in his former room. "Sonofabitch," he blurted.

"What's the matter?" Russell said.

"Did you go by the room I was in?"

Russell nodded warily. "It's posted," he said. "That's when I went down to the front. One of those brain-dead parrot-heads told me what went on."

"I have to get in there," Deal said.

"As in where?"

"My old room," Deal told him.

"That might be a problem," Russell said.

"I left something important," he said.

Russell shrugged. "Call the cops."

"It's not that simple," Deal told him.

"It never is." Russell sighed.

"I'll get in the shower," Deal said. "Go tell Stone's driver we'll be a few minutes late."

Russell nodded. "Either that or a couple extra years," he said, and walked ponderously toward the door.

"It don't look like they meant for anybody my size to walk on that," Russell Straight said, glancing down at the narrow ledge that ran along the rear facing of the wing where Deal's old room had been.

"That ledge is a good six inches wide," Deal said. "If I laid a six-inch-wide board down on the ground, could you walk on it?"

"All the way to China, man, but that ledge ain't on the ground, now, is it?"

Deal glanced out over the railing where they stood. His former room abutted the breezeway, its balcony rail visible only a few feet away. Just swing out onto that ledge, he thought, a couple of quick shuffle steps, then back over the balcony railing to safety.

If you lost your balance, he told himself, it was no more than a ten-foot drop to the stone decking below, if you missed the thorny bougainvillea plantings that hugged the building, that is. Worst-case scenario, a broken ankle. More likely, a couple of hours pulling thorns out of your ass.

"Just lean into the building, use those rocks that stick out for hand-holds," Deal said.

Russell gave him a doubtful look. "Who goes first?"

"I will," Deal said, swinging his leg over the breezeway railing. "Yell if I fall."

"I got no problem with that," Russell said.

Deal shook his head and, before he could think about it further, slid his right foot quickly onto the ledge, reaching up and finding a hold on the rough flagstone facing with his hand. He held tightly, praying the stone he grasped had been set by someone who thought in permanent terms, then loosed his hold on the breezeway railing and brought his other hand and foot along. It took him a second to find a crevice for his left hand, and he wavered giddily, feeling all that air opening up at his back.

Whatever you do, don't go ass over teakettle, he told himself. Despite his assurances to Russell, Deal had seen a member of a roofer's crew die that way. An inexperienced laborer carrying a fifty-pound roll of roofing felt stepped out of the way of a coworker sloshing hot tar with a mop. The new guy's legs hit the low parapet behind him and the weight of the felt took him over headfirst. He'd only fallen a dozen feet, landed on grass, and had been wearing a hard hat that was still on his head when they got to him, but none of that had mattered.

The guy had speared the ground headfirst like a rookie safety trying to take out the world itself. Everyone on the roof had heard the crack. At least the guy had died quickly, Deal thought, as he felt his fingers dig into a crevice. He got himself steadied, shot another glance at a doubtful Russell, then pulled himself along. In seconds he was swinging himself up over the railing of the balcony, relieved to see that the glass doors had not been sealed.

"I can probably handle things over here," he called softly back to Russell.

"Fuck it," Russell replied. He swung one of his thick legs out over the railing, then the other, and glanced at Deal with a look that suggested he'd be asking for a raise soon.

All his grumbling aside, Russell moved along the ledge like an experienced second-story man, ignoring Deal's outstretched hand to pull himself onto the balcony with ease. "Pretty impressive," Deal said.

"Don't try to sweet-talk me," Russell said. He pushed past Deal and tried one of the sliding doors. It jiggled in its track but didn't move. "What's next?"

Deal wiped his palms on his pants then flattened them on the glass of the door, leaning heavily toward the inside of the room. "Get your side, just like this," he told Russell. "Now push up."

Russell did as he was told and Deal felt the heavy door slide upward. He put the toe of his shoe beneath the exposed bottom frame and motioned for Russell to do the same. In seconds they had levered the heavy slab out and were easing it to the floor of the balcony.

"Damn," Russell said, stepping back from the leaning door section. "You must have been a criminal in your other life."

"I put about a thousand of these things into a Hyatt one summer," Deal told him. "They're good to look through, but they're not much for security."

Russell examined the dislodged door. "Sure as hell seems that way," he said.

"It was one hell of a boring summer," Deal said, pausing to catch his breath. "I told my old man if I ever saw another sliding glass door I'd quit."

Russell glanced up. "What'd he say?"

"He told me to suit myself," Deal said.

"Well, there you go." Russell nodded. Laughter from a party on a distant balcony drifted toward them, and he sent a nervous glance over the nearby grounds.

"Wait out here," Deal said. "You see anybody coming from the front, let me know, especially if they're in uniform."

"You sure a couple pieces of paper are worth all this?" Russell asked.

Deal shrugged, the image of the folded label clutched in Dequarius's stiffened fingers swimming up clearly in his mind. "Dequarius Noyes must have thought so," he said. "It's all there is to go on, anyway."

Russell nodded, then turned his gaze back over the lush grounds laid out below. "Go on," he said. "I see any cops, I'll be the first one out."

"Thanks," Deal said dryly, then turned and pushed his way through the billowing curtains and inside the shadowed room.

The worst of the smell was gone, but even in the dim light, the crusted stains were still visible on the carpet and the chair. It didn't take much for Deal to conjure up Dequarius Noyes still sitting there with his thousand-mile stare, waiting endlessly for him to arrive.

He felt a chill come over him and shook off the image, then moved quickly toward the foyer closet. He pulled the door open and groped about in the darkness until one of his knuckles banged against a ragged edge on the undercarriage of the metal ironing board, lifting what felt like an inch-long flap of skin.

"Sonofabitch," he said, drawing his hand back as if he'd been bitten by a snake. He could already feel blood trickling down his fingers. He brought his hand to his mouth and sucked at the wound, while he used his other to search out the edge of the ironing pad. He dug his fingers under the slick fabric and groped about, then stopped, feeling nothing.

He pulled his bleeding hand away from his mouth and squatted down, running his fingers along the edge of the board, all the way to the bottom, then peeled the padding away and shook it. He glanced down at the floor of the closet, but saw nothing.

For an instant, he wondered if he'd broken into the wrong room, but a glance at the grisly chair reassured him. The envelope had simply stuck to the padding, he told himself. He'd carry the whole thing out by the light where he could get a decent look.

He was trying to lift the ironing board out of the hooks on the closet caddy, when he felt the arm lock around his throat.

## 23

DEAL TRIED TO get his feet under him, but whoever it was that held him was tall enough to keep him levered off the ground. His assailant had one arm hooked under his own, using Deal's body as a fulcrum. The harder Deal struggled, the quicker it was going to end, he thought. The pressure on his throat had cut off his airway and bright stars were pinging in the ever-growing darkness before his eyes.

"Where is it?" a voice hissed in his ear. "Where'd the little fuck put it?"

The pressure on his throat eased momentarily and Deal kicked straight out. His feet drove into the mirrored bifold doors of the closet, caving them inward, showering the narrow hallway with a rain of glass. Definitely not to code, he thought as a falling shard of glass sliced cleanly through his pantleg. Maybe he could sue, if stupid dead men had legal standing in Key West, that is.

He'd gotten enough leverage from the kick to drive them back against the other wall, though, and he heard a rush of breath and the satisfying sound of a skull popping off concrete block. At the same time, Deal jerked his head back as hard as he could manage. It was only an inch or two in terms of range of motion, but coupled with the fact that his attacker's skull was rebounding forward off the block wall, it was enough.

Deal had a moment's stab of pain at the back of his skull, but it couldn't have been much compared to what the guy must have felt when his teeth caved in. He heard a curse—or what he supposed it sounded like when someone tries to curse around a mouthful of blood and bone fragments—then felt the grip at his throat loosen. In the next instant he was free and breathing, falling on hands and knees to the glittering shoals of glass.

Before he could move, there came another gargling curse from above him, then a stunning rush of pain as a heavy-soled shoe drove into his ribs just below his breastbone. The blow sent Deal into the closet, taking out what was left of the flimsy doors. A good thing he'd already kicked the glass out, he was thinking, as his shoulder cracked into the wall.

"You fuck," he heard, then a hand had him by the hair and was pulling his face up to meet a palm that felt like a lead skillet exploding at his cheek.

Deal felt himself being readied for what might have been the backhand swipe to follow when he heard a shout from somewhere and caught a glimpse of a form that could only be Russell Straight's hurtling through the curtains that billowed at the door. Deal felt the grip go loose on his hair, then heard an explosion and a flash of flame that seemed inches from his face.

There was another explosion and flash and Deal saw Russell

Straight's form go down on the far side of the bed, trailing the tatters of ripped curtains like a drunken ghost. There was another flash of light then, but no explosion—the door to the room flying open, he realized—followed by a thunderous sound of slamming, along with a return of the darkness and an abrupt and overwhelming quiet.

Deal probed his teeth with his tongue, raised his hands gingerly to his battered ribs. Nothing gushing, nothing broken or piercing skin, though a good part of him might be too numb to tell, he thought.

"Russell," he called, expecting the worst. "Are you hit?" He pulled himself up by the frame of the ruined closet, glass shards snapping under his feet as he made his way quickly toward the bed.

He was halfway across the room when he saw the ghostly shape rise, the arms slapping at yards of ruined cloth. "Russell?" he repeated.

The big man had managed to get his hands free and hooked at the edge of the fabric. The powerful arms jerked downward, accompanied by a sound as loud as a band saw's scream, and Russell Straight's glowering image appeared from the folds of cloth.

The two stared at each other for a moment in the reflected glow of the landscaping lights from outside. "You okay?" Deal asked.

Russell nodded. "How about you?"

Deal nodded back. Sirens sounded in the distance.

"We going out the front or the back?" Russell asked.

Deal glanced at the balcony and shook his head. "Screw 'em," he said, and began to limp across the broken glass toward the door.

## 24

THE LIMO GLIDED smoothly out of the Pier House's spacious cobblestone entryway at the same moment that a pair of sheriff's cruisers bounced across the gutter moat, headed the other way. Deal glanced back to see the cruiser doors fly open and a quartet of deputies hustle out, making their way quickly toward the tastefully landscaped entrance.

There were times when the trappings of wealth counted for something, he thought, reaching for the cut-crystal bottle of whiskey lodged in the limo's bar rack. Who'd be using a limo as a getaway car?

"You get a look at the guy?" Russell Straight asked as the scene at the hotel's entrance receded in their wake.

Deal gave him a look. "I didn't see him, but it sure sounded like our pal from the sheriff's office."

"Conrad?" Russell asked, his voice rising. "What the hell was he doing there?"

Deal stared across the spacious cabin of the limo. "Waiting for me," he said. "That's the only thing that makes sense."

*Where is it? Where'd the little fuck put it?* The words rang in Deal's mind.

Russell shook his head. "Whatever Dequarius was on to, somebody must want awful bad."

Deal was nodding agreement when the partition dividing them from the driver's compartment glided down. Balart turned, revealing his hawklike profile for a moment.

"Maybe we should find a doctor," Balart said. When Deal didn't answer immediately, he hurried on. "Don't worry about the police getting involved," he said with a dismissive wave. "I know the right person—"

"I'm fine," Deal said. He pulled a shard of glass out of his palm with his teeth, then poured a dollop of whiskey over the seeping wound. Russell handed him one of the handful of towels he'd snatched from a maid's cart on their way toward an exit. Deal poured more whiskey on the towel, then used it to staunch the bleeding. He'd already checked himself over. Maybe a couple of broken ribs and a couple more knots on his face to go with the lump on his forehead, but the rest was superficial. Especially compared to Dequarius Noyes.

Deal nodded his thanks, then turned back toward the driver's compartment. "I need to stop at a liquor store," he called to Balart.

Balart waited until he'd brought the limo to a stop at a light, then turned to Deal, a puzzled expression on his face. "Where we're going there's plenty to drink, you know."

"I'm looking for a place that sells wine. Good wine," Deal added. "You know a store like that?"

193

Balart thought for a minute. "There's one," he said. "Down the other end of Duval."

"Then that's where we'll go," Deal said.

Balart gave him an uncertain look, but the light had turned green and a taxi behind them had begun tapping its horn. "You the boss," Balart said, then looked over Deal's shoulder toward the offending taxi. "Hold onto your horses, back there," he called, and then they were off.

He swung the limo into a turn that carried them past the city's cemetery, where, on the other side of a wrought-iron fence, a luminous flotilla of white above-ground vaults stretched into the distance. *People dying to get in there,* Deal thought idly. His old man had never passed a graveyard without saying so. It made him wonder where Dequarius's body would end up.

The thought was still with him minutes later when Balart turned onto Duval Street and brought the limo to a stop by the curb. They were near the southern end of the boulevard, a spot where the shops thinned and the foot traffic was almost nonexistent.

"Tell him is Balart in the car," the chauffeur said. "He'll take good care of you."

Deal nodded, ducking out of the limo. There was a newsstand in front of him, shuttered for the evening, and beside it a narrow store-front with a sputtering neon sign that promised that LIQUOR was available inside. GONZALO FAUSTO, PROP. had been lettered in small-ish script on the storefront glass.

"What are we doing here?" Russell Straight asked, coming out of the limo behind him.

"I need some information," Deal said, pushing the shop door open. "It's a little late to try the library."

He ignored Russell's impatient glance and moved on inside, his nostrils keen to a blended smell of yeast, aged wood floors and pol-

194

ished shelving, musty cardboard, and suspended dust. A place out of time, he thought, a part of Key West that had survived progress and gentrification, at least for the time being. He wouldn't have been surprised to see a peg-legged pirate behind the long zinc-topped counter.

Instead it was a wiry, white-haired man who looked to be in his seventies, perched on a stool near an old-fashioned brass cash register the size of a safe. The man glanced up from a book propped on the counter in front of him, peering at Deal over a pair of rimless reading glasses.

"What can I do for you, gentlemen?" he asked in an accent that seemed an odd mixture of old-South and Castilian Spanish.

"I'm a friend of Balart's," Deal said.

The man's glance registered Deal's battered appearance, then traveled toward the front of the shop and out the window to the idling limo. After a moment he gave a nod of recognition. He was smiling when he turned back to Deal.

"Balart is a good man," he said. "We were in prison together, did he tell you?" The little man made the comment as casually as if he'd said, "We went to grammar school together."

Deal shook his head, glancing at Russell. "He didn't mention that."

"Oh yes," the man said, walking behind the counter toward them. "Castro's prison. Both of us." Now that he'd come closer, Deal could see that he might have overestimated the man's age. His fine features were creased, his hair gone white, but his eyes were alert and dancing behind the reading glasses.

"I am Gonzalo," the man said, extending a talonlike hand. "Gonzalo Fausto."

"John Deal," he said, feeling surprising strength in the man's grip.

"All that was long ago," Fausto added. He glanced out the windows of his shop again, then turned back. "Now what can I get you? I have an excellent rum just arrived from Haiti—"

195

"You sell wine," Deal cut in.

"Oh yes," the man said. "Indeed I do."

"Good wines, I understand."

"I have a truly outstanding Pinot Noir from Oregon," Gonzalo Fausto said, moving toward a bin behind the counter. "Domain Drouhin—"

"I really came here to ask for your help, Mr. Fausto," Deal cut in.

The old man turned, a look of uncertainty on his face. He had another look at the scratches tracing Deal's arms, then glanced toward the front of the shop again, as if to make sure it was Balart and his limo parked outside.

"What kind of help are you looking for?" he asked.

"I saw a wine label a couple of days ago," Deal said. "An old one. I thought maybe if I described it to you, you could give me some information."

The old man thought about it a moment. "It is possible," he said. "Depending on what you can tell me."

Deal nodded. He'd been trying to reconjure the image of the label he'd seen from the moment they'd left the Pier House. "It was French," he said. "And very old. Nineteen twenty-nine, I think."

The old man pursed his lips and nodded. "One of the finest vintages of all time," he said. "Would this have been a red wine or a white?"

Deal shook his head. "I don't know."

"What about the name of the winery?"

Deal gave him a bleak look. "Château something or other," he said. "It didn't register at the time." He glanced toward the bins where wines were stored. "I was hoping you might have some bottles I could look at, maybe it'd jog my memory."

The old man gave him a tolerant smile. "This is only a humble shop," he said. "For what you are looking for, you would have to go to Miami, perhaps New York or London."

Deal stared at him. "London?"

The old man shrugged. "A bottle from that vintage is rarely seen outside the auction houses and the most prestigious shops. And if the wine you are talking about was one of the four first growths—"

"Bear with me, Mr. Fausto," Deal said, holding up a hand. "Until recently, I was unscrewing the tops on the wine I bought."

The old man gave him a tolerant smile. "It is simply a way of designating the best Bordeaux wines," he said. "The system was devised in 1855. For more than a century, there were only four wineries which produced wines classified as 'first growths,' or the best of the best: Châteaux Margaux, Lafite-Rothschild, Haut-Brion, and Latour. After 1959, the distinctions became more varied." He paused. "But certain wineries can always be counted upon."

Deal's mind ticked over the names, but it was hopeless. He'd taken Spanish in school, and even that had been a stretch. As far as the French went, *oui* was a major accomplishment for him. "I don't know," Deal said. "It could have been one of those, I guess. Let's say it was, in fact. What would a bottle like that be worth?"

The old man shrugged. "That would depend upon many things: the provenance of the wine, for one thing—"

"Mr. Fausto," Deal interjected.

"Of course." The old man gave him an apologetic glance. "The ability to trace the wine's ownership," he said. "To establish the conditions under which it was stored, which of course affects its viability—"

"A bottle of wine from 1929 would still be good?" Russell asked.

"A bottle of wine from *1829* could still be good, assuming the cork had held up so that air could not enter, and that the bottle had been kept in a sufficiently cool place."

"Let's say everything was hunky-dory, Mr. Fausto. How much are we talking about?"

The old man thought for a moment. "It's not my ordinary realm, of course, but I've seen bottles of that vintage offered for as much as fifteen thousand dollars."

"You got to be kidding," Russell said.

"Of course, the bottle from which your label came would be virtually worthless," the old man said.

Deal stared at the old man for a moment. "Because you couldn't prove what was in the bottle?"

"That would be part of it. Of course, the cork could be removed and checked. Ordinarily the name of the winery and the vintage would be stamped there."

"Wouldn't that ruin everything once it was open?"

"Not necessarily," Fausto said. "Collectors quite often return rare bottles to the wineries to be recorked. But a bottle without its label attached"—he shook his head again—"that would almost be like owning a very rare stamp that had been torn in half. The value would be very difficult to ascertain."

Deal took it in, then glanced at Russell, who rolled his eyes. "All this for a worthless bottle of wine?" the big man said with a sigh.

"Excuse me?" Gonzalo Fausto asked, looking confused.

"Nothing, Mr. Fausto," Deal said, his mind already racing along. "You mentioned collectors. Is there anyone here in Key West who fits that category, persons who might own or be interested in wines like this?"

Fausto glanced out the window toward the waiting limo. "Well, there is Mr. Stone, of course. I have ordered some excellent wines for him. And there's the occasional visitor . . ." The old man's gaze drifted toward the ceiling, his thoughts seeming to wander.

Deal nodded, his thoughts racing along as Fausto searched his memory bank. Given his growing suspicions, he could hardly go ask

Stone for a look at his wine cellar. Maybe he could run an ad in the *Key West Citizen,* "Yo, all you wine aficionados out there . . ."

Deal shook the notion away and turned back to the shop owner. "I don't suppose you have a book or something I could look in?"

Fausto shook his head. "There would be a number in the library, I'm sure. You could try on Monday."

Deal was nodding glumly, wondering what the possibilities of breaking into a public library might be, when suddenly a thought occurred to him. "Mr. Fausto, you've been very helpful. Do you have a telephone I could use?"

"Of course," the old man said, turning to point toward an old-fashioned model with a dial on its face hanging on the wall behind the cash register. He moved to unlatch the gate that led behind the counter, and Deal followed on his heels, wondering just how long it had been since he had acutally *dialed* a phone.

**25**

"**YOU CAN FIND** that address okay?" Deal called to Balart through the open driver's partition.

"Is in Key West, I can find," the man said without turning. He pulled the limo from the curb into a gap in the growing evening traffic, then swung off Duval at the next intersection.

Deal had managed to track down Malloy on his cellular, the attorney about to tear into a rack of lamb at Louie's Backyard, where he was dining with an actual paying client. When he heard the brief version of what had happened at the Pier House, he agreed to meet Deal at his home in fifteen minutes.

It took less than half that for the limo to make its way to Malloy's, a low-slung single-story place, built in the Frank Lloyd Wright style, down Olivia Street, not far from the graveyard they had passed earlier.

You might not have known the house was there, Deal thought as he and Russell stepped out of the limo, what with all the lush foliage that shielded the entrance from the street.

"We won't be long," Deal told the driver, who waved away his concern.

"I tell the boss you had one more thing to see about," Balart said, holding up his phone. "He say no problem. On Key West time, down here," he added with a smile.

Deal nodded, considering the concept, then turned to unlatch the wooden gate. He led the way along a path that twisted through the vegetation and past a shallow garden pool where several huge koi flashed away at their approach.

"Those are goldfish?" Russell asked.

"Big orange carp," Deal said, glancing back where the limo idled. "Expensive ones. What do you make of our man Balart?"

Russell followed his gaze. "He's a fellow con."

Deal shook his head. "Meaning what?"

"Meaning I trust him."

"What makes you so sure?"

"He did time in one of Castro's jails, didn't he?"

Deal stared. "So what?"

Russell stared at him. "Then he was in for nothing," he said. "Same as me."

Deal let it go. He ducked under the low-hanging porch eave and was about to press the bell when the door swung open smoothly and a woman with the broad face of an Indio ushered them in.

"Señor Malloy say please come in," she said in a soft voice, averting her eyes quickly from the shallow crosshatching of cuts on Deal's forearms. "Is coming soon."

Deal gave her a smile that must have looked like something his    201 daughter had hacked out of a lopsided pumpkin, then motioned Russell inside. They followed the woman down a slate-tiled hallway and into a living room where a wall of floor-to-ceiling windows opened onto a garden that was even more artfully landscaped than the one they'd walked through.

There was a pool done up to look like a natural pond, fed by a stream that tumbled over a series of boulders placed to resemble a jungled cliffside at one end. Deal saw a fluttering of wings among lush foliage out there, followed by the screech of a parrot.

"We must of come to the wrong place," Russell observed. "This looks like the fucking zoo."

"It's just Key West," Deal said.

"The lawyers must do pretty good down here," Russell said.

Deal had to agree. There were three buttery-looking leather love seats arranged to take advantage of the view outside, their centerpiece a coffee table that looked like a cross section of a giant redwood, lacquered and waxed until it glowed in the soft, indirect lighting.

Set into one wall was a sizable salt-water aquarium that provided an idealized rendition of marine life very nearly as exotic as the jungle landscape outside. A school of blue disk-shaped fish as vivid as neon dollars shimmered back and forth in the tank above a pink-spotted moray eel that lounged on the sandy bottom like Popeye's disembodied arm. Deal couldn't see the thing's head, and he didn't want to. The last time he'd seen a tank with an eel in it, the owner had ended up floating amidst his former razor-mouthed pets, a sight he'd never been able to banish from his memory.

At the other end of the room was a series of louvered doors that Deal suspected hid a TV the size of a theater screen from his youth, one side flanked by a floor-to-ceiling wine rack, maybe half of its slots occupied.

"Maybe Malloy knows something about this wine . . ." Russell began, breaking off when Deal formed his hand into a pistol's shape and mimed the hammer snapping down.

"One of the reasons we're here," Deal told him.

Russell nodded, and Deal turned to survey the room once more. Rusty had come up the hard way, his old man a second-generation Irish immigrant, the owner of a glass installation business that Barton Deal had used whenever he could. The Malloy home had been a modest three-bedroom ranch on a quarter-acre lot in South Miami. Rusty had moved to a different level, or so it would seem.

"Johnny-boy," Deal heard behind him, "what the hell have you done this time?"

Deal turned to see Malloy coming through the hallway passage, his show of exasperation fading when he saw the crosshatchings on Deal's arms. "Holy shit," he said. "You look like a Zuni warrior."

"I believe the Zunis cut themselves up on purpose," Deal said.

"Man oh man," he said, casting a questioning look at Russell. "Where were you when this happened?"

Deal saw Russell stiffen at Malloy's suggestion. "Leave it alone, Rusty. He was on the balcony of the room, keeping an eye out. Whoever it was fired two shots at Russell when he charged in. He could have been killed."

"Hey," Malloy said, holding up his hands in surrender. "I was just asking."

Malloy flashed Russell a conciliatory smile, then turned to Deal. "You want to explain what you were doing in that hotel room?"

Deal shrugged. "I forgot something."

Malloy shook his head. "I'm not only your attorney, John, I'm your friend. If you expect me to help you, then you've got to be up front when you explain things."

203

Deal nodded, looking around their plush surroundings. When they'd been kids, a big outing to the movies, with popcorn, Cokes, and Jujubes, might have set them back a couple of bucks apiece, but Rusty had always been one to do more than his share. If he had an extra dollar, then they'd both enjoy a milk shake on the way home. Once again, he was extending his generosity. All he wanted in return was the straight story. It didn't seem too much to ask, even if Deal had little idea of what the real story actually was.

"How much do you know about wine, Rusty?"

Malloy's glance traveled to the half-filled wine rack, then back to Deal. "Like I told you, I had to bone up or stop taking clients to dinner." He shrugged. "What's wine got to do with anything?"

"I'm not sure," Deal said. "But I found a wine label in Dequarius Noyes's hand the night he died in my room."

Malloy shook his head as if it meant nothing. "Go on."

"I thought it was a note he was holding at first," Deal said. "It was folded in half. I figured if the guy wanted me to read it that badly, I was going to take a look. Anyway, when I took it out of his hand and opened it, I saw it was a wine label, an old one."

"How old?" Malloy asked, his interest growing.

"Nineteen twenty-nine, I think," Deal said, going on to relate what he had learned from his conversation with Gonzalo Fausto.

By the time Deal had finished, Malloy's gaze was intense. "So you don't recall where it came from?"

Deal shook his head. "It was French, that's all I can tell you. I didn't have a lot a time before the cops got there. I thought you might be able to help."

Malloy paused, thoughtful for a moment. "Why didn't you show this label to Dickerson?" he asked finally.

204        "That's the question, isn't it?" Deal said.

"Not much of a question in my mind," Russell cut in. "The cops in this town are bought and paid for."

"Nonetheless, you've withheld evidence," Malloy said to Deal. "You could always call Dickerson, say you forgot, but now . . ." He broke off with a shrug.

"And there were some other things," Deal continued, glancing at Russell. "When we were at Ainsley Spencer's house earlier in the evening, I found a note in Dequarius's room with my number at the Pier House on it. He'd made some doodles while he was waiting to reach me, I guess. Most of it was just chicken scratchings, but in one place he'd written 'Vino, vidi, vici,' and underlined it several times."

"'*Wine, I saw, I conquered*'?" Malloy translated, looking at Deal in confusion.

"It being Dequarius, I thought he might have just misspelled it," Deal said. "But now, whole new theories begin to occur to me."

"That Dequarius Noyes was trying to sell you some supposedly valuable wine?" Malloy shook his head. "As they say in court, John, this is only speculation . . . and pretty tenuous at that."

"A couple of other things," Deal continued. "When I was going through Dequarius's closet, I saw a clear outline in the dust on the floor, where someone had moved a crate or a box that had been there a long time." He gestured at the wine racks. "About the size of a case of wine, I'd say."

"John . . . ," Malloy said, his protest evident, but Deal continued, resolute now.

"And later, when I went back to the old guy's house and had the run-in with Conrad, I noticed that a bottle of wine that had been in the kitchen cupboard earlier that night was missing, too."

Malloy gave him a look. "Maybe the old lady took it."

"I suppose that's possible," Deal admitted. "But why would some-

205

one go to the trouble of tossing my room, for a wine label and some scribblings by Dequarius Noyes?"

"That's what cops do," Malloy said. "Dickerson probably went through that room with a fine-tooth comb after you left.

"That still doesn't explain why someone would be waiting for me to come back," Deal cut in. "Not unless they wanted to find something that they thought Dequarius had and might have brought to me."

"A case of wine?" Rusty Malloy said, the disbelief evident in his voice.

"I don't know what, exactly," Deal said. "Dequarius told me he'd *found* something, something he obviously thought was important. Then, in short order, Russell and I find a Monroe County sergeant beating the living daylights out of the kid. Who knows what would have happened if we hadn't come along. A few hours later, someone bursts into Dequarius's home and fatally wounds him. The next thing I know, somebody's ready to kill me for information Dequarius Noyes may have passed along."

Malloy released a breath and moved toward a bar that jutted out from the wall opposite the bank of windows. He pulled a crystal rocks glass down from a rack and filled it with ice from a dispenser recessed beneath the counter. "You look like you could use a drink," he said, pouring the glass full of scotch.

"A beer, if you've got one," Deal said.

Malloy bent and fished something out of an under-counter refrigerator, then rose and deftly popped the cap of a squat brown bottle with a red-and-white label painted on its face. "Red Stripe," Malloy said with a smile. "Jamaica's finest." He slid it across the bar counter in Deal's direction.

Deal caught the bottle and raised it in a salute. Leave it to Rusty to have Red Stripe on hand.

"How about you?" Malloy asked, his gaze traveling to Russell.

"Why not wine?" Russell asked, his expression neutral.

Malloy didn't miss a beat. "Red, white, zinfandel . . ."

"Mad Dog 20-20, if you've got it," Russell said. "Otherwise, whatever's wet."

Malloy managed a smile, then turned and retrieved a bottle from the shelf behind him. The cork had already been pulled, Deal saw, as Malloy removed a stopper from the bottle and poured a glass half full of red.

"I went out and got some of that stuff we had at the Pier House," he said to Deal. "I had a glass myself before dinner. Not bad for ten bucks."

"Well, then," Russell said, lifting his glass.

They toasted, Deal waiting for Malloy to swallow before he brought the conversation back. "That's one reason I came over, Rusty. I was hoping you had some book on wine we might look in, I could spot the label that Dequarius had."

Malloy brought his glass from his lips and popped his hand against his forehead. "Why didn't I think of that?" he said.

He put his glass down on the bar, still shaking his head. "I'll be right back," he said, then turned to hurry from the room.

**26**

WHEN MALLOY RETURNED, he was carrying a thick gilt-lettered volume that he placed on the top of the bar with a thud. "*The Encyclopedia of the Grape,*" Deal read as Malloy turned over the cover. The attorney regarded the table of contents for a moment, then began to flip through the pages.

"Here we are," he said presently, spinning the book around. "Was it one of these?"

Deal found himself staring at a glossy page with a bold heading: WINES OF THE CENTURY. Beneath it was an array of bottles representing what were apparently a series of outstanding vintages beginning in 1921, then 1928, then 1929 . . .

"I'm fairly certain this is it," he said, pointing. The picture was no larger than his thumbnail, but the image of the label he'd taken from Dequarius's fingers suddenly burned clearly in his memory.

Malloy glanced at the spot where Deal's finger rested. A suitably gray-green label with the image of a French château stamped boldly upon it. "Château Haut-Brion," he said. "A favorite of Thomas Jefferson, history tells us."

"Get out of town," Russell Straight said.

"Read the caption," Malloy said, pointing.

"It's a very old winery," Malloy added, as Russell bent to examine the tiny print. "Founded in the seventeenth century, in fact." He turned to regard Deal more closely. "You're sure this is it?"

Deal scanned the page again, his eye drawn back to the ghostly, gray-green cast of the label he'd pointed out to Malloy. "It wasn't any of the others, that much I know."

"Haut-Brion," Malloy said again, shaking his head. "Sounds French, doesn't it? Actually, the family was Irish. O'Brien. They crossed the channel to France and established one of the finest wineries of all time. Got sick of whiskey, I guess. Lucky for us all." He smiled and raised his glass.

Deal nodded. "I knew you'd be the one to ask, Rusty."

The three of them toasted briefly, then drank. The beer was cool but not cold, Deal realized, a rich maltiness blooming in his mouth. Maybe six or eight of these, he thought, with another glance at the bottle, some of the aches in his body would recede to simple agony. Then he could find a big sword somewhere, go slay some dragons of his own.

Malloy had finished his own drink and put his empty glass down on the counter. He came out from behind the bar, then walked to the wine rack and pulled a bottle carefully from its nest. He came back, tilting it so they could get a look at the label, bending to blow away a film of dust. *Château Margaux,* Deal saw printed on the label, a vintage from the 1960s.

"This is the most valuable bottle of wine I own," Malloy said. "It's worth maybe a hundred and fifty bucks."

Deal tried to imagine the Rusty Malloy he'd known as a kid plunking down $150 for a bottle of wine. No wonder he was carrying the bottle like it was full of nitroglycerin, he thought. "I guess we're not having it with the hamburgers," Deal said.

Malloy gave him a brief smile. "But this is piddling compared to one of those first growths."

"They're really that good?" Deal asked.

"Forget about good," Malloy said. "From what I read, think more like superb. Heavenly. Beyond the human ken."

Deal nodded at Malloy's rhapsodizing, but he wasn't sure he'd been convinced. "So Fausto was right about that bottle being worth fifteen grand?"

Malloy shrugged. "I had a client told me he once paid thirty grand for a magnum of Bordeaux. Of course, the guy was in Raiford doing twenty years to life for cooking meth. It's possible his memory was impaired."

"Fifteen grand?" Russell was shaking his head. "Do you get a discount on a case?"

Malloy gave him a thin smile. "I check the auction websites sometimes. I've never seen a case offered." His tone suggested it was a far-flung notion.

"But say that's what Dequarius had," Deal cut in. "Would it be worth even more, then?"

Malloy looked at Russell as if they might have something in common after all. "It's possible, assuming it was in the original packaging, that it had been carefully preserved, and the rest. Then, a collector might well be moved to pony up a bit more."

"But you have your doubts?" Deal said.

"The idea of someone like Dequarius Noyes coming into the possession of a case of the rarest wine in the world does strike me as unlikely, if that's what you mean," Malloy said.

He turned, moving back to the wine rack to replace the bottle he'd shown them. "Not to cast any aspersions, mind you," he said as he came back, "but it's a bit of a stretch to imagine Dequarius even knowing the value of such a thing. As we've heard, his scams tended to run along more mundane lines."

"On the other hand," Deal said, "let's say Dequarius *did* find this hypothetical case of wine and managed to figure out what it was worth. At best, he have something worth a couple hundred thousand dollars, maybe a little more, is that about right?"

"Possibly." Malloy nodded. "What's your point?"

"I'm not sure it's a figure that merits all that's happened," he said. "Dequarius murdered, me assaulted, Russell shot at. It seems a little extreme, even for two hundred grand."

Malloy seemed unconvinced. "For Dequarius and his crowd, a couple *hundred* dollars was a big score."

"You saying Dequarius had help on these scams?" Russell cut in.

Malloy shrugged. "I spoke with Detective Dickerson at the sheriff's office earlier today. He told me Dequarius and Ainsley Spencer used to work the sunset crowds together back when the old man could still get around."

"Doing what?" Russell asked, his tone doubtful.

"Who knows?" Malloy said. "Something about the old man being a diver on a lucrative salvage operation or like that. Dickerson wasn't too

211

specific. He told me he'd hauled them in more than once when he was working that beat—the old guy would be in a wheelchair, Dequarius pushing him past the fire-eaters and the iguana trainers, looking for marks."

"Sounds pretty cynical," Deal said.

"This is Key West." Malloy shrugged.

Deal glanced around the living room. "You seem to like it here, Rusty."

"Hey, Key West has been good to me," he said. "I'm not knocking the town. There's no place else quite like it."

Deal nodded. "A long way from South Miami, huh?"

"You'd better believe it," Malloy said, raising his glass. He drained the last of his wine, then glanced at Deal and shook his head. "So what did you have in mind next? Full-blown assault on the sheriff's office? High-noon shoot-out with Chief of Detectives Dickerson?"

Deal gave him a weary smile. "I don't think my beef's with the sheriff."

"Then who?"

Deal glanced at Russell. "I've been asking myself who on this rock would have the resources and the interest in some extremely valuable wine, and I keep coming up with the same answer."

Russell nodded. "The same guy who seems to have all the cops down here in his hip pocket."

"Franklin Stone?" Malloy said, his tone skeptical.

"You don't think so?" Deal said.

"I don't know, John," Malloy said. "Stone has a lot of influence, and he might not think twice about foreclosing on Mother Teresa and the Sisters of Mercy Orphanage, but I'm not sure that murder's his style."

"Maybe no one was supposed to get killed," Deal said. "Maybe what happened to Dequarius was an accident."

212

Malloy thought about it. "That could be," he said, glancing at Russell. "Your friend here presents a formidable target. Those shots could have been meant to keep him at bay—"

"Or I was just lucky," Russell cut in.

"Whatever," Malloy said, turning back to Deal. "But it still doesn't strike me as something Franklin Stone would engineer."

"Maybe it's really good wine," Deal said, throwing up his hands.

"So what did you intend to do, go ask Stone if he's the one who's behind all this."

Deal gave him a glum look in return. "I thought about it, but I wasn't sure it would work."

Malloy gave him an exasperated glance. "Maybe you ought to call Dickerson, tell him what happened over there just now."

"Fat chance," Deal said. "He might decide to press a few charges of his own."

"We could plead temporary insanity," Malloy said. "At least you'd have someone looking for the person who assaulted you."

Deal shook his head, his gaze drawn to the salt-water tank, where the moray eel had lazily uncoiled itself, a movement that sent the blue dollar fish flashing to a distant corner. He hadn't told Malloy about the brief look he'd gotten at his assailant before the mirrors caved in. It had only been an instant, and there hadn't been much light, but Deal had little doubt that the growling voice in his ear had been Conrad's. Still, there was no need to further fuel Rusty's fears that he was a paranoiac, Deal thought, even though they *were* out to get him. . . .

He pushed those thoughts from his head and glanced again at Malloy's wine rack. Could all this have happened over a few bottles of wine?

"I was hoping I could get myself cleaned up," he said after a moment, glancing down at the ripped pocket on his shirt. He took another look at Malloy's physique. They traded clothes as teenagers; a few          213 more pounds had accrued on both sides, of course, but it still looked to be possible. "Maybe I could borrow a shirt."

When Malloy hesitated, Deal went on. "It's just a dinner date," he said. "I'll try not to get any bullet holes in whatever you lend me."

"That's hardly my concern, John," Malloy said, managing a worried smile. He turned to glance toward the entryway of the house. "That's Stone's car out front, I gather."

"We're traveling in style."

Malloy thought about it. "Maybe the best thing would be just to go on home to Miami. Let things settle down a bit. Tell Stone you'll think about his proposal and get back to him."

"It's a thought," Deal said, surprised at how vividly the mere mention of a return to Miami had sent his mind to flashing images of his afternoon with Annie Dodds. "But I owe it to Stone to hear him out about his project, at least—" here he turned to Russell. "And we haven't had dinner yet, either."

Malloy sighed. "I can't tell you what to do, John, but I'd sure as hell be careful."

Deal gave him a smile, trying to stop the run of images in his mind. "Don't worry, Rusty," he said. He meant for his words to sound full of confidence, the sort of thing that a man who knows where he is headed tosses off like a line in a film. At the same moment, though, he'd been reliving the sight of Annie's tanned back as she slithered her way down some electrified portion of his flesh, and he knew that caution had become a meaningless concept in his recently rewired universe.

The question of who killed Dequarius Noyes, and what it might have to do with fabled wine and assaults upon his person, was weighty indeed. And there was a score to be settled between himself and a man named Conrad. But there were even more important questions to be resolved before he left Key West, and how could he explain such mat-

214

ters to Rusty Malloy when he could barely comprehend their significance himself?

Besides, Malloy was already calling out to his housekeeper, making sure there were towels in the guest bathroom, and Russell Straight was helping himself to another glass of good red wine. The moray eel had recoiled itself around its fearsome head, and the electric blue fish had resumed their hypnotic glide. Deal would take a shower now, and after that, he reasoned, things would take care of themselves.

**27**

"I THOUGHT WE were meeting at a restaurant," Deal called up the long cabin as the limo made an unexpected left on Truman Street. They were headed eastward now, away from town.

"*Sí*, Forty-nine," Balart replied.

Deal stared at the driver. "Forty-nine? Is that some kind of code?"

"Is a restaurant, Forty-nine," Balart said. "Is new. And very good."

"There's a restaurant out this way?" Deal asked, his tone doubtful. They were turning onto the isolated Beach Road now.

"Oh no," Balart said. "Not the restaurant. The chef. He is coming to *do* the dinner." Balart turned with an earnest glance.

Deal started to say something else, then gave up, settling back against the leather seat. It seemed there was indeed a destination in mind and that food would be involved. He would let it go at that. There had been a second beer waiting for him when he'd finally forced himself out of the guest room shower, and he was still feeling the last of its buzz.

"You look pretty good in the dude's clothes," Russell observed.

"Glad to hear it," Deal said.

Malloy had brought him a pair of linen trousers that were a little loose in the waist, but his belt took care of that. He'd also had his choice of shirts: a crisp white oxford with long sleeves—meant to hide the scratches on his arms, Deal supposed—and a vivid green Hawaiian print with yellow parrots that seemed to shimmer in and out of view like holograms, depending on the light. In Miami, Deal reflected, he'd have almost certainly gone with the button-down, but here in Key West, he'd barely hesitated before donning the garish Hawaiian print, further proof that familiar gravity was losing its hold.

As they made another turn onto White Street, heading southward at last, light spilled inside the limo's cabin from a street lamp, and he caught a glimpse of himself reflected in the window. He'd read a short story in one of his college English classes, he recalled, in which an escaped convict had disguised himself in such a shirt, then murdered an old woman who'd spotted him.

Was that what he was doing? Deal wondered idly. Disguising himself? But from whom? And for what purpose? At least there hadn't been blood on his shoes, a fairly new pair of Top-Siders that went well with his borrowed ensemble, he thought. He felt comfortable in his own shoes. Anchored, even.

He blinked, forcing himself out of his wildly leaping thoughts. Another one of those dragon-blood beers and he'd have been dreaming himself into a plot by Wagner.

The limo was purring down Beach Road now, headed in the opposite direction from the one he and Russell had jogged along just a cou- 217 ple of days before. It was too dark to make out the spot where they'd tussled with Conrad, and the calm, reef-protected waters were hidden as well, but Deal found himself oddly comforted by all that darkness that stretched away on his right. Out there lay the unknown. He could deal with that. It was the here and now that was tough to get a handle on.

Just short of the glow that hovered above the island's airport and its surrounding facilities, the limo swung across the opposite lane of the lonely highway and jounced over the shoulder into a parking lot that had seen better days. As they pulled to a stop, Deal saw the shadow of a dark Town Car off to one side, and a light-colored panel truck parked beside that.

"What's this?" Deal called to Balart, as the engine died.

"Where the boss say," the driver answered.

Russell sat unmoving, glancing dubiously out his window. "I don't suppose the good counselor slipped any heat into a pocket of those pretty-boy slacks," he said.

"Relax," Deal said. He was already halfway out his door and had caught sight of the familiar tower that Stone envisioned as the centerpiece of his new development silhouetted against the faintly glowing skyline. There was a staggered procession of flickering tiki torches that outlined the coral pathway to the tower's entrance and the sounds of jazz drifting above the faint crash of waves in the distance. "We're having dinner now," he added, and followed Balart by torchlight.

"If a picture is worth a thousand words," Franklin Stone was saying as a waiter set their plates before them, "then how would you judge the power of this?" He finished with a sweeping gesture that encompassed the swaying palms and the other-era battlements in the background, all of it illuminated from this side by discreetly placed landscape lighting.

218        "At least a dictionary's worth," Deal said, glancing around the newly

constructed terrace where Stone envisioned a series of outdoor parties meant to tout the project once the winter season was in high gear. Even in August, with the sun down and the light breeze off the ocean, it was a heady place, Deal thought.

"I'd say the whole damned encyclopedia," Russell Straight added.

"And the food?" Stone prompted with an eager smile.

Deal nodded, glancing after the departing white-jacketed server. It was just the three of them at the linen-clad table that had been set up by the caterers, an operation conducted by the chef and owner of the aforementioned Forty-nine, who'd been on hand only briefly to supervise the preparations for the evening.

Though Deal had caught only a fleeting glance of Boussier before the man had departed, it had been more than enough. As they'd arrived, the man—a looming, hawklike presence—had been loudly berating his employees, a trio of white-jacketed men huddled before a workstation tucked away behind a screen of palms. Stone had noticed and deftly intercepted Deal and Russell, escorting them on a tour of the nearby grounds while the restaurateur concluded his tirade and stalked away toward the parking lot.

Boussier had defected from New York's *Danielle* to come south and open up his own place on the island, Stone had told them, and was using the summer doldrums to work out "the kinks" in his new establishment's operations before the seasonal hordes descended.

"François is a bit high-strung," Stone was saying, "but he's a marvel in the kitchen. We're fortunate to have lured him here. Just one more jewel in the Key West crown, Johnny-boy."

Deal nodded absently, though he suspected there might be a flaw or two in that particular jewel. He wondered idly if Stone might be backing the restaurant enterprise.

As far as the quality of the food went, however, he could hardly 219 complain. They'd worked their way through an appetizer of delicately spiced crab cakes, followed by a fresh mozzarella salad sliced tableside by an assistant. Now, Deal found himself staring down at a version of the yellowtail dish he'd had at Louie's what seemed like aeons ago, this rendition topped by a sauce that suggested béarnaise without the threat of angioplasty and surrounded by artfully carved rosettes that he realized were actually bits of lobster meat.

His only disappointment concerning this dinner had been the absence of Annie Dodds. Deal assumed she was onstage at the Pier House, but when he'd asked—innocently enough, he thought—Stone had said she'd begged off at the last minute with a headache. His manner seemed to suggest it happened often enough, and Deal didn't press the matter. He supposed it would have made for something of an awkward dinner:

*"So, Franklin, Annie and I were screwing our brains out earlier over at the Pier House, then someone tried to kill me. You know anything about that?"*

"More wine?" Stone was asking, his practiced smile glowing as he hoisted a dripping bottle from the silver holder at tableside. He'd sent a glance at the cuts on Deal's forearms, but hadn't commented. Was that because Conrad had already given him a full report? Deal wondered.

Deal held up his hand. "I'm more into the reds, myself," he said, watching Stone carefully.

Stone seemed perplexed. He raised his eyebrows, glancing from the fish plate before him, then off toward the preparation table, where the chef, waiter, and assistant all seemed busy on a dessert that promised to surpass imagination. "I chose white with the fish, but I'm sure we have something," he said, a note of apology in his voice.

"Forget it, Franklin," Deal said. "I've had more than my share this evening."

"But I'd be happy—"

"Really," Deal said. "I'm fried as it is."

Stone nodded finally, replacing the bottle of white in the perspiring bucket. "All this romping through paradise finally getting to you?" he said.

The remark sounded innocent enough, Deal thought, as he nodded agreement. Or maybe Russell was right. All this was by way of softening him up for the hit. In a moment, the chef would pull a Mac-10 from under his toque, there would be a burst of silenced fire, and he and his new crew chief would be sleeping with the fishes.

"Your father was a great champagne drinker," Stone was saying, his gaze drifting off momentarily.

"I don't recall," Deal said.

"Oh, yes," Stone said, coming back. He gave Deal a smile. "Scotch was his signature drink, but Barton never turned down a good bottle of champagne."

Nor much of anything else, Deal thought. His old man had had the constitution of a Ford truck, right up to the end.

"Times have changed, of course," Stone was saying. "Now there's all this interest in wine . . ." He drifted off, shaking his head.

"And you're not interested?" Deal asked.

Stone turned back to him as if startled by something in Deal's tone. "I've come to a new appreciation, along with many others," he said. "I was just thinking about how tastes change over the years, that's all. When I was a child, it was hard to find a nightspot that didn't use a martini glass in some aspect of its signage or decor. But by the seventies and eighties you never heard the word 'martini.' Now it's all the rage again: martini hours, martini bars, chocolate martinis . . . good God." He shuddered with distaste. "James Bond must be rolling over in his grave."

221

"I suppose so," Deal said. "But 007 knew a little about wines, too, as I recall."

Stone gave him a wicked smile. "Mr. Fleming's creation was an aficionado of many pleasures." He waved at the scene around them, then turned back to Deal. "He would have been right at home here, don't you think?"

Deal kept himself from glancing at Russell, wondering if Stone was dodging, if there might be some hidden message in those apparently casual remarks. "Who wouldn't enjoy it?" Deal said. He was looking in Stone's direction, but all he could see was the vision of Annie glancing up at him from her place at poolside, her lips parted, her long legs crossing in a motion that never seemed to end.

"Someone told me you collect wines," Deal said, forcing himself back to the point. "Châteaux Margaux, Lafite-Rothschild, Haut-Brion . . ."

Stone paused to stare as Deal lingered on the last. "Who told you that?" he asked mildly.

Deal shrugged. "A man named Gonzalo Fausto," he said. "I dropped in to buy a bottle, and your name popped up."

Stone nodded thoughtfully. "You were shopping for some rather expensive wines, Johnny-boy."

Deal shook his head. "I went in for a six-pack. Somehow Gonzalo and I got to talking about rare wines. Nineteen twenty-nine, vintages like that."

Stone considered Deal's words, then turned to stare off thoughtfully into the darkness. After a moment he turned back to Deal. "Did Gonzalo tell you about the Cherbourg consignment, then?"

Deal stared blankly. "He must have skipped that part."

Stone raised his brows. "If you were talking about the 'twenty-nines, I'm surprised he didn't mention it."

222

Deal glanced at Russell. "Why don't you fill me in," he said, turning back to Stone.

Stone had a sip from his glass. "It was one of the greatest wine thefts in history, that's all."

Deal glanced again at Russell. "When did this take place?"

"Oh, a long time ago," Stone said, waving his hand. "Shortly after the vintage had been released in the early 1930s. A shipment of Haut-Brion on its way to London was hijacked from the Cherbourg docks, some three hundred cases of one of the finest wines ever produced."

"Who took it?" Deal asked.

Stone shrugged. "No one knows. The thieves were never caught, nor was the wine ever found."

"How do we know that?" Deal asked.

"Each bottle was numbered," Stone said. "Stamped on the label as if it were currency." He shrugged and gave Deal a look. "It might have been rebottled and sold as something else, of course . . . but then why go to the trouble of stealing it in the first place?" He raised his palms in a gesture of uncertainty. "Or perhaps it was consumed by the person who stole it." He smiled. "This would have been a very contented man, to be sure."

"Three hundred cases?" Deal repeated, trying to do the math.

"And that from barely ten thousand produced," Stone continued. "A loss that makes what few bottles are left all the more valuable."

Deal nodded, thinking about the implications. "Have you ever had any of this stuff?" he asked.

Stone gave him a smile. "I can say that I tasted the Haut-Brion 'twenty-nine once, and it was excellent." He glanced away for a moment as if savoring the memory, then finished the glass in his hand. "I

223

like my wine, there's no doubt, but spending that kind of money just seems foolish, wouldn't you say?"

Deal stared back, trying to decide whether Stone was oblivious to his suspicions or simply toying with him. Suppose Stone had come into possession of a stolen case of wine and that Dequarius Noyes had somehow gotten his hands on it, pegging Deal as someone with enough money to take it off his hands? Would Franklin Stone have killed Dequarius to get his wine back and cover up the fact that he'd been trafficking in stolen property?

Interesting questions, but hardly the kind he could blurt across the table. He'd get back to Malloy in the morning, find out if there was some kind of international black market in rare wines similar to that in stolen art.

"But enough rambling," Stone was saying. "It's time we got down to business."

He tossed his napkin on the table, glancing at Deal's untouched plate, then at Russell, who was just lifting his last bite of yellowtail to his mouth. "Come on, Johnny-boy, eat up, then let me take you inside the tower and show you a few things."

Deal glanced down at his plate. He ought to have been hungry all right, but his appetite had disappeared. "I'm full," he told Stone, then turned to Russell. "You feel like taking a walk?"

Russell cut a glance at the trio working fervently at the portable serving station, then shrugged. "Why not?"

"Good," said Stone, already on his feet. "I want to show you the true Cayo Hueso experience."

Given the possible derivations of the name, the "true" Bone Key experience might be a bit more intense than he was ready for, Deal thought as he and Russell followed Stone around the curving facade of the an-

224

cient battlement tower and into the shadows near the parking area. Still, he felt certain Stone wouldn't try anything in front of witnesses, even if he did think Deal was a danger to him.

If he had any connection with what Deal suspected had gotten Dequarius killed, then Stone was being remarkably cool about it. Just as it seemed he had no inkling of what had happened between Deal and Annie. Whatever turned out to be the truth concerning Dequarius's murder, however, the latter was an issue that the two of them would face, sooner or later.

And forget Stone for the moment, he thought as the warm breeze swept in off the Atlantic and the palms rustled softly overhead. It was a matter that Deal himself would have to come to terms with. 007 might have himself a roll in the hay, then go on about his merry business, but it wasn't going to work that way for Johnny Deal. He'd had his share of Jimmy Carter, lust-in-his-heart moments over the years, but there had never been anything like what had happened between him and Annie.

And while a part of him insisted that he had done nothing wrong, especially given all that had gone awry with Janice these past several years, another part was wagging a shameful finger his way. Worst of all was his uncertainty regarding Annie's own feelings. He hadn't had much time to dwell on it since Russell had dragged him from his stupefied slumber earlier in the evening, but his mind had been nibbling at the matter all along, he realized.

Maybe it all had been just a pleasant diversion for her. Maybe she had no intention of seeing him again. Maybe he wasn't really an adult at all, he thought, but the same seventeen-year-old kid who thought he would die of a broken heart the night his girlfriend said she was leaving him for the big city.

He shook his head to chase his clamoring thoughts away as Stone brought them to a halt before the imposing entryway of the battlement

225

tower. "Every guest will enter here," Stone said, pausing to tap in a code on an alarm keypad sunk into the stone sidewall.

When the warning lights switched from red to amber, Stone reached for the lever of the massive wooden door and pulled it down. There was a heavy clanking that made Deal think of giant slot-machine gears engaging, and then the door was swinging toward them, loosing a gust of cool air that carried the odor of centuries-old stone and moisture with it.

"That's not air-conditioning you feel," Stone said proudly as he found a light switch and ushered them inside.

"Could have fooled me," Russell said, glancing around the foyer where they were gathered.

"We'll have AC installed, of course," Stone went on. "But the fact is, you could almost get by without it." He gestured at the rough-textured walls around them. "During the heat of the day, the coral absorbs the moisture in the air, then releases it at night. Combined with the natural convection that moves through all these nooks and crannies, the place practically air-conditions itself."

"I could use that in my place," Russell said.

"They don't build them like this anymore, eh, Johnny-boy?" Stone said.

"No, they don't," Deal said, glancing around. Down the hallway that curved away from them, where he vaguely remembered historical photographs and reproductions of yellowed documents once hanging, a series of artists' renderings of Stone's proposed Villas of Cayo Hueso had been hung, including one that featured Annie poised to dive into an as-yet-to-be-built swimming pool.

"You're going to get into trouble if that stays up," Deal said, pointing at the doctored photograph. He realized with a start that she had

226

been wearing the same suit when she'd come to see him earlier that day. Coincidence? he wondered.

Stone glanced at the photograph and made a dismissive gesture. "Just modesty," he said. "Besides, how could I justify taking such a picture down?"

Deal nodded. He and Stone could agree on one thing, it seemed. Then he remembered Annie with her pistol stuck in Ainsley Spencer's ear and wondered if Stone should be so cavalier. Just how well did Stone know Annie, anyway? he wondered. No sooner had that question occurred to him than it furnished an accompanying jab of pain.

Something to think about tomorrow, Deal thought hastily. Or maybe never at all.

He was following Stone down the twisting passageway that circled the tower floor, listening only vaguely to the sales pitch that was a variation of what they had heard before. Once wiring and other necessary modifications had been made, Stone had explained, there would be interactive kiosks along the way where clients might design a virtual version of their condominium, and a sales pavilion would be built adjoining the tower to house offices and support staff, all of which would be eventually subsumed into the grand clubhouse that Stone envisioned as the centerpiece of his development. The gist of it was that he and Stone would become rich and that Barton Deal would have been proud to see it happen.

And maybe he would have been, Deal thought, wondering at the same time how long this blessed collaboration would last if the events of the afternoon were laid bare, so to speak. Maybe he could work some language into their contract, Deal mused. All's fair in love—take my girl, keep my job—or some such. Again, he tried to force himself away from this line of thinking. Wasn't it about time for dessert?

227

"We'll have an observation deck up there," Stone was saying, pointing to a doorway set in an inner wall. A steel grate blocked the way to a set of stairs that curled upward, where a guard's post had once been, Deal supposed. He was about to turn away when he noticed another doorway set in a recess beside the grate, this one a solid slab of wood like the front door. There was an ancient-looking door handle with what looked like a skeleton-key lockplate beneath it, but a modern-day hasp and padlock had been added as well.

"What's this?" he asked, moving to try the knob.

Stone glanced over. "Storage," he said, a bit too quickly it seemed.

Deal turned the heavy knob and felt the door give inward. Only the padlock was keeping him out.

"The historical society's got some of their things in there," he heard Stone say over his shoulder. "I told them they had a little time until we began renovations."

Deal gave the padlock a tug as he stepped back. "Good of you," he said.

Stone gave him an odd look, nodding uncertainly. "Well," he said, pointing over Deal's shoulder. "We're back to where we started."

Deal turned to see that they had, in fact, nearly completed a circuit of the tower's base. "There's not a lot to see right now, admittedly," Stone was saying. "But you can feel it, can't you? There's a sense of history here, of rootedness. In a place like Key West, where everyone just sort of tumbles down to the end of the line and stops, you can't put too high a value on such a thing. These places are going to sell themselves," he finished with a flourish.

Deal had a vision of a long line of millionaires stumbling down Whitehead Street, banging into one another as their progress slowed, splashing into the shallow waters like so many two-legged lemmings near the buoy marking Southernmost Point.

228

"I'll have to give you that much, Franklin," Deal said. "Maybe after we're finished here, we can go on to the Dry Tortugas, turn Fort Jefferson into a time-share."

Stone gave him a dry smile. "Can I take that as a yes?"

Deal drew a deep breath. "This is a long way from Miami."

"Just my point, John. You need a change. It'd be good for you. No telling where this could lead."

Deal stared back, fighting the urge to tell him just where things had already led. "I just don't know," is what he found himself saying. "I'm going to need a little time. It's not like things have been so placid, you know."

"I understand," Stone said. He flipped off the light switch and ushered them outside, closing the heavy door behind them. Maybe he'd been wrong, Deal thought as he heard the latch mechanism reengage. More like bank vault than slot machine.

Stone tapped at the security keypad once again, then turned to put his arm around Deal's shoulder. "Sleep on it, that's all I ask. Maybe tomorrow we can take a run on the boat, get out there and blow the stink away, see how you feel."

Stone swept his arm toward the dark waters in the distance. Deal followed his gesture and saw the distant lights of a freighter far out on the Gulf Stream.

Like a floating island, he thought. Or a small city that had broken from the mainland to set sail.

When he was a kid, he had equated the sight with his most exotic imaginings. Bogart. Ingrid Bergman. Foreign ports of call.

*The wind is in from Africa,* he thought. God help us all.

"We'll see," he told Stone. "I'll give you a call in the morning, count on it." He turned toward the parking lot then, where the limo sat, its parking lights glowing, Balart's shadow visible behind the wheel.

"But if it's all the same to you, I'd like to skip dessert, just go home and get some rest."

Stone followed his gaze toward the waiting limo. "Of course," he said. He lifted his fingers to his lips and issued a whistle worthy of a Park Avenue doorman. In seconds Deal heard the sound of the limo's engine starting.

"Go on. Get some rest," Stone said, his arm encircling Deal's shoulders. "We'll hash all this out by the light of day."

# 28

"I WONDER WHAT that dessert *was*, anyway," Deal heard Russell say at his side.

Deal shrugged, his eyes on the departing catering van. "I'm sure it's on the menu at Louie's," he said.

"Probably can't get it in jail, though," Russell said.

Deal ignored that one. When the van's lights had finally disappeared around the bend far down Beach Road, he started the Hog's engine and pulled out from behind the screen of palmetto scrub north of the tower site, where they'd been keeping watch for the past half hour. He drove a hundred feet without turning on his lights, guided by the light of a pale, if nearly full, moon that had risen since their first visit to the tower that night.

He glanced up at the glowing orb—a macular moon, wasn't it, just like the one in the song?—then swung the Hog back off the deserted highway and into the lot, parking near where the limo had been earlier. When they got out and the sound of the Hog's doors had died away, he stood for a moment to listen: no shouts of alarm, no guard dogs barking, no distant sirens. Just the sound of the waves lapping at the shore across the highway and, down the strand, the clatter of the palm fronds above, the ticking of the Hog's engine nearby.

"I hope you know what you're doing," Russell said.

"Me too," Deal said. He moved around to the bed of the Hog and opened the toolbox he'd checked before they left the parking lot of the Pier House. He took out what they would need and handed the items to Russell, then led the way to the tower entrance.

No security lights popped on at their advance, no whooping warning alarms switched on. Stone was right, he thought. This was a long, long way from Miami.

He held a penlight in one hand and punched in the code he hoped was correct. As red lights danced about the panel in response, he couldn't help but glance Russell's way.

The big man was nodding. "Same numbers I remember," the big man said.

Deal felt himself break into a smile that was only part nervousness. "I hope we're right," he said.

Abruptly, the red lights stopped their dance and switched to amber. "A pair of born thieves," he said to Russell, then pulled the heavy door lever down. Jackpot, he found himself thinking as the wooden door swung open and no warning Klaxons sounded.

"Could still be wired to the station," Russell observed.

"That's why you're going to stay out here," Deal said. "You see trouble coming, tap the horn. You keep the lights off and drive away, I'll close up and leave that way," he said, pointing in the direction of the salt marsh. "I'll meet you back at the hotel."

Russell shrugged. "Last time I was a lookout it didn't work out so good."

Deal pointed inside the dark tower. "There's no one inside there, Russell," he said, extending his hand for the tools. "I'll be in and out in a flash."

Russell handed the things over and turned back for the Hog in what seemed a minor huff. Deal glanced down the lonely beach road once more, then hurried inside, guiding himself with his tiny penlight.

He rounded the first curve to his left, in deep shadow now, running the slender beam along the rough inner wall until he found the grated stairwell. A door that was fit to have a groaning prisoner or two behind it, he thought, though he could see only a set of dusty stone stairs leading up on the opposite side.

It only stood to reason that there was a matching set of steps that led downward behind the padlocked door before him. He reached down and turned the knob until the latch was free, pushing to get as much play behind the padlock hasp as possible.

He thought about using the hammer first, but took another look at the hasp and decided to try the heavy pry bar. He set the hammer down headfirst on the floor, leaning it by its handle against the jamb. He straightened and slid the flattened tip of the pry bar toward the hasp, grunting with satisfaction when it slid beneath the shiny metal.

There would be no covering up the signs of what he was about to do, he realized, but if he was right, it would hardly matter. He took a deep breath, then gripped the end of the bar and jerked backward with all his strength.

There was a shriek that sounded almost human as the hasp gave way, and he staggered back a step. The pry bar slipped from his hands and went down to the floor with a clang.

Just screws ripping free of wood, he assured himself as he caught his balance and moved quickly back toward the wavering door. A sound a carpenter might hear every day of his life.

He clutched the doorknob again and leaned his weight into the heavy slab, feeling something behind it grinding on stone as he shoved. *A wooden crate? Was it possible?*

He fought his growing excitement as the door swung inward. *For Christ's sake, you'll have a heart attack,* he told himself as whatever was holding the door finally gave way and he staggered forward.

He swung his penlight up as he stumbled, still clutching the doorknob with his other hand. Then he saw it, the glint of the eyes first, and in the next instant the sharp tip of the sword, and nearly dropped his light in shock.

He was backpedaling automatically, moving for all he was worth, cursing himself for his brave statements to Russell, groping wildly on the floor behind him for the pry bar or the hammer, anything for a weapon. . . .

He felt a pair of arms encircle him from behind and realized that what he had hit this time was anything but a jackpot.

# 29

"**WHAT THE FUCK** *was* that, anyway?" Russell Straight asked as Deal piloted the Hog resolutely northward along Beach Road.

"A marlin," Deal said.

"I thought that was baseball players," Russell said.

Deal stared. "That's where the nickname comes from, Russell. It's a kind of swordfish."

"Whatever it's called," Russell said, shaking his head, "I'd hate to pull something like that into my boat."

Deal glanced at him. The big man had been the one who'd caught him as he came backpedaling out of the closet, like some scared-stiff heroine from a horror film. It hadn't taken long to realize that Stone had been telling the truth about what was inside: just a dusty, cobwebbed nook beneath the staircase, crammed full of boxed records, a few moldering Audubon prints, and the enormous stuffed trophy fish propped atop some filing cabinets, with its bill pointed toward any unwary intruder to come barging through the door.

"They're usually dead before they come over the gunwale," he said idly, still trying to come to terms with what he'd found, or rather, hadn't found. He'd been so sure. Some detective, he thought.

"Dead of what?" Russell was asking.

Deal shrugged, ready enough to divert his thoughts. "Somebody might lean over the side and club it," he said. "Or pop a bullet in its brain."

Out of the corner of his eye Deal saw Russell shaking his head again. "Puts a whole new wrinkle into being a fish," he said finally.

Deal nodded. Not long after he'd recovered from his fright and disentangled himself from Russell, he'd gone back to check inside the closet, gradually coming to realize he'd actually seen the gigantic stuffed marlin before: For years the trophy had graced a wall above the bar in the Full Moon Saloon, a once-favored locals hangout long since closed. One of the regulars had landed the near-record game fish in the waters just off Cuba and had brought the carcass home as proof.

The last time Deal had seen the thing, there had been a Florida State gimmee cap smashed on its head while a boisterous crowd cheered a college football game on the bar's television sets. How it had become part of the historical society's holdings, he couldn't quite imagine.

"So maybe your buddy Malloy is right," Russell said, glancing at Deal through the greenish glow cast by the Hog's dash lights. "Maybe we ought to beat it out of Dodge, let things sort themselves out."

Deal raised an eyebrow in response. "You think Malloy's right? All this is just some fantasy I've dreamed up?" After what had just happened, of course, he couldn't blame Russell for feeling that way about his cockeyed theories. He was beginning to have doubts himself.

236        Russell shook his head. "Not what I said at all."

Deal glanced at him. "Then what?"

"Far as I know you're absolutely right about Dequarius having something somebody else wants," Russell said. "But this somebody already killed one dude. No reason for them to stop now."

Deal slowed, bringing the Hog around a curve and past the entrance to the airport. No traffic at this time of night, of course, but the vapor lamps still glowed orange above the parking lot, and strings of red and blue runway lights winked in the distance. In a few hours, they could board a plane, be back on the mainland for breakfast, have someone—Balart maybe—drive the Hog up in due time.

"You could be right," he finally said to Russell. "But just going back to Miami wouldn't put an end to anything. If I'm right, whoever jumped me back at the Pier House thinks I know where Dequarius Noyes stashed a valuable case of wine—or maybe thinks I have it—that's the bottom line."

"Yeah, but you're a fish out of water down here, my man. You could end up stuffed and mounted like that marlin."

Deal considered it a moment. It was true that paradise tended to cast a certain rosy glow on things. Spend enough time in cozy Margaritaville, you could end up thinking that calamity meant running out of rum before the sun was up.

And Russell was right. He didn't know Key West well enough to be certain that anything he saw was the same as what was real. Take what had happened between himself and Annie, for starters.

He turned back to Russell finally. "This isn't your show, you know. There's no place in the DealCo handbook that covers gunfire or breaking and entering."

"Yeah, well, why don't we take that up at the next contract talks," Russell said. "I came down with you, I'll go home with you. Whenever you say."

Deal stared at him for a moment, then nodded, piloting them around another curve, leaving the airport and its lights behind. They were at the far eastern tip of the island now, traveling north, with the waters of Cow Key Channel on their right. Across the cut was Stock Island, the first of the coral stepping-stones that dotted the shallow waters northward to the mainland. A mile or so ahead was a bridge that carried the traffic of Highway A1A across the channel and up the line that connected all the dots. In less than a minute, he could be hanging a hard right turn, they could be back in Miami before the sun rose.

"And pigs might fly, too," he mumbled. The asphalt surface of Roosevelt Boulevard was rolling through the headlamps of the Hog before his eyes, but what he saw was Annie Dodds's face as she reached to pull him down to her breast.

"Pardon me?" Russell Straight said, at his side.

"Just one more stop," Deal answered, and abruptly nudged the Hog off the boulevard. They were traveling on a narrow access road now, one that led down to a set of rickety docks where houseboats were tethered, and had been, as far as Deal knew, since the beginning of time.

238

## 30

"**WHICH ONE OF THESE** you figure belonged to Dequarius?" Russell said, joining him at the prow of the Hog.

Deal had pulled to a stop, cutting the engine and the lights before they'd gotten too close to the line of bobbing craft. No sense getting any jittery residents riled up. One of the reasons people lived out here was for their privacy.

Deal glanced up at Russell, then back toward the docks. "Probably not that one," he said, pointing to a boat tied up near the far end. That craft was ablaze with light, where raucous party chatter underscored Jimmy Buffett's voice booming into the night, proclaiming himself to be the son of a son of a sailor.

There was a certain raspiness to the rendition, a hint of the been-there, sung-this-to-death that suggested to Deal it might actually be    239

Buffett himself down there leading the revelers' charge, but that was probably just his imagination. For that matter, maybe there wasn't a party going on at all. Maybe the boat was just a glittering mirage.

"I never understood that music," Russell said.

Deal glanced at Russell, feeling reassured. "That's probably what some people say about Destiny's Child."

Russell snorted. "You think black people listen to Destiny's Child?"

By that time, Deal had spotted what he'd been looking for and was moving off through the darkness. He reached the jerry-rigged post-and-shelf construction that held all the mailboxes for the docks, saving the mailman from the trouble—not to mention the potential peril—of visiting each craft individually. He pulled his penlight from his pocket and ran it over the names on the front of the boxes, which dipped and rose on the swaybacked cross-plank like the waves that lapped at the nearby seawall.

*Stone,* he read. *Feathergill. Thomas. Galliard. Dobyns. McGrath. Fuck You. Catanese.*

There was a blank face plate next in order, followed by *T. Martin, Whitehurst,* and *Tucker.* The last, the party boat, was apparently occupied by someone named Pacheco.

Deal switched off his light and regarded the gently bobbing silhouetted rooflines before them, ticking off names on his fingers. "I vote for blank," he said, turning to Russell.

"I'm not going on board Fuck You," Russell said. "Not without a gun, anyway."

"Of course Dequarius could have been using an alias," Deal said, moving along the docks now.

"None of *those* names," Russell said, keeping his voice low as he hurried after.

240    Deal slowed, pointing at one of the more tidily maintained boats,

its whitewashed planks glowing in the moonlight, its gangway flanked by a pair of potted Queen palms. "That's Catanese," he said, and turned to the next in line.

"It looks like our man, all right," Russell said at Deal's shoulder.

Deal turned to regard a listing craft with a roofline that bobbed and dipped as erratically as the swaybacked plank that held up the floating community's mailboxes. A jagged crack ran diagonally across an un-curtained window in the wall that faced them, and a toppled plastic trash can shifted idly on the deck. There was a plank missing from the boat's gangway, and the lines that tethered the craft to the dock cleats looked frayed and ready to burst.

Deal heard a creaking noise as the tide shifted and glanced across the narrow gap separating dock and deck. The cabin door had swung open slightly, then settled back as the tide shifted again.

"Don't look like no one's home," Russell said.

"I guess we'll go see," Deal said.

He raised one foot to the gangway and tested it, then stepped as lightly as he could across to the houseboat's deck. He felt the surface tilt slightly as Russell came quickly aboard behind him.

He knocked softly on the aluminum door frame. "Anyone here?" he called, then knocked again, harder this time.

They stood in silence for a moment, listening to the slap of water at the seawall behind them. Down the docks, the Beach Boys were lamenting the loss of the Sloop John B., their voices as confident and cheery as ever. Not a celebrity party, then, Deal found himself thinking. Not unless it was a doozy.

He turned to glance at Russell and saw the big man's shoulders rise in a shrug. Deal took his penlight out and pulled the door open. He had a quick, insane thought as a musty cloud of disuse and mildew swept out of the cabin toward him: The case of priceless wine had been

241

here on Dequarius's abandoned boat all right, but someone headed for the party had already spotted it and now it was down there being guzzled by a horde of merry parrot-heads, yo-ho-ho and a bottle of rum.

"The man had absolutely no housekeeping skills," Russell was saying now at Deal's shoulder.

Deal wanted to nod agreement, his penlight beam sweeping over the wild disarray before them. It was one big common room they'd entered—kitchen, dining, and living area combined—with a doorway that led down a short hallway to what was likely the bedroom and bath.

God only knew what those looked like, he thought. Here the galley doors were all flung open along with those of the oven and refrigerator, the contents strewn about the floor. Wire shelving, pots and pans, a half-filled plastic milk jug, shattered plates and glassware, cereal boxes, a lolling head of lettuce gone way past wilted and on to brown. A tabletop microwave had been dashed to the floor, its door bent awry like a twisted limb.

A Formica-topped dinette had been upended, the rug it had been resting on kicked into a wad, as if someone had been searching for a trapdoor beneath it. *Sure,* Deal thought. *Straight to Davy Jones's locker.*

There was a couch and chair in the living room—or what had once been a couch and a chair. Now their cushions had been slashed and torn and the stuffing erupted, great clumps of it shuddering with the movement of the tides like giant dust bunnies from hell.

"Do we need to check the rest of it?" Russell said, gesturing toward the hallway.

"Not unless you're a masochist," Deal said. He switched off his penlight and turned to step past Russell, suddenly desperate for a breath of fresh air. He'd also had an unreasoning flash of the interior of his own apartment back in Miami, the furnishing trashed, Isabel's things mounded into an obscene pile, and though he knew it was only his

242

imagination, he felt his jaw clench, his hands tighten at his sides. It wouldn't be the first time in his life that he'd managed to step into the path of a train unawares, he reminded himself, but that didn't make the possibility that it had happened again one bit easier to accept.

No way he could slink away in the night, run home and pull the covers up over his head and hope it would all blow away with the tides, he thought. Even if there'd been no Annie Dodds in the mix. That's what he was telling himself as he headed out the door, full of rage and certainty. . . .

"You won't find what you're looking for," came the voice out of the darkness, stopping him as he came across the threshold onto the deck. "Not here, you won't."

He gaped into the darkness toward the prow of the boat to find the tall and slender figure looming against the faint glow of the sky like a wraith risen from the waters, an apparition and a voice that changed everything.

**31**

"I WATCHED THEM take the place apart," the old man said as Deal approached, his tone flat but firm. "They didn't find anything."

"Who did you watch?" Deal said. He was close enough to see Ainsley Spencer's face clearly now, but his heart was still racing from the shock of finding him there.

The old man shook his head, though it wasn't clear if he hadn't seen or if the question simply meant nothing to him.

"Fucking-A," Russell Straight said, cutting in as he joined them on the warped and rolling deck. "You could get your ass killed, skulking around in the dark like this."

The old man paid no attention. It was the Stones drifting mournfully in the background now, *"You can't always get what you want . . . ,"* as if choreographed by some cosmic DJ.

"Waste of energy, kill an old man like me," he said, with the trace of a smile.

"When were they here?" Deal asked him.

"Earlier." The old man shrugged.

"Where were you?" Russell cut it.

The old man gestured out past the rail of the houseboat. There was a motorized skiff tied off there, Deal saw, though he couldn't recall seeing it when they'd come on board. The old man must have been tied off in the mangroves across the channel, rowed over when he saw them board the houseboat.

"You know what they were looking for?" Deal asked.

"Could have been a lot of things," the old man said. "Could have been some of these."

He extended his arm and opened his palm. Deal saw several bright disks in Ainsley Spencer's palm, none larger than a quarter, though much thicker.

"Go ahead," the old man said. "Take one."

Deal glanced at Russel, then plucked one of the bright disks from the old man's palm. He could feel the bas-relief patterns on either surface, though it was the weight that suggested the thing was real.

"Gold doubloons," Deal said.

"That some of Dequarius's racket?" Russell asked.

"Take one yourself," the old man said. "Gold's good for what ails you, just holding some in your hand."

Russell snorted, but picked up one of the coins. "You're supposed to bite it to see if it's real, aren't you?"

"If it suits you," Ainsley Spencer said.

"How much of this stuff do you have?" Deal said.

The old man shook his head. "A bit," he said, his voice sorrowful. "I was one of the first to go down when they thought they'd found the    245

*Atocha.*" He shrugged. "I found a few things I decided were mine as much as theirs."

Deal glanced at him. He'd heard stories of workers in diamond mines being shot in their tracks for similar transgressions. "I'm surprised you could get away with it."

Spencer shrugged. "It was the early days of that adventure," he said, "everybody way too excited to pay much attention till they realized it was the real thing."

He glanced off again, then continued. "It was me that told them where to look, you know, me and a couple of the fellows. Most of us knew where that old ship went down, a lot of us on my island did. But it didn't matter. It was only stories. There just wasn't any way of getting to that wreck. Not for the longest time."

Deal had an image of Ainsley Spencer and his fellow Caymaners spending nights around their campfires on a Caribbean beach, swapping tales of sunken treasure, dreaming dreams of untold wealth. And then along comes Mel Fisher, the lucky high-tech salvor, and swoops up $400 million like a Powerball player with every ticket in his hand.

"You saying you had to claim your own share of the booty?" Russell asked.

Ainsley Spencer gave him a speculative look. "Not that it did anyone any good, when it's all said and done. Look what's happened." He broke off, gesturing toward the devastated cabin.

"Then you think that's what this is all about," Deal said. "Gold coins."

"I've been dribbling these things out for years, now," Ainsley Spencer said with another shake of his head. "When I started getting older, I made the mistake of letting Dequarius help." He gave Deal something of a pleading look. "He was younger, had more energy, could get out and about. He had ways of doing better, getting a little more for these trinkets, than I ever had."

246

But not trinkets at all, Deal was thinking. If he could believe what Ainsley Spencer was telling them, if he could believe the heft and the very feel of antiquity that he gripped in his own palm, then Dequarius Noyes had been out there hustling the real thing, some of the time at least. In a way, you could say that the kid had been acting as manager of his great-grandfather's pension fund. But it hadn't been pieces of eight that had brought Dequarius Noyes to his own doorstep, that much he was sure of.

"Dequarius wasn't trying to sell me any gold," Deal said, his voice subdued.

"No?" the old man said, though there was no denial in his voice.

They broke off then as voices approached from down the dock, a trio of drunks leaving the party at last, joined in a boozy counterpart to another Stones tune blasting the otherwise quiet of Cow Key Cut. *"Please allow me to introduce myself, I'm a man of wealth and taste . . ."*

Three of them, Deal saw, hanging on to each other, staggering past the houseboat with scarcely a glance. One man caught hold of the dock railing near the gangway leading to the houseboat and began to retch into the waters below, while one of his partners reached for him and missed, barely missing a tumble into the water. Instead he came careening across the rickety gangway, groping about for a handhold to stop himself.

"Get the hell gone . . ." Russell Straight began, moving for the man who'd boarded the boat—then straightened suddenly when he saw what was in the intruder's hand.

"Hands up, all three of you," the man who'd staggered aboard said, all traces of his former awkwardness disappeared. He waved the barrel of a stubby machine pistol over them, a weapon that might have looked faintly ridiculous if Deal wasn't well aware of what it could so rapidly do.

247

The man who'd apparently been blowing chum into the dockside waters was right behind the man with the automatic, producing a cellular phone from his pocket as he came aboard. He pressed a single button, then waited a moment as his connection was made. Mobile to mobile, Deal thought. Probably secure.

"We're on the houseboat," the man with the phone was saying. "The old man's here." He broke off to glance at Deal, then continued. "Yeah. The two dickwads from Miami."

Deal glanced at Russell, who was turned toward the prow of the houseboat, his jaw set, his hands upraised. Hardly the look of the contented man Deal had seen roll out of a pretty cocktail waitress's bed what seemed like ages ago. And whose fault was that? Deal thought with a pang. He heard the sounds of powerboat engines starting in the distance and noted that the party music had died away.

"We'll take care of it," Deal heard the one with the telephone say, his gaze gone out over the dark waters. Odd, Deal found himself thinking. Here was a killer who didn't want to look his victim in the eye.

"I'm sorry," Deal said to Russell.

"Not your fault," Russell said gruffly. Deal could see a muscle twitching at the side of the big man's jaw.

"Shut up, both of you," the man with the phone said. He folded the little clamshell unit and put it in his pocket. "We've got business with this man that doesn't concern you," he said, nodding toward Ainsley Spencer. He'd affected a tone, meant to sound conciliatory, just a man trying to get a job done. "What I'd like you and your friend to do is go inside and wait."

He glanced at Russell and gestured toward the yawning door of the houseboat. When Russell hesitated, the man turned to the third of his party, a heavyset man still standing on the dock, a pistol with a long suppressor held across his chest. An assassin ready to deliver the Pledge of Allegiance, Deal found himself thinking, the sort of giddiness inspired by imminent death, he supposed.

"Bobby?" the phone man said. "You help these gentlemen inside, okay?"

Bobby nodded—a bit too readily, Deal thought. Why couldn't the order have been one too many? Why couldn't Bobby have told his scuzzwad buddy to go fuck himself? But no such luck. Bobby was already stepping off the deck onto the gangway, his pistol cocked straight up now, like the tail of a hound keen to the scent.

Deal knew they'd have to try something, he just wasn't sure what. He could see by the tension in Russell's posture that he felt the same. A few moments more and they'd dance whatever dance they could.

The thought had hardly cleared Deal's mind when there was a sharp crack from the direction of the gangway and he turned to see that a second plank had given way at eager Bobby's weight. Bobby gasped in surprise, his free hand clamping onto one of the lines as he plunged down toward the water.

There was a chuffing sound as Bobby's bulk jerked hard against the hand on the line and a tiny penumbra of flame blossomed just beneath his chin. His eyes bulged as if in disbelief as the back of his skull lifted away, flying into the darkness with most of what passed for a brain. In the next moment, his hand relaxed its hold and he disappeared into the dockside waters with a splash.

Everyone on deck stood frozen for a moment, even the guy with the automatic. It looked as if he were about to ask Phone Man a question when Deal heard something behind him and turned. The old man had flung open the emergency chest stowed beside him at the prow and rose now with what looked like a giant derringer clutched in both his skinny hands, its hammer snapped back at full cock.

The man with the automatic was swinging his weapon into position when Ainsley pulled the trigger. There was a loud click, and an instant's hesitation, as if the odd-looking weapon in the old man's hand was nothing but a toy.

Then there came a whooshing sound and a tiny flame-tailed rocket shot from the flare gun, bursting against the gunman's chest in a Fourth of July crescendo of sparks. The gunman went down with a scream, clawing at the huge glowing ember that had lodged in his throat.

Phone Man lunged for the fallen automatic pistol and was swinging it toward Russell when Deal caught the stubby barrel and shoved it aside. Deal felt a scorching pain in his palm as a burst of fire blew out the cracked window in the houseboat cabin and careened about the galley. One of the slugs ripped through the propane tank, followed by an explosion that sent Deal sprawling, blowing window glass and whatever else hadn't been fastened down far out into the channel.

Deal rolled up on his hands and knees, groggy from the blast. He found his gaze locked with that of Phone Man, who struggled to his feet just a few feet away, bleeding from a sizable cut on his forehead. The bad news was that the man still held the automatic and was bringing it back into firing position, this time aimed squarely at Deal.

So it goes, Deal found himself thinking, as the flames from inside the houseboat's cabin grew to illuminate the surreal scene on deck. One gunman still clawed weakly at a giant smoldering ruby lodged in his throat, and a second struggled to bring his weapon to bear.

Deal had given it the old college try, gone for the gusto, shot the moon, left nothing for another day. He'd spent a few hours in the presence of a woman who had reconstituted his soul, and while he would of course have preferred a bit more of that unearthly pleasure, there'd been that much at least.

LES STANDIFORD

So shoot, you sonofabitch, he thought, pushing himself up for a charge across the deck that he'd never finish.

Too far to go, no way to get there, but he'd die on his feet at least . . . that's what he was thinking when he saw a fist crash against the face of the man who meant to kill him. There was a snapping sound and a groan as Phone Man flew the deck, his jaw shattered by Russell's blow. His back slammed against the flimsy siding and he came forward again in time to meet a second blow to his midsection that folded him like a ventriloquist's dummy. The uppercut that followed was probably a waste of energy, Deal thought, but it was still a pleasure to watch.

He'd seen Ali, Frazier, Foreman, and Tyson punch, of course, all of them powerful men. But he'd never seen any of them do what Russell's blow did. Phone Man's feet left the deck of the houseboat a foot or more, the upper part of his torso snapping back as quickly as he'd folded up a moment before. He landed halfway through the window he'd shot out a moment before, his hands flung up as if he were signaling a successful score somewhere in his dreams.

Deal felt Russell's hands beneath his shoulders then, pulling him toward the forward rail of the houseboat, heard the raspy voice urgent at his ear. "Come on, now, chief. This sucker's going up."

Deal shook his head vaguely, knowing he was in no shape to swim. "Can't," he mumbled as Russell lifted him over the rail. He saw reflected flames dancing on the shallow wave tops, heard sirens in the distance.

"Can't do it," he repeated as he toppled forward.

"Sure you can," he heard as strong hands took him from below.

He blinked, caught sight of Ainsley Spencer easing him to the floor of his idling skiff. Then he saw Russell Straight climb quickly down to join them.

251

There was a comforting rumble growing under his ribs then, and the sudden sensation of movement over water. Deal felt wave tops bouncing hypnotically beneath him, stared up at the silhouette of a tall, slender black man standing above him, his ancient hand at the tiller of his tiny boat, and it occurred to him that he might well have died, in fact.

You die and then they take you across the water—wasn't that the way it worked? He saw the sky light up in a sudden glow then, saw the old man lean forward as if an unseen hand had lent a helpful shove.

Embers traced the darkness all around like fireworks, and sirens whooped and echoed a distant counterpoint. If it was this good here, what lay on the other side? he wondered, then laid his head down to find out.

252

**32**

To Deal, the story came as if in a dream. An old man talking while he drifted somewhere in the shadows above as a disembodied presence. It was almost as if he'd become the old man as the words rolled out, the power of the events coming to grip him as the old man insisted they had always controlled his own life.

And not just because Ainsley Spencer had cheated death that day. As a seafaring man, he had managed that feat more than once, and never mind the particulars. Sails torn to tatters by some fearsome blow, or cast adrift from a storm-scuttled ship, whatever the near miss had been, he'd made his way back to harbor without so much as a second thought as to his good fortune.

But the day the senator had called was different. Perhaps it was because he'd led those others to their unjust end. Perhaps it was his sense that he'd done nothing to merit surviving. Whatever the reason, he'd never been able to shake the feeling that he hadn't really escaped his fate that day.

There was a bill still owing, perhaps that was it. Even after all these years. A debt to be repaid before he could rest, before the curse could be lifted. But for the life of him, he could not figure just how it could be managed.

Ainsley's worst fears had come to pass that awful night. With the roof of the warehouse gone and the skies pouring like a water skin split from overfilling, the cellar where he huddled would have filled soon enough. But hardly had the storm brought the roof crashing down to crush the gunman who meant to kill him than it brought another threat that seemed even more cruel.

As Ainsley stared up at the grate now blocked by a body and a massive chunk of wooden-planked roofing, there came a new kind of rumbling sound, followed by a crash that sent water cascading down upon him. He'd covered his head with his arms to shield himself from the deluge, then glanced up again, just as a second wave crashed down.

Water was gushing down the stairwell now, a virtual river pouring into the room that had come to resemble a cistern more and more. He saw the fallen revolver on the step near where he stood and reached to pick it up in reflex, even as he thought about how futile the gesture was.

What could he do with a pistol? he wondered. Empty it into the dead man who'd trapped him here? Shoot the sea that threatened to drown him?

There was a blinding flash of lightning then, accompanied by an ear-splitting clap of thunder. The water was halfway up the staircase now, lapping at the soles of his shoes, in the next moment sloshing at

LES STANDIFORD

his ankles. He moved up one step, having to crouch down now, and wedged his shoulders tight against the grate that blocked his escape. He tried to straighten his legs and drive the grate up, but it was like pushing at a boxcar or a mountainside.

He would drown here, he realized, his face pressed against the steel grating inches from the sightless stare of the dead man, gasping until the last breath of air had been displaced by the rising water. Drowning was the threat that every seafaring man lived in the shadow of, he thought, glancing around his fast-shrinking prison, but never had he imagined it occurring in such circumstances as these.

He glanced once more at the pistol in his hand and thought of yet another mode of escape, but dismissed it as quickly as it had come. He knew little of matters spiritual, but whatever lay on the other side of breathing—if anything at all—was surely closed to those who took such a route. He'd die with his last breath held and his shoulders pressed to the immovable steel above his head, he thought, and was about to fling the pistol away to avoid temptation, when he remembered the other stairwell that rose at the far end of the room where he'd been working.

He glanced down at the waters that had risen to his shins where he crouched and knew that the passage to that stairwell lay underwater now. He'd have to take one breath and hope that would be enough to make his way along the narrow passage he'd left while stacking. Otherwise, he'd die down there in that twisting blackness.

What would be worse? he wondered, as seawater continued to cascade around him. But he did not wonder for long.

He forced himself to calm, drawing a series of breaths that were increasingly deeper, at the same time rehearsing the route he would take. To the bottom of the steps, then right, he told himself. Then twenty feet—or was it more?—along that narrow passage to the place where

255

he'd seen those steps. He took one last glance upward, past the motionless form silhouetted by the green-glowing sky, then took his last breath and dove.

He forced himself down, down through the cool water, fingertips brushing the rough-hewn steps as he went, the pressure in his ears growing fierce. He swallowed to equalize the force and felt the pain subside, at the same time he felt a hand swipe itself across his face. He fought back a surge of panic and shoved the drifting body aside. No way to tell who it might have been, and what did it matter now? He groped about until his own hand found the edge of the passage leading to his right.

He pulled himself around, kicking steadily but not frantically, his right hand pressed to the wall of the passageway for purchase, his left clawing crablike over the stacks and stacks of submerged crates, finding a crevice here, a handhold there. He sensed the crates tumbling crazily in his wake as he shoved himself along, a tangle that would jam the narrow passageway, sealing off any hope of retreat. A useless notion anyway, he thought. One breath was all he had.

His hand found a cleft in the stone on his right, his left dug into a seam between the stacks. He threw himself forward with a mighty shove and felt his head slam instantly into something hard.

Bright stars and comet trails erupted in the darkness. He was stunned, felt himself twisting sideways in the water, lolling backward, drifting down. He would die that way, he told himself, and fought the blackness that was even deeper than all that surrounded him.

He forced his legs to scissor once again, willed his hands to move. He found the crate that had toppled over to block the way and jerked back and upward with everything he had. Aided by the water's buoyancy, the crate gave way, bringing a second backward with it.

256     He felt the rough wooden sides brush against his legs as he flung

himself through the passage he'd made, felt the fire in his lungs growing toward eruption. He was past the last of the crates now, his dizziness replaced by bright pain at the crown of his head.

That pain was good, he told himself, and fixed upon it in an effort to drive out the agony growing in his chest. He felt his hands strike mossy stone then; one rigid angle beneath his groping fingertips, then another.

Another second, he begged his body. Just one. Two or three at most. What's that against a lifetime?

His knees were on the sunken steps now, his nails raking stone. Lungs turned to cannonballs, to flaming fountains already burst.

His mouth flew open, all pleas disregarded, all abject bargaining tossed aside. The last of his breath blew upward, and seawater rushed down his throat. He was strangling, wondering why he hadn't used the pistol when he'd had the chance, caught a glimpse of his wife's lovely face as she bade him farewell and, in the next moment, burst up from the water at last.

"I threw up water till I thought I'd drown myself again," Deal heard Ainsley Spencer say. He gave a shake of his head as if shedding decades-old water, then pointed off into the gloom behind him.

"The water rose a bit more in that chamber, but by then I knew I was safe," he added. He paused and stared through the dim lamplight at Russell Straight, who sat on a pair of stacked crates across from him. For a moment their gaze held, then both men turned to look down at him.

"He's back with us," Ainsley Spencer said.

"About time," Russell said, nodding.

"Mind your head now, son," the old man added.

Deal raised his hand to his forehead and felt a bandage there. Flashes of a firefight on the deck of a houseboat strobed through his

257

mind, interspersed with images of a dark and slender fish-man swimming effortlessly along a network of subterranean caverns.

"Where are we?" he asked blearily, pushing himself to a sitting position on what he realized was a dusty pile of burlap sacking. He had a surreal memory of a great concrete slab swinging up like the maw of a graveyard crypt, of himself being carried deep down into the earth.

Russell seemed to find the question amusing. "Can't you see? This here is King Solomon's Mines."

The big man reached for the smoking lantern that sat atop a crate next to him and held it aloft. Deal blinked as his eyes adjusted to the yellowish light.

They were in a windowless room that seemed to have been chiseled out of stone, a set of carved steps angling down the wall behind where Ainsley Spencer sat. Subterranean, Deal thought. A cellar from another era. He'd never been here before, but still, the place had a dreamlike familiarity.

Stacked against the opposite wall were what seemed an endless series of wooden crates, stretching past the circle of light cast by the kerosene lantern, many of them stamped with the likeness of an imposing French château. "You were looking for a case of wine," Russell said with a humorless laugh. "I guess we came to the right place."

Deal stared silently at the series of stacked crates. Four crates high, a dozen stacks, he saw, as far as the light allowed. He tried to do the math, but his head was throbbing too painfully.

He turned back to Ainsley Spencer. "This is what Dequarius wanted to tell me about."

The old man nodded. "I suppose it was," he said, his head bowed between his narrow shoulders. "And it's what got him killed, as well."

Deal shook his head, still coming to terms with what he was seeing. "But why did he come to me?"

258

"That's easy," Russell said. "Because everybody else in this here place is crooked as a dog's hind leg. It's pretty clear what Stone's willing to do to get his hands on all this. Dequarius probably heard about you and your high-rolling old man from Stone and figured you for someone he could talk to, at least."

Deal stared at Russell, a fresh twinge of guilt come to nag at him. But even if he'd discovered what Dequarius had in mind, what would he have done? He turned to regard the stacks that stretched away into the darkness. "It must be worth a fortune."

The old man glanced up suddenly. "It's cursed is what it is. Everybody that's ever had anything to do with it is dead: the senator, the ones that meant to steal it from him—" he broke off for a moment. "Except for me, that is."

Deal got a knee beneath himself and with a hand from Russell rose unsteadily to his feet. He waited for the room to right itself around him, then glanced at the staircase.

"Nobody answered my question," he said, turning back to Russell. "Where the hell are we?"

Russell nodded at the staircase. "What used to be the navy base, that's what the old man tells me. He brought us here in his boat while you were out. We're tied up to one of Stone's docks, right outside."

Deal turned to the old man. "That's Truman Town, up those stairs?"

The old man glanced at him as if it scarcely mattered. "We're underneath where some of the old fort used to be. They used this place to store ammunition a hundred years ago." He broke off and glanced around them. "Maybe they kept prisoners here, too. It has the right feel for that, don't you think?"

Deal glanced at the stacked cases again. "How long has all this wine been here?"

259

The old man glanced up at him. "Ever since Senator Rafferty told me to bring it."

"Senator Rafferty?" Deal said after a moment. "Douglas Jacobs Rafferty?"

The old man shrugged and began to repeat the story that he'd already related to Russell. As he listened, Deal put a hand against a nearby stack of crates to steady himself, the sense of a disembodied presence among them growing with every word.

In a state whose history was studded with a long list of scoundrels and discredited public officials, Rafferty was perhaps the most illustrious. He'd made a fortune selling underwater lots during the frenzy following the completion of the Florida East Coast Railroad early in the twentieth century and had gone on to amass an even larger fortune running rum during Prohibition. He'd rubbed shoulders with presidents, celebrities, and gangsters alike, and though out of office when he'd been cut down in a hail of bullets outside a Manhattan speakeasy in the thirties, he still held the distinction of the only U.S. senator thought to be the victim of a gangland hit.

By the time Ainsley Spencer had gotten back to the point where he'd escaped the water's clutches, Deal sensed the ghost of Rafferty among them as keenly as if the draft coursing the chamber were the senator's whispering breath. He glanced down the dimly lit passageway trying to imagine it filled with murky seawater, the old man swimming madly for his life.

"The stairs are still back there?" Deal asked, feeling the chill draft on the back of his neck.

"Stairs are, but they don't go nowhere now," the old man said, following his gaze as if he might still be envisioning how he'd popped up from the top of that rear stairwell directly out into the hurricane-lashed landscape like something shot up from a storm drain.

260

He'd discovered the entire dockside building where they had labored leveled by the storm, every speck of wreckage carried away by the tidal wave that had swept ashore. Even the heavy truck that had brought them had disappeared.

He'd fought his way home through the backside of the storm, then returned by first light to search the nearly drained chamber for the bodies of his friends. He weighted the bodies before he gave them back to the sea. The corpses of the senator's men he simply dumped over the side of the seawall at the nearby docks. The body of the man who'd tried to kill him was nowhere to be found.

He'd swung the cover that had hidden the heavy steel grate back into place, then filled the entrance to the back stairwell with rubble. He then made his way back through the wreckage-strewn streets to the quarter and told the story of the great wave that had swept him and his comrades and their truck out to sea. And then he had settled in to wait.

Deal looked more closely at the old man. "You didn't tell anyone what had happened?"

"I worked for the senator," the old man said. "He was the only one to tell. Sooner or later he'd send for me, that was the way it worked. When I found out that he was dead, I knew I could end up that way, too." He glanced up at Deal. "That's just how it was."

Deal nodded. "But you could have made yourself rich a long time ago," he said, gesturing at the stacked cases.

"It might seem that way to you now," the old man said. "But back then, I figured there'd be somebody coming along for it, sooner or later. And before long, there did come an end to Prohibition. After that, there was booze everywhere. This was just a bunch of wine in a hole in the ground, something that didn't belong to me, something that I wanted nothing to do with."

"So how'd Dequarius come to find out about it?" Russell asked.

261

The old man looked over at him and drew a weary breath. "There was a box of it in the house," Ainsley Spencer said, his voice mournful.

"Just the one I took. Had been there forever. Me and June Anna opened a bottle of it once, one anniversary. But we didn't much care for it. June Anna kept what was left to cook with. I kept the rest in the closet. I shouldn't of, I know." He gave Russell a hopeless look.

"One day a couple of months ago Dequarius was rooting around like he was fond of doing and come across it." The old man was staring off now, talking as much to himself as to them, or so it seemed.

"He started asking questions. I loved the boy, you know. He had a persistent turn of mind." He turned back to Deal, his eyes flashing. "One thing just led to another, you know. Once he had it on his mind, he was determined."

Deal nodded his understanding. "Who else did he tell about all this, Mr. Spencer?" he asked gently.

"That's Ainsley," the old man said.

"Ainsley," Deal repeated patiently.

The old man registered the correction, then shook his head. "I wouldn't know. I didn't want to know. I told him to be careful, that's all."

"How about Franklin Stone?" Russell asked. "Maybe Dequarius was tired of dribbles and drabs. Maybe he thought a guy like Stone had the bucks for a big score, he could unload the whole thing."

The old man shook his head. "Maybe, but I don't think so. It was the same as fooling around selling those coins. If anybody knew there was a lot of it somewhere, who knows what might happen? I think Dequarius was smart enough to understand that much. He'd have never let on about all this." The old man swept his arm at the treasure stacked around them, then stopped, an odd look on his face.

"What is it?" Deal asked.

"Forty-nine," the old man said. A hollowness had returned to his voice, as if he were talking to himself again.

"Forty-nine?" Deal repeated, shaking his head. Why did that number seem significant suddenly?

The old man's eyes regained their focus. "It's a restaurant, a new one, place one of those chefs from New York opened up, some Froggy fellow, I think."

"Boussier," Deal cut in, feeling his pulse spike. Stone's pet pit bull of a chef.

The old man glanced up and shrugged. "Maybe that's the name. Anyways, when things slowed down with Stone, Dequarius got him a side job busing tables there. He used to go on about the prices, what they sold their wine for. I couldn't believe it. Maybe he tried to sell this Boussiy-waz something and just didn't tell me."

"We'll find out soon enough," Deal said, his gaze turning toward the stairs. "Do you know where this restaurant is?"

"Just the other side of Old Town," Spencer said, naming a street that Deal had never heard of. "Across from the power plant."

The latter was a city landmark Deal was well aware of. He'd noted its steam-belching stacks towering above the gumbo-limbo trees every time he'd driven in and out of the Pier House's parking lot. He checked his watch, amazed to see that it was nearly six.

"I was out the whole night?" he said to Russell.

Russell shrugged. "I didn't see the point of waking you."

Deal nodded, then felt an answering throb at the base of his skull. He glanced at the old man, trying to digest everything he'd heard, order it inside a head that seemed ready to crack open with uncertainty. So Dequarius Noyes had been trying to lead him to this treasure trove all along, because he'd thought him a less dangerous go-between than Stone in some scheme to sell this cache. Then again, maybe Dequarius

263

had tried to unload the lot on a restaurateur who'd decided to take negotiations to an unexpected level; perhaps that's why he'd come to Deal for help.

Whatever had set this chain of events into action, Deal realized that once again he had stepped inadvertently into the path of a train intent on grinding him to gut and gristle. They'd managed to escape the debacle on Dequarius's houseboat, but they'd left three bodies and the Hog behind. He doubted he'd get a free pass from his friends in the sheriff's office this time around. For all he knew, in fact, those were the very people who'd been ready to put them away. He drew a breath that threatened to split his aching head, then turned to Russell.

"We're going to need a car," he said, checking his watch again. "Probably best we get moving before it's light."

Russell nodded and started toward the stairs. Deal started after him, pausing to put a hand on Ainsley Spencer's shoulder. "All this is no more your fault than it is mine," Deal told him. "We'll find out who killed Dequarius."

When the old man glanced up at him with a doubtful look, Deal added the bitter truth. "We'll damn well have to," he said, then followed Russell up.

# 33

**IF THERE'D BEEN** anyone in the maintenance area of Stone's Truman Town marina awake at such an hour to see them, it might have seemed as though three men were climbing up from an open crypt, Deal thought. He paused to steady himself as he emerged into the predawn air, waiting for a slight giddiness to dissipate as he surveyed their surroundings.

There was a hint of sulfur off the exposed flats, along with the familiar tang of a salty breeze, helping to clear the fogginess in his brain. Maybe he'd picked up a concussion back there on the houseboat, or maybe it was just his brain's way of signaling overload. A couple days ago, all he'd been worried about were the depths of some pilings at a construction site in Miami. And, for all the trouble that now surrounded him, what a trifling life that suddenly seemed.

He turned at the sound of Russell lowering the door to the chamber back into place. There was a scudding cloud bank passing over that reflected the distant lights of the city, casting enough of a glow for him to get his bearings. They were at a secluded spot near the seawall at the far end of the marina, on the other side of a cyclone fence that separated Truman Town from the grounds of Fort Taylor, another piece of the nineteenth-century network of fortifications that had been constructed when Key West was presumed to have a position of strategic military importance.

Decomissioned for more than a half century now, the place had been turned into a state park, underfunded and barely developed, a fact which probably accounted for Ainsley Spencer's cache lying undisturbed for all these years. Fifty acres of prime waterfront property that Stone would love to get his hands on, Deal mused. If he knew the man, there was probably a long-range plan outlined somewhere to accomplish that very mission.

He glanced down at the slab in which the doorway had settled, saw nothing to distinguish the entranceway. Even if you bothered to come back to this lonely corner, you'd never suspect what lay beneath your feet.

"Phone's right down there," Ainsley Spencer said, pointing along the seawall past a low-slung maintenance building. Rigging clanked dully on the masts of sailboats moored down that way, and waves slapped quiet counterpoint nearby.

Russell nodded and started off along the seawall. Deal turned to the old man. "Where will you be?" he asked.

The old man rolled his palms upward in a "who can say?" gesture. "I'll be close by," he said. "I see anybody come looking around these parts, I'll let you know."

"How?" Deal said.

"Don't worry," the old man said with a grin. "This here's just a little island." And then he was scurrying away toward his tied-off skiff.

Russell spent a few minutes with Deal, making sure he understood the plan, then went to make his call to Denise, speaking softly into the receiver while Deal listened to the receding hum of the old man's skiff. Farther out in the channel, he saw the lights of a lone shrimper on its way out of port. At the horizon a slender golden band had already wedged its way between the dark Atlantic waters and the even darker cloud bank above. Another day on its way to paradise, he thought as Russell hung up the phone. Anything could happen here.

"She'll meet us in ten minutes," Russell said as he walked to join him. "Right where you said."

"Good," Deal said and led them off.

The walk took a bit less than that, a few blocks inland from the marina to the other side of Truman Town, along a series of quiet streets that might have been picked up from a New England village and dropped down in the Tropics, a couple hours' Donzi ride from Havana harbor. Neatly manicured lawns laid out in front of Cape Cod clapboard homes with wide verandas and dangling wooden swings. The picture of the safe, secure lifestyle, Deal thought. He pictured his daughter rolling around on one of those patches of dark emerald lawn, wrestling a Lab or a golden retriever into submission, then tried to fit Annie Dodds into that same vision.

"Anybody live in these places?" Russell's voice cut through the silence and into his reverie.

Deal glanced at him. "A few," he said. "Most of these are third and fourth homes for snowbirds. It'll be different come December."

Russell nodded. Automatic porch lights were winking off here and there as dawn filtered down through the thick canopy of banyans and ficus above them. "Hardly looks like the same town in here," he said.

"This is Franklin Stone's vision of the perfect life," Deal said.

Russell nodded. "Compared to where I grew up, it just might be," he said.

"He's got even bigger things in mind for that property out by the beach," Deal said.

"I seem to remember something about that," Russell said.

"We'll talk to Stone yet," Deal said.

"Expect we will," Russell said, nodding at something up ahead.

Deal turned to see the tiny white coupe idling just outside one of the pedestrian gates up ahead, its exhaust puffing luminously into the morning air, Denise's profile visible through the open passenger's window. She turned when they came through the gate onto Fleming Street, her gaze flickering immediately past Deal toward Russell.

Deal felt a pang. Whatever had transpired between the two of them in a few short days, that moment's gaze had been something to behold—a woman who had her sights locked down, beside whom a loon's mate would seem fickle. He wondered if Russell had noticed, or if it was just something that the one who *didn't* get such glances could see. He wondered if Janice had ever looked at him that way. He tried to recollect if Annie had.

"I'll get in the back," Denise was saying, unfolding herself from behind the wheel as Deal approached the car, holding up her hand when he started to protest. "You guys would never fit." She was out—wearing little besides an oversized T-shirt, it appeared—and had climbed into the backseat in a second.

"Appreciate you doing this," Russell said, as he wedged himself behind the wheel. Deal would have turned to add something, just for another glimpse of her legs, but the close quarters and the pounding in his head held him to a nod and a murmur of agreement.

"Hey," she said. "You want to take over the payments, you can keep the damned thing."

Deal glanced in the rearview mirror to see her smile, run her hand through her tousled hair. She'd looked good in her perky Pier House getup, but in this guise she seemed absolutely spectacular. No wonder Russell didn't care when he got back to Miami, and never mind that studied show of indifference.

"Turn here." She pointed, and Deal glanced up as Russell obeyed, the front porch he'd seen a couple of nights before emerging from the early gloom up ahead. He got out of the car and waited for her to extricate herself from the tiny backseat, trying to keep his gaze mildly discreet. For his part, Russell sat staring forward stolidly, as if he were a cabbie dropping off another fare.

Denise seemed to think about something for a moment, then reached into the tiny bag she was carrying and came out with a tiny, nickel-plated pistol. Deal stared at the weapon. Did every woman in Key West pack heat?

Denise, oblivious to his surprise, leaned into the car and thrust the pistol at Russell. "You might need this," she said.

Russell stared at the weapon for a moment, then reached to take it from her. He turned it over in his hand a couple of times and glanced up at her, something of a smile on his face. "Any rabbits come after me, this just might help."

"It's better than nothing," she said, then glanced at Deal as she started away.

"Try not to get any bullet holes in my car," she said. "It knocks the shit out of the resale value."

Deal managed a nod as he got back into the passenger's seat. "Thanks again," Deal called to her, but her gaze went back to Russell, passing Deal as if he were a ghost. In the next moment, they were off.

## 34

"**WHO WOULD PUT** a fancy restaurant across the street from a factory?" Russell Straight asked as he pushed himself to a standing position beside the tiny coupe. He worked his head and rolled his shoulders like some giant version of a hermit crab who'd been trapped in too small a shell.

Deal followed Russell's gaze toward the towering stacks of the power plant, at the huge white columns of steam and smoke belching high into the air. "At least it's not a paper mill," Deal said, glancing around the quiet side street where they'd parked. He pointed at the plant's superstructure. "That's all lit up at night," he added. "Maybe if you have enough drinks it looks like there's a cruise ship moored across the street."

Russell nodded, but he didn't seem convinced. "Even dumber, why would you want to live there?"

Deal shrugged. "Maybe he got a good deal." Denise had already confirmed what a glance at the Key West phone directory seemed to suggest. François Boussier had remodeled the upper two floors of the three-story turn-of-the-century mansion he'd bought to house his restaurant, creating a pleasure pad said to go beyond even jaded Key West standards for moneyed bachelor's quarters. The windows he could see on the upper stories seemed to be clad in stained glass, as a matter of fact. Maybe all of them were.

Russell checked his watch as they crossed the street. "This guy doesn't sound like one of your early-to-bed, early-to-rise types."

"Why don't you ask me if I care?" Deal told him as he mounted the opposite sidewalk.

There was a pair of stone lions perched on pedestals beside a staircase leading up to the broad front porch, where a massive beveled glass and oak door gave access to the restaurant during normal hours. There was a tasteful brass plate bearing the street number beside it. Probably the mean price for entrees on the menu, given the look of the place, Deal thought.

He walked down to the end of the porch where a smaller door was set in an alcove, a buzzer and intercom mounted nearby. Deal pressed the buzzer and held it, releasing it for a second before jamming it down again.

"What is it?" a clearly annoyed voice cut over the speaker. "Release the buzzer, please."

Deal kept his thumb pressed tight for an extra beat, then flipped a little toggle switch from "Listen" to "Talk."

"I'm sorry to disturb you, Mr. Boussier, but I need to talk to you. It's important."

"Impossible," Deal heard on the other end, and immediately jammed the buzzer down again.

"This is outrageous," he heard when he flipped over to "Listen" once again. "Who *are* you?"

Deal hesitated. "Gene Dickerson," he said. "Detective Dickerson, Monroe County Sheriff's Office."

There was a pause at the other end. "Who is that with you?"

Deal stopped, startled by the question. He glanced up, finally noticing the surveillance camera mounted high up in the porch eaves. Something he'd hardly anticipated, to be sure. He was confident that Boussier had not gotten a good look at them the night before, but he was less certain the two of them looked sufficiently like cops.

He'd removed the makeshift bandage Russell and the old man had fashioned, brushed his hair down over the seeping gash high on his forehead, but a close look might still suggest doubt. On the other hand, he reassured himself, that was one of the things about Key West—there was virtually no way to distinguish the wealthy from the penniless, the scammers from the sincere, the good guys from the bad.

He turned back to the intercom, mustering his confidence. "That's Detective Conrad," he said, his voice firm. "He's assisting me."

"You'll have to come back this afternoon," Deal heard. "You can find me in the kitchen anytime after four."

Deal turned back to the camera. "If I come back at four, I'll have the Health Department supervisor with me, along with someone from INS," Deal said. "If you're lucky, you'll be open again by Christmas, which wouldn't necessarily be a bad thing. Maybe it'll give you a chance to get all those kinks worked out of your menu."

Deal raised his hands in a "let's be friends" gesture. "Or you could come down here and open your door right now."

Deal flipped the speaker back to "Listen," but he didn't hear anything, unless that background hissing was really the sound of synapses short-circuiting in Boussier's brain. After a moment, there came an an-

LES STANDIFORD

gry buzzing noise at the formidable-looking door plate, accompanied by the sound of a lock snapping free.

Deal pushed the door inward and turned to gesture to Russell. "After you, Detective."

"Fucking-A," Russell said after a moment. Finally, he shook his head, moving past Deal with an expression that might have been mistaken for a smile.

"I'd like to know what is so important it could not wait for afternoon," Boussier demanded once they'd ascended the staircase to his living room. His gaze flicked from Deal to Russell in a way meant to convey intense disdain. Certainly there was no hint of recognition there. For once he felt comfortable before such a presence, Deal thought. Given Boussier's native imperiousness, they probably could have brought along Charles Manson, passed him off as a deputy.

"Don't worry," Deal said. "This won't take long."

Boussier was a tall man, with an inch or two—maybe even a few pounds as well—on Deal, and a way of leaning in close to claim more than his share of negotiating space. He had a wild head of tightly curled hair, intense dark eyes, and a sizable hooked nose that he'd obviously used to great advantage, homing in on hapless underlings.

Boussier was barefoot, wrapped in a jade-green silk robe that reached halfway down his calves, exposing a pair of legs that looked as if they'd never been in sunlight. He'd headed the two of them off at the top of the stairs, but Deal could see past him into a chrome-and-steel living area, a granite-topped kitchen bay opening just beyond, and above that, the railing of an elevated loft, where a young man with the face of a Botticelli angel leaned, a sheet slung toga-style over one shoulder, his chin propped on his hands, watching this paltry drama being played out beneath him as if such diversions appeared before him every day.

273

"He's of age, I assure you," Boussier said, noting Deal's gaze.

"I'm certain," Deal said.

"I asked you what this was about," Boussier said, shifting from foot to foot.

"Do you know a man named Dequarius Noyes?" Deal asked.

When Boussier looked blank, he went on. "Wiry little black guy, bused tables for you sometimes."

There was a spark of recognition in Boussier's eyes. "I know who you mean," he said after a moment. "I fired him for stealing. What's he done now?"

"He's dead," Deal said. "Someone shot him."

Boussier faltered, his gaze swinging up toward the young man poised at the railing. When he turned back to Deal, he'd regained something of his imperiousness. "I'm sorry to hear that, though I'm hardly surprised." He sighted down his nose at Deal again. "In any case, what does it have to do with me?"

"It's about the wine," Deal said mildly.

Boussier stopped again. A gut shot this time, Deal thought. "The wine?" He shook his head. "I found that Dequarius had struck up a deal with my meat purveyor. If he was stealing wine, I knew nothing of it."

Deal glanced at Russell as though to convey great tolerance. "I'm talking about the wine he wanted to sell *you*," Deal said, turning back to Boussier.

"I assure you—"

"Mr. Boussier, you've got a gram of cocaine chopped up on that coffee table over there and a sixteen-year-old kid upstairs in your bedroom—"

"This is outrageous," Boussier tried, but there was a pale line of fear tracing his flapping lips now. "You have no warrant—"

274     "I don't need a warrant," Deal said mildly. "This is Key West." He

waited a moment but Boussier was quiet now. Apparently his few months in the city had taught him a few things. Deal had seen it often enough in Miami over the years, hotshots down from the big city to run roughshod over the natives in paradise.

"Besides, I don't care about any of that." Deal waved, mildly. "All I want you to do is tell me about this wine you bought from Dequarius Noyes."

Boussier glanced again toward the railing, then at Russell Straight, who stared back at him like the Buddha incarnate. Deal thought he saw a smile cross the features of the kid at the railing.

"I can't see the importance of this," Boussier said, turning his sour gaze back on Deal. His lip curled in a way that suggested impatience. "It was just one bottle of wine, for God's sake."

Deal felt his heart beginning to race, but he simply nodded, as if what Boussier had just told him was the most natural thing in the world.

"Why don't you tell me about it?" he said. He sensed that Russell's posture had shifted ever so slightly, a tiny forward pitch that suggested a great mass ready to come thundering down.

"There isn't much to tell," Boussier insisted with a nervous glance at Russell. "Dequarius showed up in my office one afternoon about a week ago, already late for his shift. I thought he was there to make some excuse, possibly beg off work for the night. It had happened before and I—"

"Why don't you stick to the point, motherfucker?" Russell Straight cut in.

Boussier gave Deal a pleading look, but Deal simply shrugged. "We've been up all night," he said. "You'll have to excuse my partner."

Something seemed to register inside Boussier at that moment. He looked closely at Deal, drew himself back, as if he might be poised to

275

run. "I'd like to see some identification," he said. He glanced up at the boy leaning at the railing. "Tommy, dial nine-one-one. Ask for the sheriff's office. I—"

He broke off when Russell Straight's big hand flashed out and caught a fistful of his hair. Russell jerked him backward off his feet, pulling Boussier's face close to his own. "If you don't tell us what you know, Tommy'll be calling for an ambulance."

There was no turning back now, Deal thought, ready to go for the stairs that led up to the loft bedroom, yank the phone out of the wall. He needn't have worried, though. The boy at the railing never moved a muscle. Either he was stoned to the gills, Deal thought, or he was mightily pleased by what was transpiring. Possibly both.

"You'd better be careful," Tommy called down in a dreamy voice. "He's got a knife."

"Is that right?" Russell asked Boussier, whose hand had already darted toward a pocket of his robe. Deal started forward, but Russell caught Boussier's hand easily.

He wrenched upward, squeezing, and Boussier uttered a gasp of pain. A slender, pearl-handled switchblade tumbled to the floor, and Russell bent to snatch it deftly, his hand still buried in Boussier's thatch of hair.

"What you use this for?" Russell said to Boussier, flipping the knife open an inch from the man's bugging eyes. "Carve up quail in your fancy kitchen?" He glanced at Deal, then pressed his thumb hard against the side of the extended blade. The blade snapped like a Popsicle stick.

"Finish your story," Deal said. "And we'll be out of here."

"Who are you?" Boussier gasped, his eyes leaking tears now. His head was twisted back, exposing white crusts that ringed both inflamed nostrils.

276

"Concerned citizens," Russell said, ratcheting his grip a notch tighter. "We've got a need to know."

Boussier's knees had buckled, but Russell held the man off the ground as easily as if he were made of straw. "He had a bottle of wine with him," Boussier said, his pleading gaze on Deal's. "He wanted to know if I wanted to buy it. I started to throw him out, then I got a look at what it was."

"Bordeaux," Deal said. "First growth. Nineteen twenty-nine."

Boussier tried to nod, but it was difficult, given how he was held. "I couldn't believe it," he said. "I assumed it was a counterfeit, some kind of fraud . . ." He broke off, wincing as Russell gave another yank on his hair.

"Let him talk, Russell," Deal said.

Russell gave Deal a glowering look but relaxed his grip a fraction. Boussier ran his tongue over his pale lips. "I told Dequarius I'd have to be sure it was genuine before I paid him a cent. I expected him to walk out, but he told me to keep the bottle, 'give it a taste,' as he said. There was plenty more where it came from, he told me. If I liked it, he and I could work out an arrangement."

"So you conned him out of his wine," Russell said, wrenching the knot of hair once again.

"It was his idea to leave it with me," Boussier protested, his face twisting in pain.

"What happened next?" Deal said, signaling Russell to ease off.

Boussier swallowed, speaking more quickly now. "Once I'd gotten Dequarius out of my office, I examined the label more carefully, then checked the ullage—"

"Speak English," Russell said, giving another twist.

"It's the space between the bottom of the cork and the level of the wine," Boussier managed with a pleading glance at Deal. "Can't you get him off me?"

"Soon enough," Deal said. "What's so important about ullage?"

"It's one measure of a wine's actual age," Boussier explained. "Over time, the wine shrinks back toward its natural solid state. That's what creates the sediment. As the wine settles, the ullage increases."

"I *am* getting an education," Russell said, popping the fat part of his free hand off Boussier's forehead. Deal thought he saw the ghost of a smile cross the blissed-out features of the kid at the railing above.

"Wouldn't the label be proof enough?" Deal said, the picture of that folded scrap of paper in Dequarius's stiff fingers still clear in his mind.

"Any garden-variety criminal could find a book, scan a copy of a label in a few minutes," Boussier said. "An examination of the cork is a much truer test."

Deal shook his head. "To see if the wine's turned?" he asked. "I don't get it."

"That's not why the cork is presented," Boussier said. "You're to read what's stamped along the sides, to be sure of what you're getting. The name of the château is printed there, along with the date."

Deal rolled it over in his mind for a moment. "Couldn't you phony up a cork, too?" he asked.

"Of course," Boussier said. "But it would be far more difficult, a much more sophisticated operation to find the right diameter, the proper length . . . and then you'd have to simulate the effects of age, the printing style—"

"Way beyond the capabilities of some loser like Dequarius," Russell said, giving Boussier's forehead another pop.

"I didn't say that," Boussier moaned.

"Get to the point," Deal said. "What happened to the bottle Dequarius gave you?"

278

"I thought about opening it then and there," Boussier said, looking ever more forlorn, "but I had a special party that evening. I thought I'd wait, kill two birds with one stone, so to speak. If the bottle was what Dequarius claimed it to be—"

"You'd sell it for a fortune," Deal said.

"And give Dequarius his cut," Russell added. He pulled Boussier's head back so the man's frightened gaze met his own.

"Who was in this 'special party'?" Deal asked, though he suspected he already knew the answer.

"I can't tell you that," Boussier said.

"You think you're some kind of an attorney?" Deal said. "That's your privileged information?" He nodded at Russell, who yo-yoed Boussier's head savagely toward the floor.

Deal gave Boussier a moment to stop howling, then asked, "It was Franklin Stone, wasn't it?"

Still Boussier hesitated, tears leaking out of his eyes.

"Tell me," Deal said, glancing at Russell once more.

"Yes," Boussier said as Russell's grip tightened, his voice sounding broken now. "He was entertaining a group of important investors from New York. I thought he'd be open to the suggestion."

Deal nodded, his eyes on Russell's. "So how was it?" Deal said, aware of a hollowness in his own tone. "How'd the wine go over?"

"Mr. Stone was as enthusiastic about the prospect as I hoped he'd be," Boussier said. "To a man like that, price is no object."

"Do tell," Russell said, but kept his hands still.

"The moment I pulled the cork, I knew," Boussier continued, perhaps grateful to have escaped further injury. "Everything was right. The bouquet, the color . . . the very presence of the wine itself." He made it sound like a living thing, Deal thought, as Boussier went on. Apparently wine could raise passions he had never imagined. "I filtered

279

it into a decanter and tasted it myself before I brought it out. It was as good as wine gets."

"What did you charge him for it?" Deal asked.

"We agreed on twelve thousand," Boussier said, "but when I suggested there might be more of the vintage available—"

"You made a different kind of arrangement," Deal cut in, his anger rising, along with his distaste. "You told him where the bottle came from and that Dequarius Noyes had a case of it stashed away somewhere. You and Stone decided there were other ways to get ahold of the wine and conspired to kill him for it."

"I swear to you," Boussier cried, trying to shake his head. But Russell's grip had tightened once again, Boussier's scalp going white at the hairline.

"Stone took me aside to tell me that Dequarius worked for him, that he'd handle the matter. I had no idea . . ." He stared up in terror, tears flowing freely from his eyes now. "You might as well kill me now," he choked out. "I've told you everything I know. If Stone killed Dequarius Noyes, this is the first I've heard of it."

Deal pondered what he'd just been told. He glanced up at the kid, who had his chin propped in his hand, looking a little bored by now. Perhaps he'd been hoping for dismemberment, or at the very least, gunfire. Boussier might be a scumbag, he thought, but he doubted the man had the stomach for murder. Then again, that's what someone had said about Franklin Stone as well.

"What do you want to do with him?" Russell asked.

Deal turned to see that a dark stain was growing at the front of François Boussier's dressing gown. The man looked up at him with brimming, red-rimmed eyes, as if he expected to die.

"Let him go before you catch something," Deal said, and then he turned for the stairs.

280

# 35

"YOU THINK HE'LL call the cops?" Russell asked, glancing in the rearview mirror as he piloted the tiny coupe down Simonton Street. The sun had yet to clear the rooftops and the Sunday morning streets were still deserted.

Deal glanced over. "Would you?"

Russell made a grunting sound that was somewhere between a laugh and outright dismissal. "I don't know what that dude used on his hair," he said after a moment. He sniffed his fingers again, then grimaced, holding his hand out his window as if he might be signaling a turn. "I'd call it French cathouse."

"Maybe you ought to wash your hands," Deal said.

"Maybe I will," he said. "Maybe Franklin Stone'll let me use his bathroom."

Deal nodded, watching idly as Russell made a left on Southard and took them across Duval Street, looking as lonely as a Christmas morning hooker at this hour. There was a Monroe County sheriff's cruiser parked down the block, across from Sloppy Joe's Bar, but it stayed just where it was as they moved on through the intersection and out of sight. They turned again on Whitehead, and Deal stared all the way down the tunnel of overhanging limbs to where the street butted up at Stone's mansion.

What Boussier had told them should not have come as any surprise, he thought. On some level, he supposed he'd sensed it all along. Maybe part of his unwillingness to believe had been his natural contrariness: If most of the known world believed Franklin Stone to be a scoundrel, then Deal would find a certain duty in refusing to side automatically with the crowd.

Another part of it might have had to do with Stone's long-standing ties to his old man, he mused. Given the résumés of some of the bad actors his father had done business with, Stone was a veritable choirboy, or so it had seemed.

And, he thought with a certain pang, there had been the matter of all that business the man had been poised to throw his way. Had that prospect blunted his suspicion in any way? he wondered.

And as far as Annie Dodds's connection to the man, he was not even prepared to go there at this moment. That was a matter that could wait for another day.

"Pull over here," Deal said as they approached the Hemingway house, which loomed beneath the trees on their left. Russell nodded, bringing the coupe to a halt well short of the stop sign.

What would Papa have done? Deal thought idly as he got out, closing the door gently. Gone through Stone's door, guns blazing? Or handed him his shotgun and a bottle of whiskey and left him to do the right thing?

Russell Straight was at the other side of the coupe now, staring across its dew-streaked top. "There must be people we could call," he said. "State cops or something."

Deal gave him what passed for a smile. "That's not where we are," he said.

Russell nodded. "How we going to do this, then?"

Deal shrugged. "I guess the way Vernon Driscoll would," he said.

"What's that?"

"Go to the front door and knock."

Which is exactly what they did. Several times, in fact. Deal listened to the echoes of the heavy brass knocker fading away for what seemed the fourth or fifth time before turning to Russell.

"Maybe they're heavy sleepers," Russell said.

"Let's check the garage," Deal said. He glanced down the broad overhang of the porch toward the water, expecting to find boiling thunderheads poised there. But it was just a mass of grayness drifting in. No worthy portent of doom in sight.

As they rounded the back of the house, he felt the first drops of rain on his face, then saw that the garage door was up. Stone's limo was parked inside, the driver's door ajar. Deal glanced at Russell, then broke into a run toward the car.

As he neared, he caught a glimpse of a shoe, a pants leg jutting from the partially open door. He rushed to the front of the car and glanced inside. It was Balart, lying halfway across the driver's seat, the back of his head blown away by a shotgun blast. His face was twisted sideways, one eye staring sightless at the glowing dome light.

283

Deal turned, barging past Russell and out toward the back of the house. He cleared the steps leading to the broad rear deck in a bound, hearing the thud of Russell's footsteps close behind. He was headed for the broad French doors that opened into Stone's office, ready to take them out with a kick, when he saw it wouldn't be necessary. The doors were already unlatched, the filmy curtains drifting inward at the press of the approaching storm.

Deal slowed, then turned to caution Russell. He pointed silently at the doors, and they stood listening for a moment. There was no sound, nothing but the rustling of the palms overhead, the hiss of the fine rain that had begun to fall.

Deal motioned Russell to the side, then stepped forward and nudged one of the door panels with his toe. It swung open, clearing the corner of Franklin Stone's massive desk, thudding softly against the inner wall. Deal stepped through the opening in a crouch, ready to dive for cover, take on whoever might come after him.

But there was nothing. Just the same ominous silence and a curiously familiar odor that filled the room. He glanced quickly over his shoulder, saw the shadowy shapes of the chairs where he and Russell had sat just nights before, then swung back to Stone's desk, the sound of his own breath harsh and uneven in his ears.

Someone was sitting in Stone's chair, he saw with a start, but the occupant was swiveled away from him. He saw the elegant shock of hair, the pale outline of a hand clutching one armrest. Images were flickering on a notebook computer screen sitting atop the credenza behind the desk, Deal realized.

"Stone?" Deal said, as he stood and started forward.

There was no response from the man in the chair. Russell was coming through the doorway now, the pistol Denise had given him held high in one hand.

284

"Stone," Deal repeated, his hand going for the chair.

He caught a corner of the high, padded back and tried to spin the chair around, but Stone's feet tangled in the kneehole of the credenza and he fell sideways, his torso twisting as he went.

Deal staggered back, then caught himself with a hand on the desk. He was staring into Stone's upturned and vacant gaze. There was a wide gash across his throat, a second mouth frozen open in a scream. Blood bathed the front of the man's shirt.

"Sonofabitch," Deal heard Russell's soft curse at his side. The same series of images Stone had treated them to in the presentation of the Villas of Cayo Hueso were flickering across the screen. He saw Annie's form poised to dive once again into that glittering, virtual pool, then he spun back to Russell, snatching the pistol from his hand.

"Upstairs," he said simply to Russell, then turned and hurried from the room.

He moved quickly but silently down the long hallway toward the staircase that descended to the foyer, stepping across the marble entryway as gently as a ghost. He paused at the foot of the stairs, scanning the stairway, the rail above, his ears keen for the slightest sound.

Russell was at his shoulder now, and Deal turned to whisper. "Keep some space between us," he said, nodding up the stairwell. "I'm not sure which room up there."

Russell nodded, waiting until Deal was almost at the top of the stairway before he followed.

As Deal's head came up even with the long hallway, he paused again, the tiny pistol in his hand only the vaguest reassurance. An awful dread consumed him now, fearful images of Annie that he refused his mind to blank. Worst of all was the silence, he realized. He would have almost preferred screams, the sounds of an ongoing struggle.

At the end of the hallway on his right, he saw an open sitting room that overlooked the Atlantic. Palms tossed in the gathering storm and distant whitecaps flecked the water. No sign of anyone there to appreciate the view.

He moved up onto the landing, his back turned to one wall to present a smaller target, then quickly edged down the opposite hallway. He passed what he presumed was a linen closet, then the open doorway to what must have been a guest bathroom. The lights were doused inside, the cool tiles and marble tops glowing dimly in gray light reflected from outside. No sign of anyone inside. No sign the neatly arranged room had ever been used, for that matter.

There was a bedroom door looming at his shoulder, ajar, offering him a view of the foot of a primly made bed and a gleaming dresser with nothing on its top. The bedroom for the ghost that used the bathroom opposite, he thought, moving on quickly.

The master was at the end of the hallway, he reasoned, glancing toward another open doorway a few feet ahead. But there was some kind of entryway partition that kept him from a clear view inside. He'd have to make his way all the way down there to find out.

One more doorway lay in between, this one on the opposite wall, and firmly closed. He hesitated opposite it, wondering if he should check the master first.

He glanced back at the stairwell landing, where Russell was creeping up in the gloom like a cautious bear. He gave a signal to his partner, then moved quickly across the hallway and grasped the cool porcelain globe of the doorknob.

The knob gave at his touch, and he moved inside quickly, ducking low as he went, the pistol braced to fire. Shoot without hesitation, he was thinking. Otherwise you'll die.

Her scent struck him first, a hint of tropical fruit, extract of citrus, the barest fragrance of rose. Her room, he understood, his gaze swiveling about in the dim light for any trace of her form.

A bed there, the sheets and covers rumpled . . . but no one in it. A dresser on an adjoining wall, drawers pulled out as if someone had been looking for something. A closet door flung open, a couple of dresses dangling on hangers. But no one in the room. No one asleep, no one waiting to attack.

He straightened slowly, glancing again at the tousled bedclothes, then moved quickly toward a door that opened into what he presumed was a darkened bathroom. He felt inside, flicked on the light switch, keeping his back to the intervening wall for cover. After a moment, he swung inside, pistol at the ready.

He caught an image of a dark towel crumpled on the white-tiled floor, a plastic razor tossed in an empty tub, a row of toiletries strewn about a granite vanity top. As well as the sight of a sun-bleached, broad-shouldered man before him, a crazed look on his bruised and swollen features, a nickel-plated pistol cocked in his hand.

An ordinary person turned assassin and looking for a target, Deal thought fleetingly, staring at himself in the steam-streaked mirror. It was the image of someone who might need locking up for his own good, he realized, a man who might do anything if the wrong set of circumstances arose.

He heard something behind him then and spun, the pistol leveled, and saw that he was ready to blow away Russell Straight.

"What you doing with that?" Russell said, staring at Deal with mild disdain.

"Sorry," Deal said, lowering the pistol. He started to shoulder past Russell, but the big man put a hand up to stop him.

"Take it easy," Russell said. "I already checked the master."

Deal stopped, staring to be sure.

Russell was shaking his head. "She ain't in there. This house is empty, man."

Deal pushed on past him anyway, hurrying out through Annie's room and down to the doorway of Stone's room. He glanced inside, at the enormous canopy bed that sat unmussed, at an array of ghostly furniture in a sitting area, at the vast, empty bathroom that lay open at one end of the room.

"I checked the crapper, the closets, under the bed," Russell said. "There's nobody here. Even the houseboy's gone."

Deal stared at him, trying to get his breathing under control. He hadn't been running, he was certain of it, but he felt as though he'd just finished a marathon.

"Why don't you let me hold that gun?" Russell said, pointing.

Deal stared at the pistol in his hand, then finally nodded and handed the thing over. Russell snapped the safety on, then jammed the pistol into his belt.

"What now?" he said. Deal thought he heard a note of apology in Russell's voice, as if there might be some presumption in asking such a question of an addled man.

He closed his eyes briefly and took a deep breath before releasing it. "I'm okay," he said to Russell as he reopened his eyes.

"I know," Russell said with a nod. "Just say the word."

Deal hesitated, then glanced up as realization swept over him. "The wine," he said to Russell. "The fucking wine."

Russell stared back until his gaze lit, too, and in the next moment, they were gone.

LES STANDIFORD

**36**

"**If it wasn't** Stone, then who?" Russell asked as he piloted the coupe, its wipers flapping wildly against the rain, back toward Truman Town.

Deal shook his head. He'd been asking himself the same question, but his ability to reason seemed more and more an aspect of a former life. "Maybe one of those 'important New York investors' Boussier mentioned," he told Russell.

Russell nodded, ignoring a red light as he swung left off Whitehead Street.

"We're not walking in," Deal said, pointing at a guard shack that loomed beside the gated traffic entrance to Stone's development.

"Don't worry," Russell said. He brought the coupe to a stop beside the tidy guardhouse, a miniature version of one of the Cape Cod cottages within. A rent-a-cop with a wooden-gripped .38 holstered at his side came out of his shelter, a section of newspaper held over his head against the rain. He'd been reading the Sunday comics at their approach and seemed annoyed at being forced out into the weather.

"You boys need something?" he said, peering inside as Russell rolled his window down. The rent-a-cop had his free hand poised on his hip, as if Harry Truman himself were inside the compound and he might have to go for his sidearm at any second to head off a national crisis.

Russell held up a scrap of paper in his hand. "We're looking for this address," he said. "Somebody told us it was in Truman Town."

The guard screwed up his face and leaned closer. Russell's left hand shot out and caught the rent-a-cop by his shirtfront, snatching him forward. His mouth formed an O of surprise at the same time his forehead slammed into the coupe's door frame.

"How about the gate?" Deal said as the cop toppled quietly over.

"Piece of cake," Russell said, flooring the coupe. "Or plastic, actually," he added, as the flimsy gate arm hit the windshield and snapped away.

The coupe's tiny engine whined as they raced down the quiet streets toward the waterfront. A woman in curlers stood at curbside before one of the larger homes, holding an umbrella over a squatting cocker spaniel at her feet. She shook her fist and shouted something angrily as they sped by.

"Hate to shake up your morning, lady," Russell muttered, leaning the coupe into a tire-squalling left turn. They were bearing down on the marina parking lot now.

A guy wearing Top-Siders, khaki shorts, and a double-billed fishing cap—his day sail scuttled by the rain, or so it seemed—was struggling to fit the convertible top of his vintage Porsche into place as they

290

roared to a stop in the lot. He glanced up as the two of them jumped from the coupe and ran toward the marina complex. Deal heard the sound of a revving sports car engine in their wake.

"You head for the cellar," Deal called, peeling away from Russell as they approached the deserted maintenance building. "I'll check the docks."

Russell gave him a quick wave of acknowledgment and pounded away down the seawall as Deal hurried across the wooden planking of the central pier, splattering puddled rainwater with every stride.

The gate that barred entrance to the city-block-sized network of docks had been propped open by a 55-gallon drum, where a huge pelican sat, its head tucked into its chest against the rain. At Deal's approach, the big bird lifted grudgingly into the sky, its wings pumping a series of ever-diminishing V's against the scudding clouds.

The rain was pelting now, the skies gone evening dark. Deal held his hand up to shield his eyes, scanning the docks for Ainsley's skiff amidst the welter of sailboats and fishing craft and cabin cruisers. Pleasure craft, he found himself thinking. All these buttoned-up boats brought to Key West for the prospect of enjoyment. What an alien concept it seemed.

He was about to give up, turn and head back to join Russell, when he caught sight of something just ahead and stopped as abruptly as if he'd been gaffed. He slid to a halt on the rain-slick planking, his hand clutched at a piling for support.

She stood wrapped in a dark blue rain slicker at the rear of an old yacht, a teak-studded double-decker, with its big inboard engines rumbling at idle, her gaze directed across the marina, it seemed, where he and Russell had left the tiny coupe at the curb. She wore dark glasses and her hair had been pulled up and tucked beneath a long-billed fisherman's cap, but Deal would have recognized her if she'd been dressed in a clown's suit. He'd ingrained her very presence, he realized, had memorized the psychic fingerprint of her being.

"Annie," he called. And she turned.

At the front of the boat, a man clad in bright yellow foul-weather gear glanced up from untying the forward line, but Annie made a motion with her hand and he went back to what he was doing. Deal realized he was moving across the dock again, though his legs felt leaden suddenly.

"Annie," he repeated. He glanced behind him at the deserted docks, sheets of rain obliterating the shore where Russell would have been. "What are you doing?"

She held up a hand to caution him. "You can't come on board," she told him.

Deal stared at her, shaking his head. "What the hell is going on?" he said. "Stone's dead—"

"I know," she said. She glanced over her shoulder toward the boat's cabin.

"You *know*?" He started forward again and saw the door of the cabin swing open behind her.

"John, don't," she called as a heavyset man wearing a watch cap emerged, his hand inside the flap of his jacket. She had swept off her dark glasses, her face a mask of concern.

She turned to the man who'd come out on deck. "It's all right," she said. "Just give me a minute."

The man raised his chin a fraction in acknowledgment, then turned to say something to someone inside. Annie turned back to Deal, her hands clutched to the rail.

"I'm all right, John," she said. "These are friends of mine."

"Friends? What friends? Killers?" He felt rain streaming down his face, his mind a senseless jangle of speculation.

"No," she called. "They didn't kill Franklin." She shook her head violently. "I don't know who did. They're helping me, that's all. I can't explain everything right now, John. I have to leave." She cast another glance behind her, then turned back to him, her face twisted in anguish. "I don't want to, but I don't have the choice."

He stared back, dumbstruck, still gauging the distance that separated the dock from the deck of the boat where she stood. "I'm supposed to stand here, wave goodbye like I'm your uncle Harry, have a good time on your cruise?"

"You're not my uncle Harry," she managed, trying to smile through her tears.

Deal heard mumbled conversation from inside the boat's cabin and the revving of the engines increased. "But you're in danger, too, John. You should leave Key West now."

He stared at her, blinking water out of his eyes, his mind beginning to numb itself. Too much to consider, too much to bear. "If you wanted to brush me off," he said, "you didn't have to bring goons with guns. All you had to do was say the word."

"I'm not brushing you off," she said, her tone vehement. "I'll call you. When it's safe." The guy holding the forward line must have caught a signal from someone on the bridge. He turned and tossed the heavy rope toward the dock. It landed with a slap. The boat had begun to sidle from the dock. Two feet between them now, then three.

"Don't do it, John," she called. "I love you. Don't do it. You'll die. Listen to me."

He blinked, felt the tension leaving his legs. Five feet, then six, then it might as well have been a mile. He felt something being pulled out of his gut, every foot the boat receded bringing with it another jolt of pain.

She raised her hand as the boat's engines began to roar in earnest. He felt his own hand go up in response. He watched a moment more, then turned and made his way back to shore, reeling like a drunk.

# 37

THERE WAS NO sign of Russell as he approached the fence that marked
the edge of the marina property. The hidden door to the vault where
they'd spent the night had been thrown open to the rain, a dark stain
splashed across the concrete entrance, a lighter penumbra washing
down to the edge of the seawall with the rain's runoff. Though his
mind was still numb, his pace quickened automatically.

"Sonofabitch." Deal heard the familiar voice then and hurried toward
the gaping doorway in the earth. Russell had stopped halfway down
the rough-hewn staircase, Deal saw, frozen by something he'd seen.

"What is it?" Deal called. He'd already seen that the dark stain at the
top of the staircase was not at all what he had thought. Heavy green
splinters of bottle glass littered the concrete. Already, the rain had
washed much of the spilled wine away.

Russell glanced up. "Take a look," he said, pointing down into the darkness.

Deal hurried down the steps, ready for almost anything. Almost.

What he saw should not have been a surprise, of course. If he hadn't been so exhausted, if he hadn't been so preoccupied with other thoughts, he would have known before he'd reached the bottom of the long flight of stairs.

"Gone," he heard Russell say behind him, his voice weary beyond reason. "Every fucking bit of it."

Deal stared at the blank walls before him, then glanced down the passageway to his right. He couldn't see very far in that direction, but he'd already heard the echo of his footsteps, could sense the presence of all that emptiness before him. He noticed something in a gloomy alcove near his foot and bent to pick it up.

He held the bottle to the light, nodding at the label he'd seen once before. A gray-green patina that seemed almost to blend into the dark green glass itself. A tasteful drawing of the French château beneath the legend Haut-Brion, and below that, the promise that this was a wine of Premier Grand Cru Classe. The year was 1929. The bottle even had its own special serial number, printed discreetly down one side.

Deal glanced at Russell, who had joined him at the foot of the stairs to stare glumly at what he held in his hands. "One frigging bottle," Russell said, with a sorrowful shake of his head. "That's all there is left."

Deal hefted it. The bottle seemed extraordinarily heavy, as if whatever was inside had been brewed on a far more massive planet.

"One bottle was all it took to get Dequarius killed," he said absently.

"What the hell are we supposed to do now?" Russell said.

Deal shrugged. A Vernon Driscoll shrug if ever there was one. "I'm not sure," he said to Russell, hating the look that he got in return.

296    "Maybe call Rusty . . . ," he began, struggling to find some direction

that made sense. He might have gone on from there, might actually have stumbled onto something reasonable to send them toward, when he heard the voice from above.

"No need," he heard in tones that seemed outright cheery. "No need for that at all."

**38**

DEAL SAW CONRAD FIRST, the grim-faced cop descending the stairs with what looked like a modified M-14 in his hands, its stubby barrel swollen at the tip by a suppressor. When his gaze landed on Deal's, his lip curled into a momentary smile.

"Well, look who's here," he said.

Malloy followed closely on Conrad's heels, looking fresh in a crisp white shirt, khakis, and canvas boating shoes. "Do us the favor of toss-ing that pistol aside, won't you, Mr. Straight?" Malloy said, pointing at the weapon in Russell's waistband.

When Russell hesitated, Malloy patted Conrad on the shoulder. "Shoot him if you don't like the way he does it," Malloy said.

"Do it," Deal urged Russell.

Russell's gaze held steady on Malloy's as he reached two fingers toward his midsection and pried the weapon out by the butt. "Put it on the ground," Malloy said, his eyes glittering.

Russell bent carefully and did as he was told. "Now kick it over this way," Malloy said. Again Russell obeyed, though the look he sent Malloy and Conrad would have etched glass.

"Thank you," Malloy said, squatting on his haunches to gaze at them, a guileless smile on his face.

"If you're thirsty, you're a little late, Rusty," Deal said. "All the wine's gone."

"Looks like you've got your share," Malloy said. "Château Haut-Brion, unless I miss my guess." He smiled, then threw his head back as if to catch some scent in the cool damp air. "Quite a bouquet there. I'm going to say 1929. An excellent year."

Deal stared back at him wordlessly. Rusty Malloy. His good pal, the glasscutter's son.

"Where'd you take the wine, Rusty?" Deal asked. Malloy widened his eyes. "Me? I didn't take it anywhere. I sold it to some associates of Franklin Stone." He gestured behind him. "I believe they're on their way out of the country with it as we speak."

"Stone's dead," Russell cut in.

"Is he now?" Malloy asked as Conrad tweaked the barrel of his weapon Russell's way. "How do you suppose that happened?"

Deal could only stare, all the disparate pieces of the puzzle flying apart, then rearraning themselves in his head. "You were at the dinner that night when Boussier brought the wine out, weren't you, Rusty?" Deal said.

"I may have been." Malloy shrugged.

"And Dequarius was there, too, waiting tables or busing dishes or whatever, wanting to see how his wine went over." Deal swept his arm around the empty catacomb. "Dequarius knew he couldn't sell Stone what he'd regard as his own property, so he came to you. Once you realized what Dequarius had stumbled onto, you decided to take it from him."

Malloy pursed his lips as if he were critiquing Deal's summation. "An interesting concept, Johnny-boy—stealing abondoned cargo." He made an idle gesture. "I'd say it's the law of the sea that applies in this instance. To the salvor go the spoils."

"Once you found out where the wine was, you killed him," Deal continued.

Malloy made a deprecating sound with his lips. "Did François tell you this? The man simply doesn't know when to stop talking. We just dropped by to see him, didn't we, Albert? He's holding his tongue now, quite literally."

Conrad grunted agreement, his eyes flickering back and forth between Deal and Russell, as if uncertain which target he yearned for more.

"That's what Dequarius was trying to warn me about the night he died," Deal said, his anger growing. "You knew he'd been in contact with me. He wanted me to know I was next in line. The only thing I haven't figured out is why he came to me in the first place."

"A good question, isn't it?" Malloy nodded. "Stone was in an expansive mood that night, telling a number of war stories, most of them having to do with one or another development scam he and your father had perpetrated. He told us all he had high hopes that you were about to step in where Barton Deal had left off. Stone said you'd been holding him up for a bigger piece of the kickbacks he arranged with the city, but he felt confident you'd come around."

"That's bullshit," Deal said.

"I thought about telling him you were a true-blue Boy Scout, but what would have been the point?" Malloy shrugged. "I suppose Dequarius overheard some of Stone's talk and decided you were a man he could reason with."

Russell glanced at Deal. "So much for my thoughts on the matter."

Deal shook his head glumly. "Then Dequarius came to me because he thought I was a crook." He took a deep breath. How long was his old man's legacy going to hound him anyway? Then he caught a glimpse of the weapon in Conrad's hands, which suggested something of an answer to the question.

Deal turned his gaze back to Malloy. "Who else was there that night?" he asked.

"Some very astute businessmen," Malloy answered. "Men who understand the concept of pricelessness." He nodded at the bottle in Deal's hands. "What you're holding there has considerable historic significance, you know."

"I'd call it evidence," Deal said.

"So you might," Malloy said, "if you were in a position to do anything with it." He smiled benignly, waving a hand around the sunken chamber. "Certain people have been searching for this wine for years, you know."

"So I've learned," Deal said and hefted the bottle, calculating his chances of going up against Conrad and his automatic with such a weapon. Somewhere in the sub-zero range, he thought. But at least as long as Malloy kept talking, they'd stay alive. Anything might happen.

"Some three hundred cases of one of the finest wines ever bottled. Vanished, without a trace," Malloy said. "When it didn't turn up on the European black market, speculation turned to America. It being Prohibition, a certain gangster of Italian extraction was rumored to have financed the job, but that wasn't the case." He shook his head and

301

BONE KEY

glanced around the room again. "Who could have ever figured that our own Senator Rafferty had been involved?"

"Never sell a Florida politician short," Deal said.

It brought what seemed a genuine smile from Malloy. "You were always good with a quip, John. Too bad you're so goddamned honest."

Deal shook his head. Something that Malloy had said had begun to nag at him. There was no way he could have known of Rafferty's involvement unless, of course, he'd gotten his hands on Ainsley Spencer. The thought chilled Deal, but he kept his gaze level on Malloy's.

"Did the old man tell you about Senator Rafferty?" Deal asked.

Malloy looked at him strangely. "What old man? What are you talking about?"

Deal shrugged. "I was just wondering how you knew so much about all this." He waved his hand around the dank cellar. It seemed as if the temperature had dropped several notches since Malloy and Conrad had entered. It seemed cold enough to store almost anything here for a good long time.

Malloy, meantime, was smiling. "Now there's the interesting part." He reached into a back pocket and held up what looked like a slender, leatherbound notebook. "It's a ship captain's log," Malloy said, flipping the cover open. "It belonged to a Captain Michael Gavin Malloy."

Deal stared back at him. "Let me guess. A family heirloom."

"It's a fascinating story," Malloy said. He glanced at his watch, then up at the sky. "We've got a minute or two if you'd like to hear it."

Deal shrugged. "You're the boss, Rusty."

Malloy nodded. "So it would seem, Johnny-boy. So it would seem." He replaced the diary in his pocket, and then he began to talk.

**39**

CHERBOURG

1931

"THAT IS THE last of it," the man beside Gavin Malloy said. Being French, the man put an unnatural emphasis on the *of.*

Malloy glanced at the bulky pallet that was being trundled across the dimly lit dock planks and nodded. Never mind that he had spoken to this man in fluent French when the trucks had first pulled up. He was an American in the eyes of the man, and he would be spoken to in English.

Of course, Malloy was no more an American than the wine being loaded aboard his ship was made of table grapes, but he was not about to waste his energy in that kind of debate.

"You can certify the count, then?" the Frenchman said. He sounded impatient.

For that much Malloy couldn't blame him. It was cold and the mist had thickened, muting the scattered incandescent lamps to weak, parchment-tinted halos, shrouding the men moving the pallet, boiling up beneath the trucks, obscuring the contours of the freighter that loomed above in the night like a rusting storm cloud. A chilly vision of Hell, he thought.

"You wouldn't cheat me," Malloy said. He wiped his hand across his face, felt a trickle going down his neck, diving beneath the collar of his coat. Just September and wearing a coat, for God's sake. Inside a week, he'd be back in Florida, and so much for coats.

The Frenchman stared back as though Malloy had delivered an insult. Well, Malloy thought, perhaps he had. Or perhaps the Frenchman had read his mind and knew where Malloy and his cargo were bound. Perhaps it was jealousy that made this Frenchman so dyspeptic.

"Everything is as agreed, then," the Frenchman prompted.

Malloy shrugged. "I didn't taste the wine."

The Frenchman made a sound that was something between a laugh and a clearing of his throat. "Too bad for you," he said. His intonation suggested the opposite: Too *good* for the likes of you.

The cargo net dropped to the docks with a liquid thud, a sound not unlike that of a body falling from a considerable height, Malloy thought. The men on the dock moved to the sodden tangle and pulled it toward the pallet they'd dragged from their trucks.

The knowledge that this rare freight was destined for Prohibition-blighted America, for delivery to some wealthy but undistinguished swine, had not stopped the Frenchman from stealing it from his employers, however. Such considerations had not prevented him from removing from exactly three hundred cases of one of the finest Bordeaux vintages in history from its rightful cellars, shortly before its release to

304

his infinitely more tasteful countrymen. Situational snobbery, Malloy thought. But it was a waste of energy even formulating such judgments.

The net, swollen by its catch, was rising from the docks as if by magic now, its cable hidden in the dark, the characteristic squeaks of the winch muffled by the gathering fog. *Deus ex machina*, Malloy found himself thinking. *Machine of the gods.*

In Dublin, once, he had studied theater. Though it was a fact, such a thing now seemed impossible.

"You'll be here until morning," the Frenchman said, waving his hand before his face as if there were too much moisture there for breathing.

"We'll sail tonight," Malloy replied.

The Frenchman stared at him, saying nothing. Perhaps he fancied the image of the *Magdelena* foundering on the channel rocks—as long as he'd been paid, of course.

"Then you and I are finished," the Frenchman said finally. His men—tight-lipped one and all—stood near the doors to their trucks, ready to depart. They were more than three hundred miles from Bordeaux and while Malloy was sure that every official who might have been a bother on the Frenchman's route had earned a few francs this night, one was always anxious to leave the scene of a crime.

"We are indeed," Malloy said. He turned and gestured, and his purser hurried from his place near the bottom of the gangplank, a dark leather satchel in his hand.

"Give the man his money, Avi," Malloy said.

Avi was a dark-eyed little man who looked like he'd been born to the counting room. He looked up at Malloy from beneath the watch cap mashed over his ears, then handed the dripping satchel to the Frenchman.

The Frenchman snapped open the clasp, peered inside, shook the contents. He removed a bundle of bills, held it to his nose, then up to the light as he riffled the stack. He dropped the packet back into the satchel and flashed Malloy his humorless smile. "You wouldn't cheat me," he said.

Malloy gave him the slightest bow in return. He had always appreciated irony.

"I'd be careful if I were you," the Frenchman said, moving off toward the lead truck. "That channel is tricky, even in good weather."

Malloy pursed his lips and glanced out toward sea. He caught a whiff of rotting weed, borne, he hoped, on a gathering breeze. "There *is* good weather in Cherbourg?" he asked, turning back.

It drew what might have been a genuine smile from the Frenchman. "*Au revoir*," he said and raised his hand as he climbed aboard the truck.

"*Au revoir*," Malloy replied, and went with Avi toward his ship.

Malloy had reached the ship's rail at the gangway deck when the first explosion sounded. He turned as a blossom of flame flew into the sky above a nearby warehouse roof, and in moments a second explosion came, followed by another massive fireball. Seconds later, Malloy heard shouts, and the popping of rifle fire. He turned to Avi, who shrugged, then led the way quickly down the gangway.

By the time they reached the docks, Malloy had his pistol drawn. He swept past his purser, motioning him to take a post behind the shelter of the gangway. Malloy hurried to the passage between the warehouses where the Frenchman's trucks had left. He heard footsteps pounding toward him in the darkness and stepped into a shadowed alcove at the corner of the building nearest, his weapon ready.

A man burst from the passage, his breath ragged, a pistol aloft in his hand. Malloy smelled cordite and the tang of fear.

306     When he realized where he was, the man stopped short, cursing the

sight of the ship. He glanced down the dock to his right, then to the left, where Avi was hidden behind the gangway canvas.

More footsteps thundered in the distance—his own men, Malloy knew. He'd have a word with them, letting this one get so far.

"*Merde!*" Malloy heard the Frenchman mutter. How he had managed to survive the blast, Malloy could only wonder.

From the distance came the wail of sirens, a noise that was obliterated by yet a third explosion. That blast had taken out the only bridge that connected the nearby town with its port, or at least it better have, Malloy thought.

He knew exactly what the Frenchman's arrangement with the local authorities had been, for it was no mistake that Malloy had seen to it Cherbourg was their rendezvous point. He had lived in the town for a time shortly after fleeing Russia, and he had paid an old associate now working within the city's ministry handsomely for the information he would need.

Once the trucks that had delivered the wine had passed back across the bridge, the authorities would hurry out to the docks, there to impound Malloy's ship, arrest his men—or more likely kill them—then confiscate the wine. A neat plan, the sort of thing Malloy might have devised himself, were he on the other side.

As the echoes of the bridge explosion died away, he heard the sound of a motor starting somewhere in the nearby harbor. Which would be the local patrol boat, coming to cut off Malloy's escape by sea. Of course, he thought. Well drawn. Moments later, a fourth explosion rocked the harbor, and the sound of the patrol boat was no more.

"Drop your pistol," he called, waiting for the man in front of him to turn.

Gavin Malloy had never shot anyone in the back. He was not about to begin with a Frenchman.

307

# 40

"So Gavin Malloy was your grandfather?" Deal said when Rusty had finished his account.

Malloy nodded. "He was killed himself in an explosion that sank the *Magdelena* a few miles off this very coast." He swept his arm in the direction of the sea. "My grandmother was living in Miami by then. Someone found his seabag washed up on Summerland Key a few weeks later and sent it to her. The diary was among his effects. Neither she nor my father ever told me what was inside, of course. I found it in my father's house after he died."

"And you've been looking for the wine ever since?" Deal asked.

Malloy gave a humorless laugh. "Wouldn't it be nice to think so," he said. "It did spur an interest in the subject." He glanced around the empty cellar. "Living in a place like Key West, you have time for such things." He gave Deal a smile. "You might have come to discover that yourself." He stood and stretched. "But the fact is, until very recently I hadn't wasted a minute searching for the wine. I assumed the shipment of wine my grandfather carried had been lost when the ship went down. Until that night I went to dinner with Stone, that is."

Deal shook his head. "I never would have figured you for something like this, Rusty."

Malloy shrugged. "I'd call it my due, Johnny-boy. Someone killed my grandfather over this wine, my grandmother drank herself into an early grave, my old man worked himself to death in turn. Why the hell shouldn't I turn a profit here?"

"And kill half a dozen people while you're at it?"

Malloy gave him a disdainful look. "I didn't set out to harm anyone. If Dequarius Noyes had been willing to listen to reason, he'd still be alive. He was a penny-ante crook sitting on a multimillion-dollar treasure, way out of his league." He gave Deal a look that assumed an understanding of the situation.

"That wine was valuable enough in its own right. A spectacular vintage, so few bottles produced. But this cache"—his eyes widened as he swept his arm around the room again—"it was like stumbling across Amelia Earhart's airplane in a hermetically sealed room."

Deal shook his head. "It's stolen property, each bottle numbered. How could it be sold?"

Malloy stared as if Deal were an idiot. "If anything, that makes it even *more* valuable to a collector. Doled out bit by bit, the value here is incalculable. That's why it was necessary that Dequarius Noyes be removed from the equation as quickly as possible."

So much for Malloy's earlier pleas of innocence. And so much for their prospects of survival as well, he thought glumly, his eyes on the pistol that Russell had kicked away. Conrad would cut him to shreds before he got halfway to it.

He glanced back at Malloy. He didn't want to ask the next question, but he knew he had to. "How about Annie Dodds? Was she at this dinner party?"

"There is no such person," Malloy said, his gaze level, not a trace of irony in his voice. "A woman by the name of Anita Dobbins was with us, if that's who you mean. She's the one who introduced those men who were at dinner to Stone, in fact."

Deal felt himself rocking ever so slightly backward on his heels. The "New York investors," friends of Annie's all along, then? The vision of a dark, slender form standing at the rearward rail of a speeding cabin cruiser came to him briefly, then vanished just as quickly into the dark.

"I wouldn't blame her for any of this, Johnny-boy," Deal heard Malloy saying. "She had no way of knowing what would happen, but it would hardly do for her to stay in Key West, under the circumstances." Malloy broke off, giving him a look that was supposed to seem sympathetic.

"In fact, if you'd kept your nose out of things, none of this would have happened. Stone would still be with us, as would the lovely Ms. Dobbins. You'd be on your way to a fat contract, he'd probably have been willing to turn his head every now and then so you could knock off a little something on the side."

Deal started forward, but felt Russell Straight's powerful hand clamp on his shoulder. "He'll shoot you dead," Russell said quietly in Deal's ear.

"He'll do it anyway," Deal said, his eyes murderous on Malloy.

"You're an old friend, John," Malloy said. "I'm sorry to see it end this way."

310

His sorrow sounded genuine, Deal thought. The notion only added fuel to his fury. He'd go for Conrad with his bottle of wine, regardless of the consequences, he thought. He doubted Malloy was armed. With any luck, Russell would survive to finish the job.

Malloy, meantime, was checking his watch. He stood and stretched luxuriantly. "I hate to think of that wine you're holding going to waste, John," he said. "Why not be a good fellow and set it down before Conrad does what he has to do."

"I don't think so, Rusty," Deal said. "This is going to cost you, one way or another."

He started forward then, his grip firm on the heavy bottle, cocking his arm back across his chest, his aim at Conrad's jaw. The big deputy smiled as he saw how it was going to be, and swung the tip away from Russell Straight.

Deal heard a strange thunking sound from the top of the stairwell then, along with a shout from Malloy. Conrad's glance wavered momentarily, but Deal was on the move. The big deputy was bringing his weapon into position to fire when there was another strange noise—this one wet, and thudding—and Conrad's eyes suddenly lost their focus.

An enormous arrow, Deal thought at first, gaping at the impossible sight before him. In the next instant, he realized. Not an arrow, but a metal spear from a diver's gun that had pierced Conrad near his jawbone and glanced out through the crown of his head, its tether line still taut and holding the man upright.

Ainsley Spencer stood at the top of the stairwell with the speargun in his hands. He loosed the tether line from the spear he'd sent through Conrad and began loading another projectile into the stiff elastic firing mechanism.

As Conrad toppled over, Malloy jumped from the stairwell to the floor of the chamber, going for the pistol that Russell had earlier kicked away. He had his hands on the weapon and was lifting it to fire at Ainsley when Deal strode forward and backhanded him with the bottle.

The edge of the heavy bottom caught Malloy like a mule's kick just above the ear. There was a popping sound as his skull gave and the pistol tumbled free from his grasp. He spun around, staring at Deal with a look that suggested some great betrayal, then he went over.

Deal stared down at Malloy's unmoving form, then at the still-unbroken bottle in his hand. Ainsley Spencer stood at the top of the stairwell with the loaded speargun braced in his hands. Russell Straight moved quickly past him, bending to check Malloy.

Russell stood after a moment and came back to Deal, lifting the bottle gently from his hands. "This here's some righteous stuff," he said.

And then they were all moving up toward the light.

# 41

"A LITTLE CLOSER to those mangroves, now," Ainsley Spencer said as Russell Straight's cast plopped into the quiet water a good dozen feet from an array of roots that resembled a tangle of tarantula limbs, constituting what passed for shore in these parts.

The first cold front of the season had slipped through the Lower Keys the night before, leaving behind a few ragged cirrus high up in an otherwise unblemished sky and dropping the temperature all the way down to the high seventies, cool enough to send most of the flats-loving mosquitoes into a momentary nod.

A perfect day to be out on the water, Deal thought as he sat on a sling chair on the deck of the houseboat, watching Russell madly winding in his reel. Just a moment before, they'd seen something roll in the waters just short of that tangle of roots. Maybe a tarpon, maybe a school of mangrove snapper.

They'd rented the boat from a marina in Key West, a smallish, shallow-draft craft designed for easy maneuvering in the waters of Florida Bay. They were about an hour and a half out of port to westward, he supposed, though he hadn't glanced at his watch since they'd left. The plan was to putter along the coastline until they found one of the thousand and one sandy beaches scattered at the tip of the mainland peninsula, a place to put in for lunch and a swim.

He could see a likely spot from where they were right now, as a matter of fact, a thin slice of white against the ragged Everglades coastline a few hundred yards to the northwest. But at this very moment, they were nudged close to an islandlike outcropping of mangroves just offshore, another priority at hand.

Russell Straight had reeled in now and was struggling to untangle his leader when Ainsley Spencer left the wheel of the houseboat to come lend a hand.

"Let's try us another shrimp then, what do we say?" The old man pulled Russell's ragged-looking bait off the hook and tossed it over the side. Deal saw a swirling motion just beneath the surface as something took the free lunch.

Russell waited for the old man to thread on a fresh shrimp, then turned back to his target and whipped the rod back, and once again forward, in a far too rapid motion.

"Damn," Russell said, watching the flight of his cast.

"I didn't say *in* the trees," Ainsley Spencer said, gazing off at the result.

"What now?" Russell said, looking in dismay at the shrimp that dangled from a mangrove branch.

"Wait for whatever's down there to evolve," Deal suggested. "A cou-

314

ple million years, it'll be a shrimp-loving squirrel to climb right up out of that water."

"Somebody must have said you were funny once," Russell said.

"Let me see that," Ainsley Spencer said, taking the rod from Russell. The old man switched the rod a few times. There was a plop over by the mangroves as the tangled line came free. Seconds later the rod bent, as something took the bait.

"Here," the old man said, handing the rod to Russell. "Don't be herky-jerky, now."

Russell snatched the rod up and leaned back as if he'd hooked a marlin. Seconds later the line had parted and the big man turned to them with a crestfallen look.

"It got away," he said.

"That's one way of putting it," Deal said. He absently fingered the scar near his hairline, a lasting souvenir of the last time he'd been aboard a houseboat. The hair had grown back, but he knew what marked it now: a neat wedge of white in an otherwise sun-bleached shock.

"Lunch is ready," an authoritative voice called from the cabin. A screened door swung open, and the broad brown face of Minerva Betts poked out. "We eating here or someplace else?"

"I thought over by that bit of beach," Ainsley Spencer said, pointing toward the sliver of sand glinting in the distance.

"Then why we be waiting here?" Minerva Betts said, her tone indignant. "Get us going there, old man."

As she ducked back inside, the door swung fully open and Denise emerged, wiping her hands on a dish towel that surely contained more fabric than the bathing suit she wore. "Lost another one, I see," she said to Russell, who stood examining the snapped end of his line with a

315

**BONE KEY**

mournful expression. "If it wasn't for Deal, it'd be peanut butter for lunch," she added.

"He used all the good shrimp," Russell said.

"The man knows how to fish," Ainsley Spencer cut in. He turned the starter and the motor of the houseboat grumbled to life.

"You caught all the fish, Daddy?" Deal turned as his daughter, Isabel, pushed herself up off the cushions of a canopy-shaded settee where she'd drifted off. She was yawning, rubbing sleep from her eyes with her knuckles.

"Every last one of them," Russell Straight said.

"Don't listen. There's plenty more fish, sweetie," Deal said. He put out his arms as she came to snuggle in his lap.

The boat was moving now, lumbering over the gentle swells toward the beckoning stretch of beach. "I want to catch one," she said as she nestled close.

"You will," he told her, nuzzling her hair with his chin. "You'll catch a million of them."

"Are you going to stay in Key West forever?" she asked then, her gaze averted.

"Who told you that?"

"Uncle Russell said *he* was," she said.

Deal glanced toward the railing of the boat, where Denise and Russell leaned at the rail, their heads bent in close conversation. "Did he, now?"

"He did," Isabel said. "He said you have all this work to do in Key West now, and somebody has to watch over it."

Deal nodded, glancing involuntarily back over the placid surface of the bay in the direction they had come. Shortly after Detective Dickerson had dropped by his rooms at the Pier House with the news that he and Russell had been cleared of charges, a delegation composed of the

316

mayor, the director of the chamber of commerce, and the head of the Monroe County Development Commission had arrived, bringing with them the Islamorada attorney who was the executor of Franklin Stone's estate.

Their proposal contained many of the same terms as those outlined in the paperwork that Stone had stuffed in his pocket earlier, sweetened a bit by the common desire that Deal carry out the environmentally amended plan that Stone had agreed to before his death. In that way, argued the city fathers, the project would be withheld from normal probate, thus ensuring there would be no takeover by some outside, far less sensitive interests.

For once, Deal mused, the politics of expediency seemed justified. It would mean considerable shuttling back and forth from Miami to Key West, of course, but at least he would have an able project manager in place.

He cut another look at Russell, who had his arm around Denise's shoulders, then gave his daughter a hug. "Don't worry, sweetheart," he said. "I'm not moving to Key West."

"Good," she said, giving him a kiss on his cheek. "You need to shave," she added as she snuggled in again.

Deal smiled, running a hand over his cheeks as Ainsley Spencer brought the houseboat into a turn fifty feet or so off a stretch of brilliant white beach and cut the engines. The water off the side of the boat was as crystal as that of a spring.

"Are you going swimming, Daddy?" Isabel called.

Deal nodded. "Sure," he said. "How about you?"

"Of course," she said. "That's why I'm wearing my suit. Aunt Denise, too," she added, pointing.

Deal smiled and helped her down from his lap. Isabel started away, then stopped and came back to him. "Daddy?" she asked.

317

"Yes, sweetheart?"

"Don't you wish Mommy was here?"

Deal stared back into her innocent gaze for a moment, some minuscule portion of the million or so words that an answer to that question would require flashing briefly through his mind. An easterly breeze had sprung up the moment they'd stopped, traveling the same course that hurricanes used, in a different season, of course. *The wind is in from Africa,* he thought, and made his way to his feet.

"Sure I do," he told his daughter, who accepted this answer with a nod.

"Lunch is served," Minerva Betts called, pushing her way through the screen with a formidable hip, platters of freshly grilled snapper arrayed down each of her arms.

"Looks good," Ainsley Spencer said. "Looks mighty good."

"Back off, old man," Minerva Betts scolded him. "Let these others eat." She was slapping platters down on the picnic table that took up most of the rear deck space.

"How about a little wine with lunch?" Deal said. He reached into the duffel bag that he'd stowed beneath his chair and pulled out a bottle.

Russell Straight glanced at what was in his hand. "Maybe you ought to save that one," the big man said.

Deal glanced down at the label and shrugged. There had been no trace found of the missing cache of wine, but then again, perhaps his description of two bright red and overloaded Donzis headed hell-bent for leather out of the port might have had something to do with that.

No reason to do otherwise, Deal had told himself, as he'd once again lied to a detective named Dickerson. The men who'd bought the wine from Rusty Malloy were simply businessmen. And they'd been kind enough to give a lady a lift out of a jam.

318

He hefted the heavy bottle in his hand, bothered not a bit by what he'd once used it for. Without it, he thought, they might not have been here at all.

"Save it for what?" he said, turning to Russell. He pulled a Swiss Army knife from his pocket and flipped the corkscrew out. As he worked the point into the still-firm cork, he nodded toward a stack of plastic cups that Minerva Betts had plopped down in the middle of the picnic table.

"Get yourselves a glass," he called as the cork popped and a trace of something like smoke appeared and vanished as quickly as a genie's track.

Deal held up the bottle and glanced off to eastward once again, thinking of toasts he might have otherwise proposed, and wondered if someday, somehow, he might yet have that chance.

"To life," he said as the song began to cycle through his mind once again. And finally he began to pour.